welfth prophecy

BOOK TWELVE

A.D. CHRONICLES®

twelfth prophecy

Tyndale House Publishers, Inc.
Carol Stream, Illinois

BODIE & BROCK
THOENE

Visit Tyndale online at www.tyndale.com.

TYNDALE and Tyndale's quill logo are registered trademarks of Tyndale House Publishers, Inc.

A.D. Chronicles, the A.D. Chronicles logo, and the fish design are registered trademarks of Bodie Thoene.

Twelfth Prophecy

A.D. Chronicles series designed by Rule 29, www.rule29.com

Interior designed by Dean H. Renninger

Edited by Ramona Cramer Tucker

This novel is a work of fiction. Names, characters, places, and incidents either are the product of the authors' imaginations or are used fictitiously. Any resemblance to actual events, locales, organizations, or persons, living or dead, is entirely coincidental and beyond the intent of either the authors or the publisher.

Library of Congress Cataloging-in-Publication Data

Thoene, Bodie, date.
   Twelfth prophecy / Bodie & Brock Thoene.
     p. cm. — (A.D. chronicles ; bk. 12)
   ISBN 978-0-8423-7540-5 (hc)
   I. Thoene, Brock, date. II. Title.
   PS3570.H46T87 2011
   813'.54—dc22   2010050529

ISBN 978-0-8423-7541-2 (sc)

Printed in the United States of America

18 17 16 15 14 13 12
 7   6   5   4   3   2   1

For Captain Todd Mirolla, HMS Victorious
Described by Jack Aubrey as
"A master tactician and a man of singular vision,
who always says, 'Never mind maneuvers, just go straight at 'em.'"
Pace è bene!

the middLe east

FIRST CENTURY A.D.

Mount Hermon ✝

GALILEE

• Caesarea Philippi

Chorazin •
Mediterranean Sea
Capernaum • •
• Bethsaida

Magdala •
Sea of Galilee
Tiberias

Sepphoris •
• Tiberias

• Beth Shan

Sebaste •

Jordan River

• Sychar

SAMARIA

Jericho •
Jerusalem • ✝ Mount of Olives
• Bethany
PEREA

Bethlehem •
• Herodium

JUDEA *Dead Sea*

IDUMEA

↑
N

◄— to Alexandria, Egypt

Prologue

THE HOUSE ON CHURCH ROW, HAMPSTEAD VILLAGE
LONDON, PRESENT DAY

Eben Golah gazed from the second-story window of the Church Row town house as the sky turned suddenly black and threatening. The wind was steady, westerly, propelling the clouds above London like the sails of great ships. The ancient oak trees on Hampstead Heath swayed with the approaching storm. Lightning flashed. For an instant the brick and mortar of Georgian houses was frozen in silver light, reminding Eben of the monochrome blast of bombs during the Blitz.

Loralei, cheerful and excited, entered the cherrywood-paneled study. Her shoulder-length blond hair framed an oval face unmarked by age or time. She seemed to be in her late twenties, a few years younger than her husband. Her bright blue eyes were animated as the boom of thunder rattled the windows in their frames.

"Big one brewing," Loralei remarked, gathering up cups and empty plates from Eben's long night of study. "Heaven's going to open up any minute. BBC says to expect it to bucket. Going to be quite a gale. My friend Emily rang to say the lift is acting up again at the Hampstead tube station."

Eben nodded. "I hope Shimon will think to bring Alfie in a taxi. Too many steps for him."

"They're late." Loralei glanced at two stacks of documents on Eben's desk. One was labeled in her handwriting, *Book of Hours*. "That's a good sign. Traffic. Probably are stuck in a cab somewhere. I've got the kettle on, and everything prepared for when they come."

"I could use another cuppa, please." Eben sighed and turned away from the approaching storm. He sat down heavily in the hunter green leather desk chair.

Loralei rubbed his shoulders. "I've got that special blend from Harrods. Or Darjeeling."

"Plain and simple for me. Black tea, please."

"Harrods Special Blend for Alfie, then. And Darjeeling for Shimon."

Eben's cell phone offered the tune *HaTikvah*. "It's Shimon," Eben told Loralei as he flipped open the phone. "Eben here," he answered.

Shimon Sachar's thick Israeli accent was momentarily muffled by the roar of traffic. "Hello! Hello? Eben? *Shalom!* Is it you?"

"Yes, Shimon. Everything all right?"

"We took a cab. Stuck in traffic. An accident on Edgware Road." Shimon's voice sounded tinny. Lightning flashed and thunder rolled again. The reception hissed. "More fool me. If we'd just taken the tube—"

Eben countered, "No. Right choice. The lift is out of order at Hampstead tube station. Deepest station in London. Your father and I sheltered many a long night there during the Blitz. Too much of a climb up the steps for Alfie, I'm afraid. How was the flight?"

"Good. Too excited to sleep."

"You brought it, then?" Eben could not wait to ask.

"Yes. Yes. Have you completed the project?"

"Finished. Translated. Originals scanned. I've got an additional original World War II diary here for you to carry back to store as well."

As Loralei left the room, Eben rang off, then scanned anew the seven manuscripts he had translated from ancient Hebrew and Aramaic into modern English. They were resealed in moisture-proof shrink-wrap. Shimon had picked up where his father, Moshe, had left off. Guardians of the secret library beneath Jerusalem's stones, Shimon and the now elderly Alfie Halder, Moshe's friend of over fifty years, would return the documents to their original storage containers under the Temple Mount. The shuttle of ancient journals between Israel and London worked seamlessly, thanks to connections in high places in Israel. One look at Shimon Sachar's passport and the two were waved through El Al security without question.

Today Eben was particularly excited by the package Shimon was bringing to him. Until today Eben had never met the couriers at his home. But these were dangerous times. Eben suspected he was being watched. At his request the Mossad had scanned this house for electronic bugs and declared it safe. Time was growing short for London and for the world. Spiritual and political oppression was being revealed in every nation, just as the book of Revelation foretold. The privacy of these walls remained the one place Eben felt safe to accomplish the translation of the ancient accounts.

Loralei whistled as she carried up sandwiches, scones, and an array of Alfie's favorite treats for tea. "Eben, I've been fighting with myself all day, since you told me they were coming here. Alfie. He's grown so old. Before they arrive, I . . . think I'll step out for a while. I can just make Evensong at the Abbey if I take the tube. Do you mind? I can't bear to see him . . . well, you know. It breaks my heart, Eben."

"You picked a great day to go to Evensong. Grab your umbrella, will you?"

She grinned over her shoulder as she slipped on her raincoat. "Meet me at the Spaghetti House on Haymarket after?" She stooped to kiss him, then moved swiftly toward the door, slamming it behind her.

Only moments passed before the familiar rattle of a London cab's diesel engine sounded at the curb. Eben stood and watched. Loralei tucked her head against the rain and hurried up the street.

Shimon, black briefcase handcuffed to his wrist, paid the cabbie. Old Alfie lumbered stiffly out of the vehicle. Umbrella unopened, he stood, hands limp at his sides, and stared after Loralei as she jogged toward High Street. What memory was sparked in his mind as she rounded the corner?

"Come on, Alfie." Shimon grasped Alfie's arm and steered him to the front door. "Come on! The rain!"

Eben rushed down the stairs and threw open the door. "Come in! Come in! *Shalom! Shalom!*" he cried.

Rainwater dripped from hats and slickers and puddled on the black-and-white checkered tiles of the foyer.

Alfie blinked at Eben and muttered, "I'm not surprised by nothing no more." He struggled to remove his coat.

Shimon slapped Eben on the back. "A good trip. Mossad watching over us all the way. On the plane. Until we got into the cab."

"It's working well, then." Eben hung their coats on the rack and led the way to his office. "There's tea. My wife prepared it."

Alfie sniffed. "Where was she going, then, in such a hurry?"

The old man stood before a black-and-white photograph of Eben and Loralei. He picked it up and held the frame in his hands.

"Jet lag hasn't kicked in yet," Shimon said, eyeing the platter of sandwiches and desserts.

"This will see you through." Eben poured the tea. "Loralei made Darjeeling for Shimon. And Harrods Special Blend for you, Alfie."

Alfie's chin rose and fell. His eyebrows raised slightly. "With caramel. She used to send it to me . . . for my birthday." Alfie raised the lid on the teapot and inhaled the steam.

Eben eyed the old man as he picked through sandwiches and sweetened his tea with four lumps of sugar. After slathering clotted cream and jam on his scones and devouring them, Alfie lay down on the leather sofa and promptly went to sleep.

Shimon shrugged. "The trip was probably too much for him. But he said he wanted to come. See you one more time."

"Sixty years of friendship and more. A good man, always," Eben remarked. "We shall miss him."

"Miss him?" Shimon asked.

"He's come to say farewell. There are more, by far, on the other side waiting for him now than remain here. It won't be long."

The two men polished off the rest of the treats in silence. Alfie snored a bit, then slept deeply.

Eben and Shimon settled down to work. Eben summarized and reviewed his translation work. Shimon removed an airtight case within the briefcase and triumphantly placed it on Eben's desk.

"So, you found her. All these years." Eben stroked the box.

"My father looked for her account his entire lifetime. You told him it must be there, but he never found it. Alfie came across it in a storage room. It was sealed in a jar meant for carrying water. Unusual script. First century. Samaritan dialect."

"I knew it was there," Eben said in an awed voice as he opened the folder. "Yes, it had to be there. Abigail's story. She won an entire chapter for herself and her people. Too important to be forgotten or neglected or . . . lost."

The yellowed parchment of the manuscript was imprinted with letters barely readable: *Twelve Prophecies. Abigail of Sychar.*

Shimon remarked, "I can read enough that I'm certain this is what you were looking for. The interior pages are quite clear. The ink. Readable."

Eben's heart raced. "Like black fire on white fire. She was there in the beginning. From the first summer. Peniel remembered her writing the account. And so here it is."

"Can you translate the language, Eben?" Shimon sipped his tea and leaned forward as Eben drew back the title page.

Scanning the text, Eben nodded. "Yes. Very clear. Your father would have reveled in this. She was . . . very beautiful. Painters don't do her justice. Always in scarlet. But she wore greens and golds, as I recall . . . well, here it is. Listen. . . ."

From: Peniel of Jerusalem
To: Romanus Melodus
Constantinople, A.D. 551

Our Dear Brother Romanus Melodus,

Word of your songs and glorious hymns of praise has reached us even here in Rome in these days of great conflict and danger to the church of our Lord and Savior Jesus, the Christ.

We are brothers through the line of Abraham, Isaac, and Jacob. It is reported that you were also born a Jew. I myself am a Jew, born sightless in Jerusalem in the years our Savior walked among us. The story of how Jesus touched me, and I was healed, is recorded in the Gospels. You, yourself, have composed a kontakion recounting this true event that is sung by many among us. The beauty of your voice and the songs you have composed for worship have spread throughout the land. I have heard many true stories you have put to melody so the Gospel may be spread abroad to all inhabitants of the world through music.

In your letter to me you state:

> Truth is everything in the kontakia. The details are often so scant. Day by day and night after night the Holy Spirit brings to my mind the story of Abigail Photini of Sychar and her daughter, Deborah. You knew them, so perhaps can shed light on their story for me as I compose a hymn about her thirst for righteousness and her meeting at Jacob's Well with our Lord.

My brother, in reply to your questions, I will do my utmost to answer you. Abigail Photini, the Samaritan woman of Sychar, was perhaps among the first apostles. She was a sinner and a

— 1 —

singer of songs long before I ever knew her. She was a woman of renowned beauty. A courtesan, whose reputation was tarnished at an early age.

I first laid eyes on Abigail Photini as the disciples journeyed from Galilee to Jerusalem two years before that final Passover in Jerusalem. She sang sweetly along the dusty road toward His death. Words of victory. The song of prophecy sung by the Hebrew judge Deborah:

> Tell of it, you who ride on white donkeys . . .
> and you who walk by the way!
> To the sound of musicians at the watering places,
> there they repeat the righteous triumphs of the Lord.[1]

We passed through Samaria. I was walking beside my friend James when I heard her voice . . . the voice of an angel . . . behind us. I asked, "Who is she? One of us?"

He answered, "A Samaritan woman. There is cause for the Pharisees to slander the Lord because he allows her to sup at our table with the others. I wish she would turn back. Before your time, Jesus showed kindness to her when there was little kindness in her life. She only gave him a little water to drink. He quenched her soul's thirst with truth and forgiveness. She left her water jar behind as we left our nets and boats at the shore of Galilee. She ran joyfully singing into her town to tell her thirsty tormentors that Living Water had come to Jacob's Well."

Abigail proclaimed the coming of Messiah to those who persecuted her. It was plain to me that the twelve apostles did not approve of her. This, I believe, was not so much because of her many iniquities, but more because she was a Samaritan.

They did not understand the twelve prophecies about Messiah that were fulfilled in that meeting. They could not see then that the Word of the Lord declared what was, what is, and what will be, on that day by the well. God's love for all who thirst was proclaimed by that ordinary meeting.

Read on, dear friend. And may her song fill your heart with joy.

Peniel of Jerusalem
Once I was blind. Now I see.

FIRST PROPHECY

Invitation to the Lord's Salvation

"Is anyone thirsty?
   Come and drink—
   even if you have no money!
Come, take your choice of wine or milk—
   it's all free!
Why spend your money on food that does not
   give you strength?
   Why pay for food that does you no good?
Listen to Me, and you will eat what is good.
   You will enjoy the finest food.

"Come to Me with your ears wide open.
   Listen, and you will find life.
I will make an everlasting covenant with you.
   I will give you all the unfailing love I promised
      to David.
See how I used him to display My power among
   the peoples.
   I made him a leader among the nations.
You also will command nations you do not know,
   and peoples unknown to you will come running
      to obey,

because I, the LORD your God,
  the Holy One of Israel, have made you
    glorious."

Seek the LORD while you can find Him.
  Call on Him now while He is near.
Let the wicked change their ways
  and banish the very thought of doing wrong.
Let them turn to the LORD that He may have mercy
  on them.
  Yes, turn to our God, for He will forgive generously.

ISAIAH 55:1-7 NLT

CHAPTER 1

bigail made yet another circuit of her windowless prison. One slender hand traced the rough outline of the stone wall. Her fingertips were torn and bloodied. The other palm rested lightly on her distended, pregnant belly. She had been walking continuously, ever since being confined here the night before. There was no place to lie down, but her fearful thoughts would never have permitted sleep anyway.

The punishment for adultery was death . . . death by stoning.

Abigail was so far advanced with this, her first pregnancy, that the child was almost ready to live outside her womb. With stabs of pain, Abigail sensed what it would be like when fist-sized rocks struck her. Instinctively she wove her hands together in front of her stomach.

Of course, her baby would die as well.

Even if it lived, would anyone care for it?

Abigail tried to walk carefully. The animal pen in which she was confined, beneath Rabbi Tabor's house, was shin deep in dried manure. Any uncautious step further added to the cloud of acrid dust already filling the stagnant air. It was scarcely possible to breathe. To raise up fully was to snag her hair in the beams of the low ceiling.

There was no actual prison in Sychar. Minor infractions, like public drunkenness, were punished with floggings in the town square. After such a beating, the prisoner was released.

A greater threat than whipping was betrayal to the Roman authorities in Sebaste. The local centurion's preference was for crucifixion, so only murderers and habitual thieves were ever delivered there.

But outside the town, between Sychar and Jacob's Well, was the sunken stone ring of a winepress. Abigail had no doubt it was there she would be stoned. Once, as a young girl, she had witnessed such a punishment. She was not supposed to be present but, being a headstrong child, had hidden in the vineyard atop the hill to watch.

The sights and sounds sickened her dreams ever after. They forced themselves on her again now: the prisoner's screams of protest, his upraised hands pleading for mercy, the scarlet gashes in his scalp and face as his life poured out. . . .

Abigail could not close her eyes and so escape the vision, but neither did opening them drive it away. In the gloom of her cell it hovered ever before her, as if drawn on the gritty fog that hung in the air.

"Oh, baby, baby," she crooned, rubbing her stomach in desperate, circular motions, "will you fly away with me to *olam haba*? If not, who will take care of you? Who will love you if I am gone? Will he? Will he claim you? But no, then he would die as well. Dear one. Sweet one! I'm so sorry . . . so very sorry!"

When she reached the stout, barred oak panel that marked the only exit from her imprisonment, she paused. Was that a tiny fragment of light around the edges? Where there had been only darkness before, was there now a glimpse of dawn?

Abigail shuddered. The coming of the sun might bring light but would also bring death. No escape from imagined horrors with this sunrise. Fearful night was poised to become terrifying day.

She began another stumbling circle of grief, fear, and shame. The baby within her, responding to the violent emotional chafing, kicked vigorously. Always before, Abigail had replied to her child's inquiries by crooning a lullaby, a love song, or a hymn of heroic deeds, like Miriam's or Deborah's.

But not now. No words would come; no tune could pass her teeth, chattering with apprehension and not cold.

By the time three more circuits of the cell had been completed, the truth of dawn's birth was undeniable. Gray light penetrated the recesses of the stable. A swath of wall, chest high, had been completely scoured of dirt by Abigail's questing fingers. In place of the dust were streaks of blood. The same bloody fingerprints also lovingly marked the shelf of homespun fabric above her baby.

Footsteps approached. Voices—hostile, self-righteous voices—neared.

Unconsciously, Abigail withdrew from the door, shrinking back to the other side of the chamber as if to hide herself. Was this room really so small? In the darkness it had seemed vast enough to get lost in. Now it seemed too small to hide an orphan lamb.

Could she flee? What if she burst out and ran toward Mount Gerazim? Could Abigail lose herself in the hills of Samaria? Perhaps she could escape to Galilee?

Perhaps her lover had a rescue planned. Maybe even now he was waiting to jump between her and her jailers, to free her and escape with her!

The outside bolt securing the door jerked backward with a snap that startled her. She clasped her arms across her belly and hunched her shoulders into the rocks.

The gate flew open, allowing light to stab her eyes.

"Come out!" Rabbi Tabor's voice demanded.

Abigail emerged into the day. Three men stood before her—a solid rank of accusers. To the left was the town's richest man, Jerash the Merchant. He was tall and lean, with long arms and long legs that enabled him to look down his equally long nose, which he did continuously.

To the right was Abel the Cloth Dyer. He was younger than the other two. His hands and arms were permanently stained dark brown from his work, his arms and shoulders brawny from stirring the vats. His eyes, narrowed to slits, regarded Abigail with a truly evil mixture of spite and scorn.

But Abigail read the most hatred and loathing on the face of Rabbi Tabor, in the center of the trio of judges. His broad face was framed by a dirty white beard below and a swath of forehead above that continued into a balding dome. The fringe of hair around his skull stood out as if every bit of the rabbi vibrated with hostility and condemnation.

"Woman," the rabbi intoned, "you have had all night to reflect. Now we repeat our demand: Name the one who shares your guilt."

Abigail, chin downward, shook her head.

"If you are obstinate," Jerash said in his reedy voice, "we will have no mercy."

What mercy had they shown her before this? What hope had she of mercy now? These three men had no mercy in them to offer.

Again, without speaking, she refused to give in to their demands.

"Then you leave us no choice," Abel said.

Roughly they tied her hands together, then dropped a loop of cord about her neck.

She was to be led to slaughter like an animal!

The lane from the rabbi's house led down a slope toward the village. At the bottom of the small hill was the main road through town. To the left was the market square.

To the right lay the outskirts of town, the road to Shiloh, and the Jordan River.

And the winepress . . . the place of stoning.

Neighbors already lined the street. Old men looked troubled at the sight of her; old women, sad.

Young men glanced away furtively or stared openly.

Married women glared at her. Each of their glances was full of venom, like the strike of an adder.

Abigail kept her eyes down. Surely her lover would step forward soon. She had seen him on the edge of the crowd.

At the bottom of the hill the procession of shame halted. The judges conferred among themselves. An argument was in progress, though Abigail could not follow the cause of it.

Only once did Abigail venture to peer up, trying to catch the eye of one man among the onlookers—just one.

He no longer stood where she had seen him. He had disappeared. Was he readying the rescue even now?

"Woman," the rabbi said sternly, "once more we order that you reveal the father of your child. Otherwise we will have no choice but to beat it out of you."

Abigail's repeated refusal to cooperate caused a delay in her thoughts. Beat? They were going to beat her, but not kill her?

The rope around her throat tightened as Jerash tugged on it, pulling her toward the market square . . . and away from death by stoning.

The town square of Sychar was its marketplace. On market days purveyors of dried fish from Joppa or dates from Jericho competed for customers with dealers in honey, or cheese, or sacks of lentils, or pomegranates brought all the way from Syria.

But not today.

Though the square was ringed many ranks deep with spectators, the only merchandise on offer was misery; the only hunger to be satisfied was vengeance.

On every side Abigail saw hatred. The menfolk might behold and turn away, but the women's eyes challenged her. There was no pity there, no sympathy.

There must be one on whose face concern glowed. After all, there was one in the crowd who truly did share her guilt. Where was he? Why did he not intervene?

The tall post rooted in the center of the square bore a pair of iron rings near its top. Abigail was marched to the very focus of the plaza and forced to stand beside the tree of punishment.

"This woman," Rabbi Tabor bellowed, "stands visibly guilty of adultery. Her lawful husband, Zakane of this city, is an honorable, upright man."

Honorable, yes. Zakane had taken in Abigail when no one else would, becoming the last of her five husbands.

It seemed ages, but had only been a handful of years, since Abigail was a cheerful young woman, beautiful in face and form, with many suitors. When her first husband was killed in the rock quarry in an accident, there had been no shortage of those vying for the widow's hand.

Even after husband number two died of a fever their first winter together, no blame attached to the sorrowing young woman.

But when Abigail's third husband was drowned at sea, all the pent-up superstition and need to fix blame crashed in on her. All those men had been good men, too. All had relatives to mourn them—parents, brothers, cousins, uncles in some part of Samaria. Either Abigail was a sorceress or she brought a curse with her to the marriage bed.

When Reen married her, becoming husband number four, Abigail did not know if it was during one of his sober moments or in his usual drunken state. Within a month, the distinction did not matter. He was never sober, and he beat her every night.

Then he had divorced her and left. It was the only kind thing Reen had ever done for her.

"Zakane ben Adam," the rabbi bawled, "has been away for more than a year. The evidence of this woman's sin is clearly written. She cannot deny it. We, his neighbors, are duty bound to uphold his honor and the integrity of our city."

Unspoken in the midst of this recital of Zakane's honorable qualities was the fact that he was forty-five years her elder . . . and incapable of giving her a child.

"Once more we adjure you: Name your accomplice in this crime."

If she named him, they would both be killed. If she kept silent, she would be beaten, but there would still be a chance to run away together. Abigail's resolve to protect her lover was stronger than ever. She shook her head.

At a gesture from the rabbi Abigail was jerked about so her nose pressed against the post. Her hands were untied, only to be yanked above her head and fastened there so she was forced to stand on her toes.

The baby! She must at all costs protect the child. Let them cut her back to shreds; she would keep her baby safe.

Jerash and Abel walked past her, deliberately showing her the birch canes with which she would be flogged. As they held them in front of her, the rabbi said, "Even now we are prepared to show mercy. Name him! Name the man!"

Abigail lowered her head and closed her eyes.

Her collar was yanked backwards. A knife blade hissed, splitting her robe and exposing her back from neck to waist.

The first rod whistled through the air, landing across Abigail's shoulders. She screamed with the pain of it. It burned like a hot iron. She squirmed aside, remembering only at the last second that she must not expose the baby to a blow coming from the other direction.

The second strike landed, splitting the skin over her backbone with the ferocity of the swipe.

"What is his name?" the rabbi demanded.

The third blow drew a scream from Abigail with the agony that started in her toes and emerged from the top of her head.

"Name him!"

The fourth stripe drove the cries completely away, to be replaced with a panting, whimpering attempt to merely get another breath.

Jerash and Abel were vying to see who could strike harder or make the edge cut deeper. In some pain-dulled part of her mind, Abigail heard the backstroke of the cane before the fifth slash of the rod.

"Stop this instant!" a commanding voice bellowed.

The expected blow landed, but it had no force behind it.

"I said, stop! And I'll crucify any man who disobeys. Cut that woman down."

When the knife hacked through Abigail's bonds, no one tried to catch her as she fell.

"Centurion Romulus," Rabbi Tabor said, "this is a religious matter. We have authority—"

"I don't care if your religion demands that you cut your own throat," the centurion responded angrily. "You'll not flog a pregnant woman."

"She is a transgressor of our law," the rabbi argued. "An adulteress."

"And she was not guilty of this crime alone. Where is the other party?"

"That's what we are going to determine."

"Not this way," the Roman officer ordered. "Let her go!"

An elderly man, limping heavily on a crutch, arrived on the edge of Sychar's market square just after the centurion delivered his command to stop the beating. Shorter in stature than most of the other onlookers, the newcomer approached the scene unable to determine the cause of the gathering.

"Pardon me, sir," he said in a hoarse voice, plucking at a witness's elbow. "But what is happening here?"

"Nothing, as it turns out," growled the other over his shoulder. Lowering his voice, he explained, "Lousy, interfering Romans."

"Interfering with what?"

The wife of the man leaned toward her husband and spoke without turning. "Giving a harlot her due, that's what. A proper flogging—that's what was called for. And we'd have had the name of the father of her whelp, were it not for the Roman."

"So she betrayed her husband?"

"Out to here," responded the woman with a snort and a pat of her own ample waist. "And him such a fine, old gentleman too."

"How was he not aware of the infidelity? Blind?"

"Gone on a journey and her cavorting in the master's bed. Poor, old Zakane."

"Who?" the late arrival demanded with an indignant croak.

"Zakane," the man repeated, pivoting on his heel. "Zakane," the man said again, the light of recognition altering his speech. "Look, Wife: Zakane has returned from his travels."

The stoop-shouldered, rail-thin man pushed his way through the crowd, which parted for him as if the murmurs of his name were a magic spell. By the time he stood in the forefront of the crowd, they had backed up, making Zakane a player in the drama instead of an onlooker.

The Roman centurion had departed.

Hand over hand, using the whipping post for support, Abigail struggled to her feet. No one helped her.

When she reached an approximation of upright, Abigail crossed one arm protectively over the baby. With the other she held up the shredded remnants of her robe.

A hawk wheeled high overhead, soaring on the winds and screaming defiance.

A dust devil swirled down Sychar's main street.

Abigail and Zakane confronted each other.

"Husband," Abigail said in a weak, quavering voice. "I—"

"Silence," Zakane returned. Two spots of high color glowed over his cheekbones, while the rest of his face was deathly pale. "Silence," he said again, stalking in a circle. He stabbed the ground with his cane like a stilted wading bird, seeking prey to strike.

"Please." Abigail staggered, then leaned heavily on the post.

Rabbi Tabor moved to Zakane's side at once. "Honored Zakane, let me help you." Dropping their rods in the dirt, Jerash and Abel joined them. "Let us assist you to your home."

Zakane shook his head violently, his entire upper body swaying with emotion. "Not until I do something here. Help me," he demanded. "Support me."

Aided by the trio of Abigail's judges, Zakane released his crutch and bent to unlace his sandal.

In the entire crowd no one moved. All were transfixed by what they were witnessing.

Shoe in hand, Zakane slapped the ground violently. "I divorce thee," he said, striking. His voice rising in both inflection and volume, he repeated, "I divorce thee! I divorce thee! I utterly cast thee out!"

His faltering energy completely spent by his outburst, Zakane sagged into the arms of his friends.

"Come, sir," the rabbi said. "Let us help you home now. The rest of you, disperse. Leave her. She is dead . . . the same as dead."

In a daze, Abigail stood at the center of the square as the crowd dispersed. Some townspeople departed with downcast faces. Others, especially a solid phalanx of married women, displayed satisfaction and scorn.

"But not nearly enough beating," she heard one of them say.

"No matter what that Roman says, this isn't over yet," another added.

Then Abigail was alone. Where was she to turn for help? Where could she go?

It was from her own home—Zakane's home—that she had been dragged by the judges.

The rabbi was her enemy. Even those in the village who had been friendly in the past were cowed by the massive display of hatred against her. At this moment she could think of no single ally in Sychar. No one had spoken up for her, defended her, pleaded mercy on her behalf.

It was certain none of the families of her previous husbands would help. This humiliation had confirmed their worst suspicions: Abigail was bad luck. She was accursed and proven spiritually responsible for the deaths of their loved ones.

There was only one who might . . . who should . . . who must . . . feel pity for her. But Abigail could not go to him, not yet. If he were found out now, it would ruin everything.

She believed he would come to her as soon as he was able. Abigail fixed her hope on that belief, clung to it as desperately as she grasped the post of her shame and punishment.

But for now, where was she to go? Even last night's imprisonment in the barn had offered shelter of a sort. Where could she turn? So many emotions trampled her thoughts: terror, despair, relief, anguish. She could not think clearly.

The baby thumped impatiently in her womb. She felt something hard and sharp form a crease across her stomach. An elbow, perhaps? A knee?

Every movement was agony. Bits of torn fabric sticking to the welts felt like shards of glass digging into her skin. When she moved the least bit, the wounds broke open and fresh blood trickled down her skin.

Abigail's head swam. She must find someplace soon.

All she knew was Zakane's house. All her belongings were there. Her clothing. Food, warmth, warm water.

Zakane had always been kind to her—treated her with respect. Perhaps this last vision of him was delirium brought on by the pain. She must go there . . . throw herself on his mercy.

Yard by painful yard, Abigail dragged herself out of Sychar and up the road toward the house that had been her home. On the way doors slammed in her face at her approach. A chamber pot was emptied in front of her path by a hard-faced matron. A stone whizzed past her ear, accompanied by the sound of laughter.

By the time Abigail reached Jacob's Well, she knew she could go no farther. Her back stiffened; her feet stumbled. Each step gave birth to a groan through clenched teeth.

The well, located on the main trading route, was home to beggars. A few homeless souls huddled beside the stone wall flanking the water supply. The well drew travelers, and such pilgrims gave alms.

Suspicious faces peered out of palm-frond shelters and lean-tos formed of broken roof slates and discarded timber. The outcasts of Sychar built their meager existence from the cast-off bits of others.

"Go away, then," one legless indigent demanded as Abigail approached.

She swayed where she stood and would have fallen had she not sat down abruptly on the lip of the well.

A blind woman, eyes wrapped in a band of black cloth, emerged from a hut. "Who are we to drive anyone off?" she demanded.

"You don't know who this is, Leah," the cripple retorted. "It's the harlot of Sychar. Her as was beat and turned out and divorced all today. She's a vile sinner—brought it all on herself."

If she leaned backward at all, Abigail would plunge into the well. Would that not be an answer?

The blind woman approached, feeling her way along the ledge. When her questing touch reached Abigail, both women flinched.

"I won't hurt you," Leah said.

"I don't want to cause trouble," Abigail said. "It's not for me. It's for my baby."

Leah gently touched the swollen belly and was rewarded with a vigorous kick. "Come with me, sweet," she offered. "Water to wash your wounds and a bit of oil. Had a blessing today. Even have some bread to share. Come on, then. Don't be afraid of Leah. I won't hurt you."

SECOND PROPHECY

Water from the Rock

At the LORD's command, the whole community of Israel left the wilderness of Sin and moved from place to place. Eventually they camped at Rephidim, but there was no water there for the people to drink. So once more the people complained against Moses. "Give us water to drink!" they demanded.

"Quiet!" Moses replied. "Why are you complaining against me? And why are you testing the LORD?"

But tormented by thirst, they continued to argue with Moses. "Why did you bring us out of Egypt? Are you trying to kill us, our children, and our livestock with thirst?"

Then Moses cried out to the LORD, "What should I do with these people? They are ready to stone me!"

The LORD said to Moses, "Walk out in front of the people. Take your staff, the one you used when you struck the water of the Nile, and call some of the elders of Israel to join you. I will stand before you on the rock at Mount Sinai. Strike the rock, and water will come gushing out. Then the people will be able to drink." So Moses struck the rock as he was told, and water gushed out as the elders looked on.

Moses named the place Massah (which means "test") and Meribah (which means "arguing") because the people of Israel argued with Moses and tested the LORD by saying, "Is the LORD here with us or not?"

EXODUS 17:1-7 NLT

CHAPTER 2

When Abigail awoke the next day, she did not know where she was or what time it was. Her eyes were glued shut with sleep, but the sunlight glowing through her eyelids made it feel late. Also the bedchamber seemed to press close around her. There was a powerful, unpleasant aroma, as if the linen had not been aired in a year . . . or ten.

It was not until Abigail rolled to her back from where she lay curled on her side that the truth rushed in. She cried out with the pain of her wounds. The skin of her back felt brittle, as if even a tiny movement would tear her flesh anew, and she whimpered.

From outside the hut she heard a voice say, "She's awake. Better get rid of her soon, Leah. Already travelers abroad."

"We've done nothing to deserve what we are," another whined. "But she made her own bed of sorrows. She isn't one of us."

Prying open her lids, Abigail stared into the palm-frond ceiling of Leah's hovel and remembered all that had occurred. Was it only yesterday?

A jug of water and a crust of rock-hard barley loaf were beside the pallet. Abigail swallowed the water in gulps, grateful for the cooling of her sob-scarred throat. She used the last palmful of liquid to wash her face. She did not feel like eating but thrust the bread into a fold of her robe.

Her robe was whole again. Someone—Leah?—had repaired it.

"Abigail," Leah called from outside the hut, "you are awake?" There was a note of sorrow, or perhaps regret, in the blind woman's tone.

"Yes, yes. Coming," Abigail returned, crawling out into the sunshine.

Leah was sitting on a stone. She was younger than Abigail had thought—no more than middle-aged.

"Thank you for the food and the water and the shelter. And someone has mended my robe . . . you?"

Leah nodded. "Before I lost my—" she passed her hand before her face—"I had already learned to sew. Eyes are not needed for a straight seam, so long as the hands are true."

"And the heart, I think," Abigail added. "You doctored my wounds too, but I don't exactly recall."

"Olive oil," Leah acknowledged. "But sleep and the mercy of HaShem are due more credit than I. But, Abigail . . ." There was a long, painful pause. "My friends here, of the well, do not think . . . you may not . . ."

Some argument from the night before reappeared in Abigail's thoughts and sang in concert with the comments overheard this morning. Even beggars, it seemed, did not want her around. "I understand," she said. "I must go."

"But where?" Leah asked. "What door is open to you now?"

The baby greeted the morning with a kicking salute, and in that expression of joy the full memory of Abigail's dream returned. "I . . . I had a vision. Mother Rebekah spoke to me."

"What did she say?"

"She said I would meet a man of mercy who would . . . pay to redeem me."

Overhearing this conversation, the legless beggar offered a snorting laugh. On a fragment of carpet he scooted his way toward the highway, rolling his begging bowl in front of him.

Excitement rising, Abigail said, "Perhaps she meant my husband! He is a good man and a kind one. Perhaps he will be merciful."

When Abigail reached Zakane's villa, no one seemed to be around. Timidly, Abigail knocked on the door. "Husband," she called, "Zakane, please hear me. Please listen to me."

The latch popped. The hope that fluttered in Abigail's heart was accompanied by a rapid ticking within her womb. Zakane would answer! All was not lost.

The door opened a scant two inches—only enough for Abigail to recognize one of the cook's pale green eyes.

"Please," Abigail said.

"The master says, 'Go away.'" The green eye blinked.

"Please," Abigail repeated. "Ask him to let me sleep in the barn. In the shed. In the cellar. Let me be as a slave. Only please . . . some shelter for the baby's sake."

"Go away," the cook hissed loudly. Then in a much lower tone: "The master says to show you no kindness. He'll turn us out, else."

The absolute absence of pity wrung a desperate plea from Abigail. "But where am I to go? Where?"

"Go with others of your kind, the master says. Go to Shechem and live with the other harlots. Go live with the beggars by Jacob's Well. But go away and leave us alone."

The door slammed decisively in Abigail's face. Dejected and frustrated, she swayed and put her hand on the wall to steady herself. What to do now? Where to go?

A deliberate, thudding rhythm finally broke through her fog of despair.

The cook's son, age six, was throwing stones at a knot on an olive tree's trunk. "Jeroboam," Abigail called, "will you carry a message to my husband for me?"

Jeroboam shook his head with certainty.

"You won't do a favor for me?" Abigail said, a catch in her throat.

"You're dead, Master says," the boy returned. "Said we're to have nothin' to do with you. Told me if I wanted I could shy these stones at you, same as you was a dog."

"Jeroboam, please look at me," Abigail said. "Don't you remember how we played together? how I read to you? Don't you?"

More slowly, Jeroboam moved his head side to side in denial. "Don't matter. You're dead. Go away. You can't be here no more. You're evil, and you bring a curse wherever you go."

Abigail's vision clouded with tears.

Abigail stumbled away from Zakane's house. Her steps led nowhere. If her path didn't slope downward, she would have been completely aimless.

Where was she to go? What was she to do? If even the beggars cast her out, how would she live?

Abigail drew the bread from her robe and gnawed on it. It tasted of dirt and chewed like a mouthful of gravel, but she forced herself to swallow for the sake of the baby.

It was not enough. She must have more food, and she must have shelter.

Through no conscious plan she wandered toward the village. If she received but a single sympathetic glance, she would beg without shame. Perhaps if she could only get a handful of coins, she could leave Sychar and find lodging in Shechem.

By now Sychar was wide awake. There were travelers on the road: merchants, families going to visit relatives, soldiers tramping, and the women of Sychar on their morning journey to draw water from the well. It was their practice to make a trip to the well before the heat of midday. There was another source of water on the opposite side of the village, nearer to the market square, but Jacob's Well had the reputation of having sweeter, cooler liquid.

The women of Sychar traveled in a pack, so their journey to the well was as much entertainment as chore. Now they were returning.

Abigail became aware of their approach just in time. Ducking around the corner of a building, she hid in the shadow of a pile of garbage and prayed they would pass without noticing her.

Today's subject of conversation was Abigail.

"Now see what her tarted-up ways have gotten her," one said. "Always acting so friendly around the men. My Manasseh says women like her are the pit of destruction."

A stray dog approached the heap of refuse. He stopped at the sight of Abigail. Owned by no one and often chased with stones, he slunk back out of sight.

"Your Manasseh," a friend returned, "used to follow her around your fabric shop with his tongue hanging out." This sally brought a burst of laughter from the group. "These water jugs are heavy," the joker added. "Let's rest here a bit."

Abigail's eyes widened. Why did they have to choose this spot to stop? How soon would they leave? She remained absolutely still, afraid any movement would give her away.

"Well," replied the wife of the cloth merchant, "don't we all recall how your Gad went out of his way to help her carry a jug of olive oil all the way to her house? I ask you, does he even offer such a thing to any of the rest of us?"

"Just what are you saying?"

"I'm saying we're well rid of her. She was a wicked, heathen sorceress, if you ask me. Used her wiles to draw men to her . . . all men! Look what happened to all her husbands! Bewitched 'em all . . . only she got caught but good this time!"

Abigail stiffened at the accusations. Was she to be blamed for being attractive or friendly? Sadly, she rested her hands on her belly. Now she really felt guilty. How could she deny any of their charges, however false or stupid?

The dog's hunger drove him forward. On his belly he crawled toward a heap of decaying chicken guts.

"Whose whelp do you think it is, really?"

This question set off a round of speculation. Some favored the tanner, known to have been to the harlots in Shechem, but this suggestion only carried weight because his wife was not in today's group.

"Since she's a witch," the cloth merchant's wife said, "it could be any of our menfolk, couldn't it?"

Every one of the matrons in the discussion vehemently denied her husband's involvement. Every denial had an edge of shrillness, as if not every wife was completely convinced of her man's innocence.

Abigail could stand this no longer. She took a step backward.

"Mark my words," the oil merchant's wife said, "the guilty party will be found out. Then they'll both be stoned! But it's up to us to do the sniffing around. Our men are too soft on her. Everyone gets addled when she's about."

Abigail took another step back, then turned to flee.

She and the dog confronted each other. He growled and barked loudly.

"What's that about?" one of Sychar's women demanded.

The dog snapped and snarled, blocking Abigail's retreat.

The pack of women rounded the corner.

"Look here!"

"It's her!"

"Spying on us!"

"Casting a spell, more like! Stone her."

The dog was less frightening than the wives. When Abigail fled toward him, the dog bolted out of the way.

"Harlot!"

"Witch!"

"Get out of here, and don't come back!"

A shard of pottery struck Abigail in the back. A handful of chicken guts landed in her hair. A gob of mud flew past her. Then she was out of range and running as fast as her weakness and awkward shape would permit.

Abigail wandered over the hills around Sychar until almost dusk. Afraid of encountering anyone, she stayed away from roads and trails. She hid in clumps of brush whenever even a single worker drew near. For food she gleaned a few handfuls of barley, left over after the fields were harvested. She shelled out the grain by hand to fill the gnawing ache in her stomach.

If only she were brave enough to go to the father of her child and ask for his help. It was the abiding hope that he cared for her, that he would keep his promises to her, that sustained her through the long, long day.

But fear of exposing him before he was prepared to care for her kept her from going to him for the aid she so desperately needed.

With nowhere else to turn, and finding herself near Jacob's Well once again, she decided to appeal to Leah the Blind Woman. Cautiously she drew near the famous landmark's plaza, approaching by a gully running down from the hills. She waited and watched to be certain that the well was deserted.

Even when assured that it was, she hesitated. Could the ravening mob of Sychar somehow know her whereabouts? Could they be waiting for her to emerge from hiding to pounce?

Her back and legs ached horribly. She needed rest, she needed water, and she needed food. Her need drove her forward.

"Leah," she called softly as she approached the blind woman's hut. "Leah, it's Abigail."

"I know, dear," Leah replied. "I heard you back in the ravine. Come here."

Almost weeping at the sound of one friendly voice, Abigail met Leah, who was carrying a torn woolen blanket, a bit of heavy sailcloth, a jug of water, and an entire loaf of barley bread.

"I don't want to cause trouble," Abigail began.

"Nonsense," Leah said. "The rest of the beggars of Jacob's Well agree not to bother you if you stay away when travelers are near. Besides, I heard the wives of Sychar when they came to draw water today."

Abigail felt herself color up to the eyes.

"I made up my mind right then," Leah continued. "Those harpies! Anyway, it's not much, but you can use this." She passed Abigail the fragments of fabric and meager supplies. "You remember the boulders back in the gully? Where two of them lean close together, you can cover the top with the heavy cloth and plug the entry with brush. There's a bit of clean straw for a bed. Mostly clean, anyway. The blanket is for you as well. I'm sorry it isn't more."

Now the tears did stream down Abigail's face. "No, no! You've helped so much. Thank you! Thank you!" She threw her arms around Leah in a mighty embrace.

Leah returned the hug, then carefully patted Abigail's stomach. "We must take care of the little one, eh? Now go on; get yourself settled before dark."

It was late. On the walls above the city gate, the watchman called the hour.

All was well within the town. In the marketplace, commerce and cruelty rested. The hawking of fruit peddlers and the envious gossip of homely women was silent, smug, and satisfied. Hatred for Abigail had worn them out. The wives of Sychar slept deeply beside husbands who did not reach for them.

The flesh and blood of Sychar's menfolk, no longer disguised in the daylight cloak of self-righteousness, was consumed with flames of secret desire. Inner lightning flashed in drowsy male brains, revealing the beautiful image of Abigail. Rabbis, judges, and unhappy husbands murmured in their sleep, dreaming they were kissing the soft lips of the woman they had lately cursed and banished.

Lust for Abigail's beauty had been forged into a determination to destroy what they could not possess.

Who was the lucky man among them all who had seduced Abigail's heart and lived out the fantasies of every man in Sychar?

Who was the father of Abigail's child?

Who was she protecting by her silence?

How could they discover him and destroy his life, as they had destroyed hers?

What cruelty would make her betray the man she loved?

Tomorrow morning works of envy, lust, and hypocrisy would be resumed. For now truth crept in quietly to reveal the secrets of each heart.

The sentry cried that all was well within the walls of the city.

Outside the gates, near Jacob's Well, Abigail lay on the bed of straw beneath the lean-to she had made. Through a gap in the blanket she watched the stars revolve above the earth. The motion made her dizzy. Did the heavens move? Or was it earth? Or was it Abigail herself who slid slowly toward an abyss and eternal death?

As if hearing the music of creation's slow dance, the baby tapped a rhythm within her womb. The signal was a reminder: Abigail carried life in her, not death; mercy, not judgment. She placed her warm hand over the infant who shared her heartbeat. Closing her eyes stopped the cold universe's spinning. Abigail regained her focus. Only the movement in her womb was real. Like the molten earth, the baby's existence had been forged as fire rushed through Abigail's veins. The heat of passion had cooled and become something greater when the child had first signaled its existence to her.

A nightingale sang to Abigail from the sage growing near Jacob's Well. *Do you see me, God? Do you see us here? We are waiting for him to come.* Abigail looked at the giant gates of the city. Would her lover come to her? Would he leave everything behind and come to her in the night to steal her away? They could go somewhere far from this place. They could live and have their child and start all over again where no one knew.

Minutes swept by. Hours passed. The gate did not open. Her lover did not come for her.

At least I am alive. We are both alive. Abigail rubbed the mound of her belly and whispered, "I love you!" She put in order the events of the last weeks. "HaShem has spared us somehow. Oh, baby. Baby! I am here. Mama is here. We are alive, you and I!"

The coarse laughter of the women of Sychar rang in the morning air as they again carried their water jars to Jacob's Well. Abigail, the object of their amusement, remained hidden in the shelter of the boulders. She recognized the voices of her tormentors.

"This has been a long time coming."

"I used to see her batting her eyes at the cantor."

"And remember that time when she was playing the role of Esther in the megillah? singing Esther's song to the children?"

"Yes, at Purim! I saw her too. She was wearing that green cloak. The color of emeralds. Oh, wasn't she the pretty thing. And didn't she know every eye was on her!"

"Flaunting herself in front of all the men!"

"Well, that's over. She wouldn't dare show herself again."

As if suddenly sensing her presence, the gaggle of gossips paused and lowered their voices.

"Where is she?"

"Licking her wounds."

"She didn't look so pretty when we got through with her."

"Or smell so nice either."

"If it hadn't been for that Roman. What's his name?"

"Romulus."

"Pagan. He calls himself a son of Mars."

"She's bewitched him too."

"She . . . wouldn't dare show her face. Harlot."

"Suppose she's run away?"

"Couldn't get far in her condition."

" . . . baby due any day . . ."

"Poor baby. You've got to pity the child."

" . . . didn't ask to be born . . ."

"Such creatures are better off dead, if you ask me."

"Zakane ben Adam. Such a husband. Too old to bother her in bed."

" . . . and rich besides. She had a fine life if she'd kept to herself."

"What I wouldn't give for a husband who went to sleep before I came to bed!"

"And rich besides."

"She tried to go home."

"Old Zakane threw her out without so much as a shekel."

"Poor fool."

"Never a real marriage."

"He's got poor circulation."

" . . . married Abigail for show. He needed someone pretty to keep his feet warm at night."

"All she's ever had is her looks!"

"Flaunting herself in front of all the men."

"Zakane should have bought a dog for company."

"He did . . . a female dog!"

"Too old to consummate the marriage."

"No fool like an old fool when it comes to a pretty woman. He thinks he's Abraham."

"My husband warned the old man before he married Abigail that she was accursed. Married four times. Three husbands die and the fourth beats her bloody before he leaves. Cursed, just like in the story of Tobit. There's a lurking demon there, mark my words."

Abigail heard the sound of sputtering as the women spit between their fingers to ward off evil.

But is the evil here with me . . . or out there with them?

"She's a sorceress. Killed them with passion. Casts a spell and—"

"What did the old man expect? A woman like her. Five husbands."

Abigail covered her face with her hands. How she pitied Zakane ben Adam this humiliation! The marriage could never be consummated. Even so, Zakane had been kind to her, treating her like a pampered daughter. When Zakane left for Antioch on business, she had missed the kind old man. Word of his illness arrived in Sychar three months later. Abigail had prayed for him to recover, waited for him to come home. But for over a year, he remained bedridden and unable to make the journey.

Abigail, alone in her home, had not suspected she could be in danger from one of the most respectable young men in Sychar. How could she know he was watching her every move? that he was consumed by thoughts of her?

She had awakened in the middle of the night with a man in her bed. His hand was clamped hard across her mouth, preventing her scream. She fought hard, but he overpowered her and forced her to yield to him. Fleeing in the darkness, he kept his secret well. She did not know who her assailant was. Fear and shame kept her silent.

A month later he approached her as she walked home from the marketplace. Confessing his love for her, he said she had bewitched him with her beauty. He told her the townswomen believed she had cast a spell on men in the town.

Before that, she had never spoken his name . . . never imagined . . .

Weeks passed. He slipped unsigned love letters beneath her door. He begged her to forgive him. Begged her to love him as he loved her. He said his heart was broken because he had ruined her life.

Then one night he returned, climbing the balcony as she slept. He had called her name and told her he could no longer live without her. She discovered a terrible truth. She loved him as much as he wanted her. Night after night he crept into her bedchamber. She fell ever more deeply and hopelessly in love.

When she told him she had conceived a child, his midnight visits came to an end. He promised that, one day, when Zakane was gone, they could be together. He begged her not to reveal his identity. She had given her word. And even now, she kept his secret safe.

The women at the well drew their household water while slicing up Abigail with their sharp tongues.

Suddenly the first contraction struck like a vise around her middle. Out of sight, Abigail crouched in the dust and hugged her belly. Her breath came in short gasps.

She silently prayed, *Oh, HaShem! Not here! Not now! HaShem, don't you see me? Am I too much a sinner for you to have mercy on me? Please then, not me, but for the sake of this innocent child! Help me.*

The gossips fell suddenly silent at the sound of approaching hooves.

"The Roman."

"That centurion, Romulus."

"He's coming here to the well."

"Don't speak to him."

"No doubt sniffing around after Abigail."

"Maybe he's the father."

"For shame! A Roman?"

"Don't look at him! Turn your backs."

The horse was very near. Abigail heard the creature snort as Romulus reached the well.

"Shalom," he greeted the women.

Their words were strained as they ignored him: "Come on!"

"We've got to get back."

"Don't speak to him."

The Roman asked, "I am looking for the woman you tried to kill."

"We don't know what you're talking about," snapped one of the women.

"The one who was wife to Zakane," he replied. "Have you murdered her and thrown her in a ditch? No one seems to know where she is. The rabbi says she's dead."

"The one you speak of is dead to our people. Work it out yourself."

Abigail heard their footsteps hurry away. Their indignant conversation retreated toward the city gates.

The horse snorted. Bridle and bit jingled as the Roman stepped down and began to draw water from Jacob's Well. Another labor pain gripped her. She moaned softly.

"Who's there?" asked Romulus.

"It's . . . it's the woman you . . . protected." She was breathless.

"Stand up. Come here," he commanded.

"I can't . . . stand. Sir, please, I'm . . . please. Help me!"

THIRD PROPHECY

Promises of Restoration
This is what the LORD says:

"At just the right time, I will respond to you.
On the day of salvation I will help you.
I will protect you and give you to the people
as My covenant with them.
Through you I will reestablish the land of Israel
and assign it to its own people again.
I will say to the prisoners, 'Come out in freedom,'
and to those in darkness, 'Come into the light.'
They will be My sheep, grazing in green pastures
and on hills that were previously bare.
They will neither hunger nor thirst.
The searing sun will not reach them anymore.
For the LORD in His mercy will lead them;
He will lead them beside cool waters."

ISAIAH 49:8-10 NLT

The shadow of Romulus fell across Abigail's shelter. Sun bright behind him, she could not see the details of his face. Broad shoulders, leather breastplate, and bronze helmet identified his rank as centurion.

He stooped and peered in at her. "You are the woman they were beating in the market square."

She managed to reply, "You made them stop."

"I am Romulus."

"You saved my life."

"Your baby?"

"I am in labor."

"So." He straightened and placed his hands on his hips. Turning his back on her, he surveyed the area for a long moment, neither moving nor speaking.

Would he leave her to face her agony alone? Another pain gripped her. A warm gush of water followed the contraction.

At last he spoke. "Woman, are you able to stand?"

She panted, "A minute more . . ." The pain eased. "Yes, I can stand."

He extended his hand to her. "Come on, then."

Pulling her up, he put his arm around her waist. His face was lined from the harsh sun of his postings, and a deep scar marred his cheek. He looked to be forty years or so. His neatly trimmed beard was streaked with gray.

He helped her to his sorrel horse. "Get on."

Abigail squinted doubtfully up at the creature. "I . . . can't."

Without waiting, Romulus swept her up and put her on the saddle. In an instant he mounted behind her. "What is your name?"

"Abigail," she answered, secure between his strong arms.

"Abigail. I've seen you many times in the town."

"Why do you help me? I'm an outcast."

There was an amused shrug in his reply. "And I'm a Roman. Even before this, I've seen how these women in your town hate you. They hide their bitter words behind their hands as you pass by. It is because you are beautiful."

As if on cue, the heads of her departing tormentors swiveled as Romulus rode away with her. The eyes of Sychar's women widened. Their gleeful outrage echoed against the stone blocks of the city wall.

"They will think you are the father."

"Does it matter?" he asked.

"No. I am anathema." She hesitated.

He laughed. "So how can a Roman make it worse?"

"I meant, I am an outcast and if they think I have—I mean—you are a Roman."

"Your lover is a Samaritan? Like you?"

"I made a promise."

"You protect him. If this were my child, I would never have stood by and let my woman be beaten. What kind of coward is your lover?"

"You don't know our people. What they would do to him," she said defensively.

"You love him, then? The man who fathered your child and left you to bear this judgment alone?" He snorted his derision. "I saw your ancient husband. He trembled like a leaf when he denounced you. He is a dry and brittle stick without the sap of passion. This custom of your race—marrying off beautiful young girls to the walking dead—invites disaster."

Another contraction clamped down. Romulus sensed it and reined his horse to a stop. He waited silently as she leaned forward. Her muscles tightened and then slowly released. Only when the pain had eased did he urge the horse forward in a slow walk along the road.

"Where are you taking me?" she asked.

"The caravansary. Only a mile distant from Sychar. You have time. Lean against me."

The caravansary was located at the crossroads between Sychar and Shechem. The innkeeper, called Weasel, was a greasy, unwashed man of mixed heritage. His woman, an Ethiopian, was more slave than wife. She spoke only her native dialect and had the good sense never to look Weasel directly in the eye. There was no pretense the inn was reputable. No Jew or Samaritan would stop there. There were rooms for travelers who wished only a good night's sleep, but for the soldiers of the Roman garrison, Weasel kept four prostitutes at work in separate quarters behind the stables.

The centurion's rank and authority sent the innkeeper and his wife scrambling. A spice merchant from Syria was turned out of the clean single chamber—a room with a high window on the second story, overlooking Mount Gerazim. Clean linens were placed on the feather mattress atop a rope cot. A brazier was set alight with coals.

Abigail's contractions came in regular intervals, five minutes apart. She lay down and closed her eyes as Romulus gave instructions to the innkeeper.

"She must have a midwife," Romulus demanded. The jingle of coins emphasized his commands.

"My wife knows the midwife of Sychar," Weasel replied.

"No!" Romulus barked. "Not Sychar. No one from Sychar is to come near her. Shechem."

"Yes, sir. Yes. Shechem, then. The midwife of Shechem shall be called for your woman, sir. As you wish."

Romulus did not correct the impression that Abigail was his woman. "Then let it be done. Send a messenger at once!"

The innkeeper shouted over the rail, summoning his teenage son to the stair and bawling urgent instructions. "Shechem . . . midwife . . . she'll be well paid. Hurry!"

The clatter of a horse's hooves retreated as Romulus counted out coins for Abigail's care.

"But sir, will you not be here for the birth of the child?" whined Weasel.

"I am summoned to Galilee. But know this: Rome will hold you and your woman responsible for her care and the well-being of the child."

"You are Rome, sir." Weasel's voice trembled.

"Then you understand my meaning."

"But, sir, how can I be held responsible for her health?"

"Trust me in this. When I return, she and the child will be alive and well. Thriving."

"But if they are not?" Weasel protested.

"Then you won't be either."

Abigail was seized with panic at the thought that her protector would not stay with her. "Sir!" she called to Romulus. "Please, sir, don't leave me here alone."

Romulus entered the chamber and towered over her. His craggy features softened with pity. "I can't stay."

"Thank you. Thank you. HaShem bless you. Twice you have saved my life."

"Be strong," he commanded. "For the sake of this child."

"Why . . . why have you been so kind to me? to us? Two lives are forever indebted to you. Not just one."

"Perhaps one day I will tell you. But the governor requires my presence."

"Sir, I'm afraid," she whimpered as the vise gripped her around her middle and bore down. "I . . . please!" She reached for him.

"I will come back soon." His voice was tender.

"But . . . sir!"

He turned on his heel. In the doorway he paused. "Abigail, my name is Romulus." With that he strode from the room and hurried down the steep steps to the stable yard.

Abigail wept as she heard the pounding of hooves vanish in the distance.

Something was wrong. Abigail was certain of it. Night fell and help did not arrive. Too many hours passed. The pains, regular and fierce, penetrated Abigail's back like twin knives. Where was the midwife from Shechem?

Weasel, terrified by the threat of the centurion's return, paced in the dark outside the door. His Ethiopian woman sat on a low stool beside Abigail's bed. From time to time she sponged Abigail's forehead.

"I . . . need . . . help," Abigail breathed as the agony became unbearable.

"*Algebanye'm.*" The Ethiopian shook her head in sympathy.

Abigail grasped her arm and moaned. "Where is the midwife?"

The woman's dark, downcast eyes looked everywhere but at Abigail's tortured face. "*Denneh nesh?*"

Abigail realized the woman did not understand what she was saying. But still the Ethiopian understood the female language of anguish. She continued to daub Abigail's forehead gently with a cool cloth. "*Aznallo.*"

"When will she come?" Abigail pleaded. The contraction was so fierce it took her breath away. The room swam around her. A wave of nausea swept over her.

"*Awo.*" The Ethiopian stood suddenly and went out to Weasel.

Voices, hollow and urgent, drifted up. "Where is she?"

Weasel clambered down the steps. "What took you so long?"

"Why didn't you fetch the midwife from Sychar?" an angry female voice replied.

"The centurion won't have it," Weasel declared. "No one from Sychar is to come near her. Romulus is the name. His woman. His child. If the woman dies, you're responsible."

The midwife countered, "He'll go through you with his short sword first, I'll wager, Weasel. We know this man. Oh yes. Romulus! He's known in Shechem." The midwife cursed and plodded up the steps. "How did I get myself involved delivering a child of Romulus?"

Abigail's fingers gripped the ropes of the bed. Head back, she groaned long and squeezed her eyes tightly closed. She wondered if she could beat her head against the wall and knock herself unconscious. "Help me," she whispered.

The midwife, a ruddy-faced, plump woman dressed in the garb of a Greek, entered. She placed a leather bag near the head of the bed. Lower lip protruding, she stood above Abigail. She snapped at Weasel over her shoulder, "I'll need more light than this. Lamps. Hot water. Now!"

She bathed her hands in wine and oil then knelt and pulled the blanket back. One hand on the small of Abigail's back and the other on her belly, she silently considered and calculated as the next pain struck.

"Worst . . . one . . . yet," Abigail gasped.

The midwife said quietly, "You're having a difficult labor. First baby?"

Abigail managed to nod. "Am . . . I going to . . . die?"

"Not if Weasel can help it." She rolled up her sleeves and went to work, probing Abigail with gentle fingers. "He hasn't dropped. Your baby is turned wrong. Faceup. That's why your labor is all in your back."

Abigail counted backwards as the pain began to ease. "Will I die?" she asked again. She had never known any agony like this. Death in the marketplace of Sychar would have been more merciful. At least it would have been quicker.

"Time for you to stop thinking such thoughts." The midwife washed her hands again. "Your man will kill us all if you die. Knowing Romulus, we'll all work a little harder to save you."

The Ethiopian reentered, bearing a large ceramic bowl of steaming water. The innkeeper followed with two additional lamps.

"Is she going to live?" Weasel's sallow face had a panicked expression.

"I will do my best," said the midwife. "Now get out. Leave me to my work. I'll have to turn the child."

"Turn? Turn?" He looked as if he would collapse. "Why? What happened?"

The midwife remarked coolly, "No doubt Romulus will blame you if the child strangles by the cord."

"Oh no. Oh no!"

The midwife narrowed her heavy-lidded eyes. Her lip curled in disdain. "Why didn't the Roman take her to his own house? I would have come. To deliver a baby in this place . . ." She glared fiercely at Weasel as he wrung his hands. "You! Weasel! Stay at the bottom of the steps in case I have need of something."

ighteen hours of labor. Abigail's damp curls clung to her brow. Cords on her neck stood out as the midwife from Shechem said in a low, hoarse voice, "You feel it. . . . That's it. Push!"

The urge was overwhelming. Silent in her effort, Abigail leaned into the contraction and bore down with all her strength. *Oh, HaShem,* she prayed.

The midwife's eyes gleamed as she worked with Abigail. "He's crowning. Once more. Once more!"

"HaShem, help . . . me!"

"Work with your body!" the midwife instructed.

Abigail was filled with a physical strength she had not known she possessed. The contraction built to a climax. Abigail gathered herself for the final effort and pushed with all her might. The warm rush followed as the child emerged into the midwife's confident hands.

"Come on, little one, breathe. Breathe! That's it!" A feeble bleating filled the room. "It's a girl. A beautiful baby girl!"

Abigail began to cry softly as she gasped for breath and reached for her baby. "Oh, let me see her. Let me see!"

"Hold her. That's it. Keep her warm while I finish." The cord was tied, and the midwife placed the infant on Abigail's chest. Her dark, wet hair clung to skin that flushed ruddy as lungs filled with oxygen. An angry little fist trembled at the intrusion of the world.

Abigail, tender and serene, forgot the pain of the last eighteen hours. She stroked the baby's cheek and gasped as she saw the unmistakable resemblance. There was the face of Abigail's lover! Surely the whole world would recognize and know who the father was.

The thought brought fresh memories of stones and curses. She covered the baby's head protectively with her palm.

Several minutes passed as the midwife worked to wash Abigail. Only then did she rub the baby with salt and oil and wrap her in fresh swaddling clothes as Abigail dozed.

She awakened when the woman placed the clean, fresh baby in her arms.

"The hardest work you will ever do. Well worth it for the prize," the midwife crooned. "What a beautiful little girl. . . . Sweet. Sleep now, my dear. I'll stay and watch awhile."

The baby's head fit perfectly in the palm of Abigail's hand. Wide blue eyes, still unfocused, were set in a perfect oval face. Baby turned toward Abigail's voice as she sang sweetly to her in the twilight of Shabbat.

Through the window a light gleamed upon Mount Gerazim where the Samaritan faithful worshiped the God of Abraham, Isaac, and Jacob with an evening sacrifice. The sight caused a twinge of longing in Abigail's heart. Cut off from her people and her God, Abigail was considered as vile as the four harlots who lived in the building behind the stable. But, somehow, this tiny infant made her feel loved. She stroked the downy cheek with her finger as the baby nursed.

"You will be a mighty woman of the Lord one day," Abigail sang. "Like Deborah, you will be. Fearless and true."

With that Abigail knew the child's name must be Deborah. First, she would ask the baby's father what he thought about it.

Abigail began to sing:

"When the princes in Israel take the lead,
when the people willingly offer themselves—

praise the Lord!
Consider the voice of the singers
at the watering places!
They recite the righteous acts of the Lord,
the righteous acts of His warriors in Israel!"[2]

Abigail held her baby close, kissing ear and nose and eyes. "You will be strong and sure. Not like me. No, you will be Deborah!"

Abigail had never known such fierce love. The baby had pushed everyone else into the shadows of Abigail's thoughts.

Foreign travelers who sheltered in the squalor of the caravansary did not seem to notice the lights on the hills surrounding them. As Abigail sang to her baby, Gentile eyes raised and heads nodded in approval in the courtyard below.

6 CHAPTER

It was almost suppertime. The clank of dishes and the aroma of roasting meat quickened Abigail's appetite. She had no money of her own to buy food. Romulus had left funds reserved for her care with Weasel. She descended the stairs with baby Deborah wrapped in a shawl. Long tables were set for a communal meal.

Male guests turned to stare at Abigail as womenfolk scowled and cast venomous glances her way.

Weasel's woman had been friendly as long as Abigail had been sick, pale, and desperate. But in the weeks since giving birth the color had returned to Abigail's cheeks. She carried her head erect, and her breasts, swelled with motherhood, added allure to her statuesque and shapely figure. Abigail was tall and slender, towering over the local females, with their broad, bitter faces perched on thick necks. Pendulous breasts and stumpy ankles made the local women seem almost a different species from Abigail. The low women who populated Weasel's establishment hated Abigail for the same reason as the respectable housewives in the town: She turned the heads of the men in the courtyard. She smiled, and the men leaned forward, hoping she would see them. The eyes of Weasel's Ethiopian wife narrowed like a panther's when Abigail passed.

Over the Ethiopian's shoulder, Abigail saw that the doors to the harlots' cribs were open. The painted-faced occupants lounged against their doorframes, hoping to become an expensive dessert after hungry men feasted on roasted pork and too much wine.

Abigail averted her eyes from the hatred. She smiled at the baby, who slept in the cloth sling around Abigail's neck. Abigail took the wooden plank that served as a plate and filled it with a mix of meat and lentils. No one here knew the Sabbath customs of the religious in Sychar. Men did not wash before eating or bless HaShem for their food. The gathering was, rather, like animals at a trough.

Abigail carried her plate to the steps leading up to her room. There she sat alone and ate her meal as raucous laughter from inside the inn filled the air and Shabbat began.

HaShem, I know it is Shabbat and that the meat on my platter is swine. I am sorry. But I am so much worse than a Sabbath breaker. I have done so many bad things . . . too many to be redeemed. I am hungry. I am sorry about Shabbat. Maybe it doesn't matter. Surely you don't hear me, anyway. She took a tentative bite of the shredded pork. It tasted good. She glanced up at the last rays of the setting sun and then down at her daughter. *Blessed are you, O Lord, who has let us live to see this day.*

As at every sunset for the past forty days, the clamor in the courtyard of Weasel's inn increased as darkness settled over the land. Abigail ate, then quickly retreated into her room. She closed the door and locked it by sliding a board through two metal brackets.

Safe from the men below, she nursed Deborah. When the little one slept peacefully on Abigail's cot, Abigail looked out the window. A twinge of longing passed through her at the signal fires on Gerazim alerting the surrounding countryside that it was yet another Shabbat, and the Samaritan observance of the holy day's laws was in effect. Was her lover there, warming himself by the observance of Torah on the sacred mountain where Joshua had pronounced the blessings upon the descendants of Israel? Though corrupted by pagan influence, the religion of Samaritans looked backward to Moses on Sinai and forward to the coming of the Messiah, called "the Restorer." The Temple in Jerusalem did not figure in the equation.

Abigail knew who she was. What she was. Even though evidence of her guilt lay in her arms, she would not change anything that had happened. Not now. The child, Deborah, was too precious—more precious than Abigail's own life.

She whispered, "HaShem, I don't desire him anymore. No. That fire is banked and covered with ash. But my heart longs for him to come and love me. Love us. If only he would come and cherish the life we made."

Behind her the door rattled. A knock followed. Then Weasel's voice. "Woman!" He demanded a reply.

"What do you want?" She moved instinctively nearer the baby.

"It's Weasel."

"I know who you are. I asked what you want."

He slurred as he talked. "What every man in the courtyard wants."

A chill coursed through her. "You're drunk."

"That's right."

"Go away."

"Not 'til you pay your bill."

"What are you talking about?"

"That Roman centurion. Your lover. He left enough cash for a month. Said he'd be back. Very late, ain't he?"

Abigail stared fearfully at the door as he rattled it again. Would it hold? "Go away."

"Look! I've got a proposition to make." He laughed.

"The centurion will crucify you if you lay a hand on—"

"He's not coming back. Some action against rebels in the Galil. I heard about it tonight. He ain't coming back for you. You owe me, see?"

She furrowed her brow and planted herself between the door and the baby. "He'll crucify you after he slits you open," she threatened.

"Ah, well. You owe me. You want to stay here, you gotta start earning your keep, see? Like the girls in the back. You know how much I could make if you was to go to work? Men'll come from Shechem and from Sychar . . . even far away as Sebaste . . . for a turn with you."

Abigail's heart beat faster. She was guilty of many things, but did her prior sin condemn her to a life of such degradation?

HaShem! I know you can't hear me. But, for the sake of my child, help me now. Please! Make Weasel go away.

The signal fire on Gerazim blazed brighter for an instant. As if in answer to her prayer, the shrill voice of the Ethiopian woman sounded. "WEE-ZUL!" A string of angry epithets in her native tongue followed.

Cowed and contrite, Weasel grumbled, "Well, all right. What am I supposed to do? Just making an offer. Employment!" His fist delivered a concluding angry blow on the door as he retreated.

Abigail swept Deborah into her arms and held her close. She knew this would not be the last time Weasel would come to her door. "Oh, HaShem! Where can I go? Where will we be safe?"

Hours had passed since Weasel's visit to her room, yet Abigail could not lie down to rest. She knew with certainty that she and the baby would not be safe if she stayed even one more day at Weasel's inn. But where could she go?

The echo of revelry faded. Drunken guests, howling bawdy tunes, staggered to their chambers.

Through the high small window the lights on Mount Gerazim dimmed and began to fade. Abigail prayed for deep sleep to topple like bricks on Weasel and pin him to his bed. She prayed for morning light to come.

"Where can we run to, HaShem?" she asked.

The gibbous moon sailed across the horizon, leaving in its wake a dark, starry sky. When a dog barked in the stable, someone cursed and shouted in a foreign tongue.

At last silence settled on Weasel's inn. But silence did not bring peace. Abigail's sense of urgency increased. A single word replayed in her thoughts: *escape!*

The wick of her lamp had long since guttered out. She groped in the dark for what few possessions she had. Tying her shawl into a sling, she put Deborah into it and prayed the baby would not cry.

Her ear against the wood of the door, Abigail listened for a footstep or any sign that Weasel might be lurking in the shadows. Only when she was sure he wasn't did she slide back the bolt. The hinges groaned as she opened the door a crack. The night air was cool and smelled like hay and horses. Coarse laughter erupted from the prostitutes' quarters, making Abigail's heart jump.

The baby was warm and still in her sling. Abigail placed a protective hand over the delicate head and stepped out onto the landing. She closed the door behind her, hoping Weasel would not notice she had fled until the sun was well up.

For now the darkness was her ally. Abigail held her breath as she tiptoed across the creaking planks to descend the steep stairway. The gate to the outside world had been closed at sundown. A sentry slept in a chair beside the pedestrian entrance.

Abigail heard a footstep. Someone was moving among the caravans. What if it was Weasel? What if he had discovered she was missing? Abigail willed herself to be part of the night, blended in with the shadows.

The steps drew closer. Abigail stifled an urge to scream. She bit her lip. Where was he? Who was he? Was he after her?

Deborah sighed and cooed. The noise, however slight, seemed impossibly, dangerously loud to Abigail. *Oh, HaShem,* she prayed, *protect us.*

A figure loomed up in the darkness. In the center of the courtyard he stood swaying, peering all around as if searching for something. For Abigail?

Just as Abigail was ready to bolt—to run back to her room and lock the door—the man scratched himself, belched, and moved off toward the privy.

It took several breaths before Abigail could get her heart back in her chest.

Drovers and camels drowsed together among packs and saddles in the open yard. Abigail picked her way through them, taking care not to stumble or awaken anyone. The smell of sour wine was strong.

Behind her a shaggy cur snarled and hit the end of its tether as she hurried just beyond reach of its fangs. The animal's master rolled over and groaned, "What? Who?"

"Nothing," Abigail replied in a quaking voice. "Go back to sleep."

The man accepted her non-reply and rolled over, pulling his blanket over his head.

Sensing someone was watching, Abigail glanced over her shoulder and quickened her pace.

The arched pedestrian door beside the main gate was hidden in shadow. By the opposite doorpost of the portal, the gatekeeper snored loudly.

Abigail's heart pounded. Even at a distance of several paces, the odors of wine and vomit reeking from the man were strong. He slept in a drunken stupor. All to her good fortune.

The darkness hid her from view, but neither could she see. Like blind Leah, Abigail groped along the stone and grasped the rough wood of the gate. She breathed a sigh of relief. Her way of escape was barred with the same sort of device used in her bedchamber. There was no lock or iron key to have to ferret out.

Just then the baby stirred and gave a small cry of protest. Abigail had accidentally squeezed her as she slid back the heavy wooden bolt. "Shh, baby," she murmured. The door swung open easily.

Abigail did not look back as she slipped away from Weasel's inn. Starlight illuminated the highway to Sychar. A brisk walk and perhaps she could be at Jacob's Well by sunrise.

The bleating of sheep guided Abigail through the dark streets of Sychar. The baby whimpered in her arms and turned her face toward Abigail's breast. Abigail felt her milk let down, and a small patch dampened her tunic. Deborah bleated as Abigail stumbled into the lambing shed behind the sheep pens of the wool carder.

The low-ceilinged structure was warm from the sleeping animals. Abigail felt her way along the wooden rail from stall to stall. At her scent, the ewes bawled. What if the wool carder heard the noise and came to search?

Abigail prayed, *HaShem! Oh, a place to sleep tonight. A quiet corner where I can feed my lamb.*

Reaching out her hand, Abigail swung a gate wide. The pen was empty. The straw was clean, as if some unseen hand had prepared a place for her to rest. She slipped down to lean against the back wall and fumbled to nurse the baby. Deborah feasted eagerly on Abigail's plentiful milk.

Abigail sang softly, as her mother had sung to her:

> "The LORD is my shepherd,
>   I shall not be in want.
> He makes me lie down in green pastures,
>   He leads me beside quiet waters."[3]

The lullaby and the baby's loud gulps quieted the milling sheep. At last, satisfied, Deborah slept, still attached to Abigail's breast.

Abigail laid her cheek on the baby's brow. "I am thirsty . . . thirsty . . . for you . . . my shepherd."

Exhausted, Abigail laid her head against the wall and closed her eyes and slept.

7

CHAPTER

Warmth penetrated her aching shoulders like sunlight on a cold day. The bleating of the flock sounded all around her, and yet it was a different flock, a different day.

"Abigail?" a young woman's kind voice called to her.

"I am . . . Abigail," she murmured.

"Open your eyes."

Abigail obeyed. The shadow of a young woman fell across her. She was a shepherdess. Her bronzed face beneath the loose weave of her head scarf seemed lit up from within, like a candle in a pierced clay jar. Gold-green eyes and white straight teeth were radiant in her smile.

"I am dreaming," Abigail said.

"Are you?" asked the shepherdess, amused.

"No one living smiles at me so."

"Life is not as you imagine. We, your seven sisters, are alive." She swept her arm toward six other young women who ringed the flock. They carried shepherd's staffs, directing and guiding their charges with taps and nudges. The six grinned cheerfully and waved at Abigail as though she was one of them.

"But . . . where am I?" Abigail looked down at little Deborah asleep in her arms. They were not in the sheepfold but rather sitting beside a well among a herd of milling sheep.

"My father's well. The well of Midian. Are you thirsty?"

"No flesh-and-blood woman would ever ask me if I thirst."

"You are thirsty. Your lips are parched, I see. Little lamb. Poor little lamb."

"Please, don't." The gentle concern made Abigail's eyes fill with tears. "Don't speak kindly to me. Please. I have managed to bear the cruelty of the womenfolk of my city when they drove me from the well of our father Jacob, but mercy will break me."

"Abi-gail. A beautiful name. It tells of your father's joy and rejoicing in your life." The woman extended a ladle of cool, clear water. "Your child is beautiful. We see how much you love her."

"More than my life."

"You must live then, Abi-gail . . . for her sake. Now, drink."

Abigail accepted the cup and gulped the water, quenching her thirst. "Thank you." She felt happy as the woman reached out and touched the baby's cheek.

"Beautiful. Sweet baby," she praised.

"No one has spoken a kind word about her 'til now. I didn't know how much that hurt my heart. Please . . . kind shepherdess, what is your name?" Abigail asked in a voice filled with wonder.

"Zipporah."

"I know your name . . . Little Bird."

"My name is Sparrow, in the language of my father's heart. Eldest of seven daughters of the priest Jethro."

"Why am I dreaming about you?"

"You will draw water at the well of salvation soon."

"They won't let me near. Their hatred keeps me away."

"Stand up, my sister Abigail, and you will know." The woman reached out for Abigail's hand and helped her up. Zipporah led her to a patch of shade beneath a date palm. "Sit here."

Zipporah moved away, wading into the flock, clucking and cooing to the sheep. The seven sisters let down waterskins into the deep well. It was hard work, drawing up the heavy skins from the depths. As they filled the troughs, they sang a song Abigail did not know in a language she could not understand. Zipporah cast a happy glance at Abigail as the thirsty animals pushed and shouldered in to drink deeply.

Abigail called, "What does it mean? Teach me this song!"

But Zipporah labored on as if she could not hear Abigail and had forgotten that she was there.

Suddenly Zipporah's youngest sister leapt onto a stone wall, pointed, and cried, "Look, Sister, look! They're coming!"

The wind shifted. The shaggy heads of the date palms hissed. The baby stirred in her mother's arms, and Abigail fought the urge to run.

Zipporah's countenance hardened. Unlike her sisters, there was no evidence of fear in her face. Her jaw was set with determination. Pausing in her labor, Zipporah raised her chin high as if to sniff the wind.

Then Abigail saw them too: rough, coarse-featured men of the desert, driving a herd of goats toward the watering troughs. Abigail counted them, saw at least a dozen bearded ruffians and a hundred goats.

The sheep scattered, despite the cries of the sisters. No efforts by Zipporah and her sisters could prevent it. The goats butted frightened lambs out of the way. "Stop!" Zipporah called. "You have no right to do this. Keep your herd back!"

The desert herdsmen laughed at her. When a ewe with a newborn lamb did not move out of his way quickly enough, the biggest of the shepherds kicked the lamb and cracked his staff across the back of the ewe.

"Clear off yourselves," he ordered Zipporah. "Before I serve you as I did this sheep."

It had taken great effort for Zipporah and her sisters to draw water from the well and fill the troughs. Now all their work would come to nothing. The sheep wandered in the gorse, bleating with thirst and fear.

Zipporah, rod in hand, approached the leader of the goatherds. "We will share this well," she said. "But only if you keep your animals back until ours have drunk their fill."

"Or what follows?" the chief of the raiders returned scornfully.

"This," Zipporah said, lashing out with her rod and catching the chieftain on the side of his head. He ducked away from the blow, but it still lashed his ear and tore it.

Abigail saw bright red blood flow.

The man reached up and touched his wound, holding his bloody palm aloft for his men to see. "For that you need to be taught a lesson," he said. "Not just you, either. All you women who don't know your places." He pretended to count his men and then the sisters. Turning to the grinning circle of leering herdsmen, he remarked, "Some of you will have to share."

Suddenly, like the roar of a lion, a male voice boomed, "You will not lay a hand on these women!"

A strong fierce man dressed in Egyptian clothes leapt between Zipporah and the bully. A shepherd's staff came down across the chieftain's head, flattening him where he stood.

Abigail had to shade her eyes against the glare of the sun. Where had this tall, bronzed man come from? His clothing was worn and ragged as if he had wandered far, alone.

Despite his tattered appearance, neither his courage nor his strength was lacking. Though outnumbered eleven to one, Zipporah's champion launched himself at two knife-wielding tribesmen. With a mighty sweep of his staff, he felled them both at once.

"Come on, the rest of you," he challenged. "If you dare. I'm Mosheh. Mosheh! I killed a man in Egypt and I'm not afraid of you. Come on!"

Three more rushed in on him. Without flinching he took two blows of sticks on his shoulders. Either wallop would have crippled Abigail, but Mosheh neither cried out nor retreated. Holding his staff like a spear, he stabbed one of his attackers in the stomach, making him collapse. Striking backwards without reversing the weapon, he smashed the teeth and dislocated the jaw of a second.

The third of the trio swung his staff at Mosheh's head. Unexpectedly Mosheh dropped his own staff and seized his attacker's. In an instant Mosheh wrenched it free. Abigail heard it whistle in an arc around Mosheh's head like the cry of an angry hawk. She heard the shrill yelp of pain from the opponent as his collarbone snapped like a twig.

Just like that the odds were reduced to only six to one. The rest of the goatherds decided they did not want a share in what their brothers had received.

"He is berserk," one said.

"He'll kill us all."

"Please, sir," they begged. "Let us take our wounded and our goats and go!"

Retrieving his staff from the ground, Mosheh leaned on it and said, "Apologize to the women and then get out of my sight!"

The desert tribesmen could not disappear quickly enough, it seemed to Abigail. Within minutes, the last of the animals, driven by limping, cursing men, vanished over a rocky, brush-choked ridge back into the wilderness.

"Sir," Abigail heard Zipporah say, "you're wounded. Let me bind your wounds."

Mosheh glanced down at a cut on his arm. "It's nothing," he said. Then sweeping a shabby cloak from around his shoulders, he spread it on the ground and invited Zipporah to sit. "Wait here," he said. "I was resting in the shade by your well. I had already helped myself to water, not knowing it belonged to you, so it's only right that I refill the troughs for your sheep."

His shoulder muscles rippling, Mosheh hauled skin after skin of water out of the well. He filled the water ditches until they overflowed and the sheep had all drunk their fill.

Zipporah, little Sparrow of Midian, smiled into his eyes. She held her finger up as if to ask him to wait. Turning on her heel, she strode toward Abigail. She stooped beside her and grasped the baby's perfect hand between thumb and forefinger. "You see, Abigail? Mosheh came to us when we most needed him."

"The deliverer."

"He was the prince of Egypt once, but he set all that aside to come here. He was here, watching over us as we worked. He saw all that took place. He heard their threats and saw their evil intent. And then he who was once a prince became like one of us. He made himself known, and fought for us."

Abigail fixed her gaze on the rosebud lips of her child. "I know your meaning. They have driven me from the well."

"No man has a right to keep another thirsty soul from the well of salvation. Every shepherd who steals the labor of another will one day face the Great Shepherd. Mosheh showed us the One who is to come. Messiah will be our Shepherd. He is called Salvation . . . Yeshua. You will not know Him when first you meet . . . but He will know you. Abigail, He has made you thirst so that you may one day drink living water and never thirst again."

"Do you know where He is?" Abigail cried as Zipporah walked away.

"Coming soon. To do battle for your sake."

"Tell me where He is."

"One day, when you least expect Him, He will be there." Zipporah reached out to Mosheh, and he returned her embrace.

A whirlwind sprouted near the well and swept between Zipporah and Abigail. And when it passed, the scene had vanished. "Wait!" Abigail called, but they had gone. . . .

A bawling ewe in the next stall drew Abigail back to consciousness. Suddenly awake, she opened her eyes. Where was she? It took a moment before the baby stirred in her arms and she remembered the dream.

Her tongue felt thick and her throat dry. "Oh, Lord," she whispered. "I thirst."

FOURTH PROPHECY

The Gift of a Well

From there the Israelites traveled to Beer, which is the well where the LORD said to Moses, "Assemble the people, and I will give them water." There the Israelites sang this song:

"Spring up, O well!
*   Yes, sing its praises!*
Sing of this well,
*   which princes dug,*
which great leaders hollowed out
*   with their scepters and staffs."*

NUMBERS 21:16-18 NLT

aShem had provided a sheep pen for her and her little lamb, but before anyone was awake, Abigail had made her way back to her little shelter, still intact, among the outcasts of Sychar. After just one day in her makeshift shelter, Abigail felt almost at home again. Now, as darkness closed in, a nightingale sang in the brush of the gulley. It was a sweet but lonely sound. Abigail closed the makeshift gate across her shelter. By the flickering light of a tiny oil lamp, she checked the baby. She had nursed Deborah less than an hour before, until a trickle of milk dribbled out of her mouth. Now the baby was sleeping soundly.

Drawing back a corner of the blanket, Abigail lay down next to her child, enfolding her carefully in her arms. For an instant before blowing out the lamp, Abigail studied the precious face. The perfect rosebud lips worked in and out, drawing sustenance in dreams.

Abigail touched her own cheekbones. She needed no mirror to know how gaunt she'd grown. Soon her looks would be no threat to the women of Sychar.

Would they still hate her enough to wish she were dead? With absolutely no reason to judge her so harshly, were they still prepared to be her executioners?

Thanks be to HaShem, the child seemed to be thriving. The little one remained plump and rosy-cheeked, even as her mother spent the coin of her life to keep her so.

Abigail nourished herself with scraps, but she fed on hope. Two things kept her from despair: the overwhelming, all-consuming love for her child and the belief that her lover would come to save her.

Perhaps he would come tonight.

If not, perhaps HaShem would send another messenger in her sleep to counsel and console her.

Both possibilities made sleep very desirable, as well as offering a few hours' relief from hunger.

The nightingale called. Abigail softly hummed the tune to Miriam's song: *"The horse and his rider He has thrown into the sea."*[4] It was a song of victory, of the triumph of God's Mercy in the face of overwhelming odds.

The fact that it appeared right before the miraculous advent of manna was not forgotten by Abigail either.

Then she slept. . . .

A voice called her name: "Abigail. Abigail?"

Was this a dream? "I'm here," she replied drowsily.

"May I . . . may I come in?"

Abigail sat upright, drawing a bleat of protest from the infant. It was her lover's voice! Her *Machama.* He had come to rescue them. "Wait! Let me light the lamp." Her heart pounded fiercely.

"No!" he returned urgently. "No light. Can't chance someone seeing."

"Then come in," she said.

Brush crackled against the rock walls as he pulled open a passage into her home. One moment a fan-shaped swath of stars filled the portal. Next the space was filled with a cloaked and hooded form. Thank HaShem for the way she warmed to his voice, because the apparition was terrifying.

Would he embrace her? Would he assure her he loved her? Was this the night they would run away together?

"Will you take us away tonight?" Abigail asked.

"No, not tonight. I can't possibly. It's . . . not time yet."

Abigail's body sagged with disappointment. "But soon?" she asked in a voice tinged with desperation.

"Yes," her *Machama* agreed forcefully. "Yes, of course. That's why I came tonight. To thank you for being so . . . trustworthy. If you gave away my—our—secret, it would ruin everything. Just wait a bit longer, and then you'll see."

"I can work," Abigail added. "If we go away together, I will work. We can have a new life together . . . with our baby."

"Not tonight," he said carefully. "But soon. You'll see. Look, I brought you some money."

A leather coin pouch landed with a soft thump and jingle on the stony floor.

"It's not much," he continued, "but enough to buy food."

"But we can't stay here." Abigail's letdown was close to overwhelming her. Her voice rose in pitch with her emotions. She picked up the baby and snuggled her close.

"Yes, I know," her *Machama* said quickly. "I'm seeing to that. Tomorrow . . . or the next day at the latest. You'll see, I really do care for you. I do."

His affectionate words coursed through her like a draught of new wine.

"Just . . . keep our secret safe awhile longer."

"I will," Abigail promised, rocking the child.

"I have to go. I've stayed too long already."

No embrace. No offer of a kiss.

"Do you want to hold your baby?"

"Can't. Not tonight," he said hastily, backing out of the shelter, his boots crushing the branches underfoot. "But we'll be together soon. You'll see."

Then he was gone.

Two days and nights passed. Her *Machama* did not return, nor did he send word. The packet of money, coppers totaling not quite a denarius in value, bought food: bread, a hard rind of cheese, a packet of olives, a handful of dates.

Abigail used Leah's connections in the marketplace to make the purchases. A beggar's coins were welcome when shopping in Sychar.

Abigail's might not be.

The first morning she treated herself to a big meal, sharing the bounty with Leah.

The second day Abigail was more cautious with her supplies, allowing herself to only nibble at the olives and bread, using every precious drop of brine to moisten and flavor the tough dough.

As the sun rose on this, the third morning after his visit, Abigail nursed the baby while eating a half dozen of the dates. The sweetness revived her energy but not her spirits.

No more dreams.

No more *Machama*.

Very little hope. Was he to prove faithless after all? Soon the lengthening days would feel the full blast of the sun's heat. Soon the nights would present Khamseen winds, dust-laden and scorching. Abigail must find better shelter for the baby.

Did she have the courage to denounce her lover to his face—to shame him into assisting her?

What if he denied the charge and sent her away, never to see her again?

A boy dressed in a ragged tunic, belted about the middle with the cast-off broken bridle from a Roman's horse, wandered into the plaza beside the well. Abigail had never seen him before. Perhaps he was a runaway slave from a great house or a newly orphaned son of some captured rebel turned out of his home.

Abigail saw him stop by the legless cripple and ask a question. The beggar waved the boy away angrily.

Persistent, the lad did not retreat completely but circled the rim of the well to approach Leah.

This time a gesture directed the boy toward Abigail's hiding place.

Abigail's pulse quickened. The lad was coming toward her. In his hand he held a packet wrapped in cloth. A message for her? A summons to meet her beloved?

The boy, who appeared to be about ten, entered the gully. "Your name Abigail?" he asked.

She nodded eagerly.

"Used to be the wife of Zakane?"

Abigail dropped her chin and stared at the ground as she nodded.

"Then I was told to give you this," he said, extending the small parcel.

"By who? What is it?" she asked, undoing the twine with which it was bound.

"Dunno his name," the courier admitted. "Never seen him before. I'm from Shechem, see? This man give me a coin to come to Jacob's Well and ask for Abigail. Said he'd give me another when he learned I'd done it. Guess I have."

The last fold of oiled fabric bent open under its own weight, spilling a slim metal rod with a double bend near one end onto the ground.

"A key?" Abigail asked. "What's it for?"

The boy shrugged. "Goes with the message, I s'pose."

"Quickly," Abigail demanded eagerly. "Tell me quickly. What did he say?"

"He said you was to go to the house of the potter."

"That's all?"

The boy nodded and began edging away. Clearly he felt the payment for his services had already been exhausted.

"Wait!" Abigail urged. "The potter in Sychar?"

"Dunno. I'm from Shechem, remember?"

"What did he look like? This man?"

"Medium, I guess. Kept his cloak on and hood up, though it was a warm day. A thief or a rebel most likely." The boy's eyes glittered as a sudden thought struck him. "You want to send a reply? For when he comes back? Do it for just—" He stuck out his lower lip and appeared to be calculating what an outcast woman could pay. "Two pennies."

"No, no reply," Abigail said, holding the key and turning it slowly while wondering what this could mean. "But thank you."

9

9

K omer the Potter was a Gentile. Neither Jew nor Samaritan, he
was tolerated in Sychar because he kept his worship of Artemis
to himself and did not flaunt pagan idols in his shop.

This toleration was partly extended because he was the only potter
in Sychar. Given that the hills throughout the Vale of Shechem were
planted thick with olive groves, Komer's tall, dark red amphorae were
in great demand for shipping the precious oil to Jerusalem, Antioch,
and even to Rome.

His place of business, managed by Athena, his wife, opened onto the
market square and they lived above it. In the space behind the building
were his kiln and the awnings sheltering his open-air workshop. Great
wooden racks, stretching up the hill, held the unfired, double-handled
jugs, as well as the other products of the potter's workmanship.

Her arrival obscured by the forest of pots and jars, Abigail made her
way toward Komer's house. She waited under the shade of an ancient
olive tree until the last of Komer's workmen left for the day, then crept
cautiously into his yard.

Komer was alone, examining the glazing on a recent batch of water
jars. He used a bit of charcoal to mark places where the glazing was

inadequate or the pots had cracked in the firing. He looked up at her approach, noting the sleeping baby carried round her neck in a sling of cloth. "Shop's closed," he said. "Come back tomorrow."

Abigail had known Komer for years. As Zakane's wife, she had made all the purchases of pottery for the old man's home and had consulted with his steward about amphorae for the groves. Komer was always gruff, but never unkind.

"You remember me?" she asked.

"'Course," he said. "All Sychar knows about you."

Abigail blushed. "I've come about this."

Reaching into the neck of her robe, she withdrew a leather string. From the end of it dangled the metal rod brought to the well by the messenger from Shechem.

Komer's eyes widened. "So it's for you. I should've guessed." He approached Abigail, extending his hand for the iron bar. His forearms and shoulders were powerful, but the top of his head did not reach above Abigail's shoulders.

Abigail handed him the object. "What's for me?"

Jerking the key over his shoulder, Komer indicated a shed attached to the rear of his house. It was no more than four paces deep, but it spanned the width of the structure and had a stout door. "My storeroom," he said. Walking on his bowed legs across the work yard, he inserted the key into a lock and twisted. A bolt snapped within. "Had it made special in Damascus." He shoved open the entry and stepped out of the way.

Abigail did not move. "Who arranged this?" Had her lover finally stepped forward? Was he openly taking responsibility for her?

The rush of pleasant expectation warming her was soon dashed. Komer shrugged. "Bit mysterious, that." Studying the baby in her arms, he added, "Not now, though. Man sends me a message. Says he wants to rent my storeroom for someone. Says he'll pay me every month. Says to leave a key under this stone—" Komer nudged a flagstone with the toe of his sandal—"if I agreed. Paid in advance, so why not?"

"You don't know him?"

"Not I. Not my business." Then he added, "Suppose you do, though."

The long, narrow space had no windows. Moving inside, Abigail saw that all four walls were lined with floor-to-ceiling shelves. Beneath the bottom rack, a thicket of amphorae leaned against each other. The middle spaces were clustered thick with water jugs and grain carriers and kneading bowls. The topmost ledges bore the weight of pinch-faced clay oil lamps in three sizes.

The valley formed by this canyon of clay was barely a pace and a half wide. A cot with a rope mattress but no padding occupied much of the remaining space. Reaching up on the topmost shelf, Komer retrieved a handful of coins. "Left this for you, too. For food, clothes. It's all here. I'm an honest man."

Her head swirling with gratitude and disappointment, with grief and relief, Abigail barely managed, "Thank you." With a shudder she added, "Aren't you afraid of what people will say? To have the infamous harlot of Sychar living here?"

"Not me," Komer replied with a grimace. "What're they gonna do? Buy their pots in Shechem? Let 'em. You just keep to yourself, and we'll be fine."

"And your wife? She's agreeable to this?"

For the first time in the conversation Komer appeared vaguely uncomfortable. He pushed up his turban, his charcoal-stained fingers leaving a pair of tracks across his forehead. "She's not one of . . . them," he concluded, repeating, "Keep to yourself, mind."

Komer returned the key and nodded his way out of the dark, cramped space.

Abigail sat on the cot and peered around her. This was the promised shelter? And he had paid in advance . . . for a month? Mindful of Komer's warning, silent tears rolled down her cheeks.

Living behind the potter's shop may have brought Abigail back into the town of Sychar, but it did not bring her back into the community. The fabric of everyday life, like going to the well for water or shopping in the marketplace, was laced with hatred and hemmed with danger.

"You," Abel's wife said at the top of her lungs when she spotted Abigail still a hundred paces from the well. "Harlot! How dare you walk on the same road with decent women? Get out of sight! Now, before we stone you."

Afraid for Deborah, Abigail scurried into the bushes. Thereafter she only went to the well when no others were likely to be there, as in the hottest time of midday, before dawn, or after dark.

Shopping was even worse. It was not possible to get the food and oil and clothing she needed for herself and the baby without venturing into the market square. Abigail adopted the habit of lurking around the corner of the plaza until a chosen merchant was alone. Then she would dash forward, plunk down her cash, demand her merchandise, and race away before the alarm was raised.

The stray dogs hanging about the garbage heaps were treated with more kindness, or at least with less hostility.

Komer allowed her the use of a small charcoal-fired brazier on which to cook, but his wife absolutely forbade giving her any of the fuel from the plentiful supply stored for the kiln. "Her room may be paid for," Abigail heard Athena say, "but nothing more. And she cooks in the doorway of the shed. Don't want her parading about."

Elam, the charcoal seller, kept his table at the far end of the square. It seemed a safe enough outing. Ten pennies would buy a bundle of fuel enough to last a week or more since it was not needed for heat. She waited until he was alone, then slipped up behind the stall. "Please," she said, "one bundle."

"Of course," he said, smiling at the dark-haired crown of Deborah's head where it poked out of the sling. He bent down and retrieved a bundle tied up with cord. "Bit heavier than usual. Broken bits, you see. But I hear you need just a small fire at that."

Abigail smarted at the reference to her living arrangements. Her life was known and discussed by everyone in Sychar it seemed.

"Can you manage it?" Elam inquired. "With the baby and all? Here, let me carry it for you."

"Elam bar Jerim," Elam's wife said as she emerged from their home, "what are you thinking? Get away from that woman! At once, do you hear? Do you want people to think—"

Elam's wife broke off the challenge as if the same accusation that might appear in the minds of others had suddenly popped into hers.

"Now, Judith," Elam said, "don't get ruffled."

"Don't tell me," Judith retorted. "Get away from my husband, you brazen . . . you scarlet . . . you slinking . . ." Words failed her as she searched for the perfect epithet.

Judith's screeching alerted the market. The ears of Sychar's women perked up at the sound. That the trouble was caused by the harlot was no surprise. What was noteworthy was whose husband had been caught by her wiles this time.

A pack of wives converged on the scene.

Abigail was already fleeing, awkwardly cradling Deborah and dragging the bundle of charcoal.

Even as she hurried, her eye was drawn to a man across the plaza. His build was familiar, his hair color recognizable, even the robe he wore . . . it was her beloved, her *Machama*.

He saw the attack brewing and turned quickly away.

Abigail's heart plummeted. He made no move to defend her.

That night Abigail built no fire, nor cooked any meal. She ate cold, dried fish and went to bed, but sleep would not visit.

Neither did her *Machama*.

Of all the cruelty leveled against her, the most painful—like a dagger plunged into her heart—was the way her lover spurned her when she was attacked in the marketplace. How could he stand by and do nothing? No, it was worse than that! He abandoned her to her fate. Besides not intervening, or even speaking up on her behalf, he didn't even seek someone else to protect her.

It was good that Deborah slept soundly, because Abigail could scarcely sleep at all.

When she did doze it was not restful, nor were her dreams kind or reassuring. Mocking faces, jeering words, angry voices, upraised fists threatening her child . . . these were the images that populated Abigail's thoughts.

She lived, she had shelter of a sort, she had enough to eat, but what sort of life was this? Was this existence the proof of her *Machama*'s love . . . or of his neglect?

There remained but a slender thread of hope. What if the meager provision was part of a greater plan? What if her lover was hoarding his funds so as to take her away from Sychar and start a new life with her?

That had to be the explanation. She clung to it with desperation, as a drowning person snatches at the most fragile reed.

And there was but a single consolation: The cruelty of the villagers had reached its climax. None of Abigail's spiritual wounds could be deepened by anything more they had to say. She had experienced the worst.

Just as she finally achieved sleep, there was a loud crash from the potter's work yard and a string of violent curses.

"Where's the light?" a deep, slurred male voice demanded. "What kind of bawdy house is this? How do we find the women? Come on, show yourselves."

Another male, this one calling in a breathy tenor counterpoint to the other's explosive bass, caroled, "Come out, my dears. Come meet some real men. Time to earn your pay! Wake. . . ."

Further drunken raving was interrupted by the crash of pottery. Apparently the men had blundered into Komer's curing racks.

Abigail was grateful for the solid door and sturdy lock between her and the inebriated sots.

"That must be the crib, there!" the bass exulted. "Come on, Ahaz. Forward march!"

Fists pounded on the storeroom's door. Bass voice bellowed, "Come on, sweet. Open up! Don't toy with us; we know you're in there. We're soldiers of Tetrach Antipas. We've been eight weeks on desert patrol with only camels for company."

"Yeah," Ahaz exulted. "Me and Samson, we're lonesome for company, even if you're ugly as a camel." The fists drummed on the door. "We heard about this place in the inn. 'The harlot of Sychar,' they said. 'Behind the potter's,' they said. You're famous. Open up! We have shekels to spend."

The door bounced in its frame. The hammering on the wall toppled a row of pots from the highest ledge. They exploded in knifelike shards on the ground.

Abigail flung herself across Deborah, who wailed in terror at the sudden awakening. Unable to remain silent any longer, Abigail shrieked, "Go away! Please, go away. Help! Won't someone help me? Please!"

A grunt of pain came through the wall as someone's shoulder rammed into the door. "Again, Samson," Ahaz cheered. "Hit it again! Another and another."

The repeated blows caused a column of amphorae to topple toward her cot. Abigail caught one with her left hand just before it smashed into her head. Snatching up Deborah, she retreated to the farthest corner of the shed.

"That's it," Ahaz exulted. "One more and down she comes."

The lock burst from the wood in a shower of splinters, and the door was yanked open. Abigail was reduced to whimpering, "Please! Don't hurt my baby."

The orange glare of a torch appeared outside. Abigail saw a shaggy head silhouetted against the light; then an upraised kneading bowl slammed down on the soldier's head. He collapsed in a heap.

"Clear off," Abigail heard Komer demand. "Drag your friend's carcass and be off."

Ahaz protested, "Watch out! What'd you do that for? We didn't mean no harm."

"Get out of here! Now!" Komer repeated.

"All right, all right. We're going."

Groaning accompanied the scraping of sandals across the courtyard. "Come on, Samson," Ahaz encouraged. "You can make it."

A torch was thrust into the storeroom, followed by Komer. He surveyed the broken pots. "Look at this mess. A whole week's inventory shot."

"It's her fault," Athena's voice announced from outside. "I told you she'd be trouble, Komer. But would you listen? Oh no. 'She's got to live somewhere,' you said. 'We need the money,' you said. Now look at what she's cost us."

"You all right?" Komer asked over Deborah's shuddering sobs.

"Yes . . . yes. We're all right," Abigail managed to reply.

"Well, heap some pots in front of the door for tonight. I'll fix the lock tomorrow." Komer left, muttering placating words to his wife.

Deborah finally returned to sleep, but Abigail sat up all night, huddled in the farthest corner from the door.

10

Abigail awoke to Deborah's cries. She jolted upright, fearful the Herodian soldiers had returned. Instead, it was morning. No one was about, but the baby was hungry.

It was still early. Abigail needed to get out of the wreckage of last night's near calamity. She needed air fragrant with ripening fruit and grassy pastures and not the stale, smoke-laden breath of Sychar.

Stepping carefully over the smashed pots and fragments of broken crockery, Abigail tucked her own water jar under her arm. Supporting Deborah with the sling, she nursed the baby as she headed for Jacob's Well.

There was much to ponder this morning.

Herod's troopers were demons in human form. There was no doubt about that. The tetrarch hired the worst bullies and cutthroats out of the souks of Jerusalem and Damascus and Petra. They were charged with keeping the peace in Herod's dominions of Galilee and Perea over Jordan, but this arrangement merely meant they were paid to continue being bullies and cutthroats.

When drunk on cheap wine, they were worse.

The residents of Samaria would never admit it, but they were fortunate to be ruled by a Roman governor rather than by Herod. Herod's men were not stationed in Sychar; they were only passing through.

And may they never return, Abigail prayed.

But if the soldiers were demons, what did that make the towns-people of Sychar, whose gossip had set the troopers after her?

Abigail had escaped being raped and perhaps killed and her baby left an orphan. But how could she escape the malevolent hatred with which she was surrounded every day?

Though she told herself it was for her baby, Abigail sang Mosheh's song to quiet her own nerves even more than Deborah's:

> *"Return, O LORD! How long?*
>   *Have pity on Your servants!*
> *Satisfy us in the morning with Your steadfast love,*
>   *that we may rejoice and be glad all our days."*[5]

Abigail thought about the familiar lyrics. Steadfast love was exactly what Abigail craved. She needed it more than food, more than shelter. Her desire for steadfast love was more akin to thirst—burning, intolerable thirst.

How long had it been since she had experienced steadfast love? None of her husbands had modeled it for her.

As a very young child, perhaps she had known it in the home of her parents.

It is, she thought, *what I want Deborah to grow up feeling. Steadfast, enduring, unshakable love. It's what I want her to be certain of always receiving from me. Like the psalm says, I want her to feel content and safe every morning of her life, because of how much I love her.*

I want her to know with absolute certainty that nothing can ever separate her from my love . . . nothing!

But where would Abigail find such love for herself? The hymn spoke of a returning Lord. That must mean when Messiah came—the one the Samaritan clergy called "the Restorer." Was love what would be restored? A belief that such a transient thing as love could actually be reliable? Was there a love so unselfish as to be never failing?

The image of going to the well was somehow linked in Abigail's mind to the psalm. She went to draw water every morning. It was satisfying to fill the water jar and have it fresh and cool to drink.

But each day required another trip to the spring . . . another journey to and from. The satisfaction was real, but it did not last.

What did the Lawgiver mean in his prayer? What sort of satisfaction could last "all our days"? Once again she crooned:

"Let Your work be shown to Your servants,
    and Your glorious power to their children.
Let the favor of the Lord our God be upon us,
    and establish the work of our hands upon us;
    yes, establish the work of our hands!"[6]

"Listen, Deborah," Abigail caroled to her baby. "Mama is asking God to show you his glorious power. May your daddy love us and want to build a home with us with the work of his hands."

"Listen to the brazen woman," Abel's wife drawled from behind her. "Singing in public when we all know how she entertained a soldier last night."

Abigail's musing had made her less than attentive on the journey to the well. Unexpectedly she was caught between a group of Sychar's women going to the water and a second cluster returning home.

In the oncoming gaggle was Jerash's wife. "I hear she took on two of them. Shameless! Despicable!"

"They attacked . . . ," Abigail began in defense.

"See," the rabbi's wife added, "next she'll claim it's not her fault. As if she didn't flaunt herself at every male over the age of ten. Wicked! Wicked woman, tell us who the father is."

"Yes, tell us!" other women demanded.

"We must and we *will* know the truth."

"It's cruel to leave suspicion on all the men of Sychar."

"Unless she doesn't even know which one it is! Name all your wicked lovers. Name them!"

Abigail's head spun as she turned about in place to try to watch the circling swarm of accusers. Juggling water jar and baby, Abigail could not manage to protect both. The clay pot fell and shattered.

"Tell us! Was it the Roman?"

"It was that potter, wasn't it?"

"The charcoal seller?"

"Tell us!"

"I won't," Abigail said. She flinched as someone picked up something and threw it. Would she and Deborah be stoned to death right here on the highway?

A handful of dust hit her in the chest, stinging her eyes, making her cough. Hurriedly she backed away, pulling a fold of the sling over Deborah's face.

Someone shoved her from behind; then another palmful of dirt struck her in the hair.

"Get away from the well. You contaminate it. You dirty it just by being near it."

The air around Abigail's head was swirling with dust. It blotted out the sun until the cheerful orb of morning was a bloodred ball hanging above an execution.

"We will find out who is guilty. We will cleanse this town."

Amid the fog of grit Abigail spotted an opening in the circle of loathing and darted through it. There would be no steadfast love this morning, no pity from HaShem for Abigail, no demonstration of glorious power for her or for her much-loved baby.

Where was the Restorer of All Things? Where was Abigail's beloved?

Abigail ran from the highway, scouring her eyes with the hem of her robe and blundering in and out of ditches. As soon as she could manage it, she reached the windswept height of a small knoll. There, beneath a welcoming olive tree, she paused to catch her breath.

If the acrid limestone dust had penetrated Abigail's mouth and lungs and clogged her eyes, what had it done to poor baby Deborah? Fearfully, Abigail shook excess dirt from the sling before peeling back a corner and peering in.

Deborah, completely unscathed, blinked at the sudden onslaught of sunlight and waved both fists at her mother.

"Baby! Sweet baby," Abigail said. "I was so worried about you. I was scared."

Deborah's hands waved in time to an unheard melody as she cooed and smiled.

Laying the child in a crook of the gnarled trunk, Abigail did her best to dislodge the grit from her hair and the folds of her robe.

To avoid any more encounters with the matrons of Sychar, Abigail went the long way around, through the fields and orchards. Eventually she arrived at the cistern on the far side of the village. She was grateful no one else was there. Dropping the well's waterskin into the depths on its length of cord, Abigail drew out a pouch of warm, stale, brackish water—the best that could be had at the moment. After drinking, she used the rest to wash her face, especially her eyes and ears. Her hair, she decided, was hopeless.

Since she now had no way to carry water back with her, Abigail would have to make another journey later. Perhaps Komer would let her borrow a jar to replace the one she had lost. With nights full of dangerous, drunken rowdies and mornings given over to rampaging housewives, it was rapidly becoming certain Abigail could only approach Jacob's Well at the height of midday, when everyone else took shelter from the heat.

It took Abigail a long time to get back to her shelter behind the potter's shop. She had been gone hours longer than she had planned, and way past time to eat. Deborah was satisfied, but Abigail was hungry.

The door to the shed still hung crookedly from its hinge. Apparently Komer had not yet attempted to repair it.

Abigail approached carefully, stepping around more shattered pots and sharp ceramic slivers.

She stopped a few paces from the entry. Why was her shawl lying in the dirt? It had not been there when she left for the well.

Stepping inside, Abigail halted in stunned dismay. The inside of the storeroom had been ransacked. All Abigail's meager belongings were strewn about the floor. Her spare clothing—a single tunic, one extra robe, and two head scarves—and all Deborah's baby things were heaped together.

Over them had been dumped a sack of flour and a jug of olive oil.

The rest of Abigail's provisions—figs and raisins and bread and dried fish—were trampled into the dirt and sharp fragments of clay.

A bit of Abigail's charcoal supply had evidently been put to use. On the wall above her overturned cot was scrawled, *Harlot of Sychar! You're not wanted here!*

Abigail sank to her knees and wept. Not wanted here. Not wanted anywhere, except back at Weasel's inn to become what the people of Sychar already believed her to be.

Her life was in shambles. Even the Restorer could never put this wreckage in order again . . . never.

By dragging the cot as far as possible from the entry to the storeroom, Abigail was able to keep Deborah in a secure location while she cleaned up the debris left by the vandals. Using a broom made of rushes and a dustpan formed from the remains of a water jar, she began clearing the wreckage.

Her clothing could not be salvaged. Neither could the provisions. All would have to be replaced. Only a handful of coins remained in her supply. It would barely be enough to buy food for the week—nothing more.

But the loss of her belongings was far from the worst thing she had to endure.

Komer's wife, Athena, hung about the outside of the room, haranguing her husband. The potter, keeping strict silence lest his wife's venom for Abigail be directed at him, repaired the doorframe and the lock.

"She has to go, I say," Athena maintained. The woman was taller and broader than her husband, the way a wine amphora lords it over a kneading bowl. The size of Athena's mouth and her bulbous shape were reminiscent of a wine container as well. "A week's worth of work destroyed. Another day's work lost while you spend time setting things to rights. To say nothing of the lost business! How many of the righteous people of Sychar shop elsewhere because of the harlot living here?"

Athena spoke as if Abigail were not even present. Abigail ignored the diatribe, but the last comment was too much. Dumping the swept-up fragments atop a heap of other broken pottery with a crash, Abigail said, "The righteous people of Sychar are the ones who did this. Soldiers hammered down the door, but your righteous customers are the ones who broke in and did the rest of this."

"Don't you raise your voice to me, harlot!" Athena bellowed. "If you weren't who you are, if you weren't *what* you are, none of this would have happened. It's all your fault. Komer, are you going to let her speak to me this way? Komer! She has to go."

Heaving a great sigh, the potter straightened up from where he crouched with hammer and chisel beside the doorframe. "If she goes, the rent money stops. Then all this—" he swept the hammer over the damages—"will be unpaid for."

"We'll demand that her keeper pay!"

"We don't know who he is," Komer said. "How do we make an invisible man pay?"

"Then we haul her into court," Athena maintained. "Sell her into debtor's prison. Then he'll pay . . . or she'll rot."

Abigail experienced a flurry of anxiety. Could that happen? What would be Deborah's fate if her mother was tossed into prison?

"What court? What judges?" Komer said. "The elders of this town are on notice not to harass this woman. Remember what the Roman centurion said? Do you think any of those gutless wonders will complain to him? And if not him, then to Lord Herod? Remember, it was me who busted that pot—" Komer kicked one of the broken jars with his foot—"over the soldier's head. No, Wife. She stays here for now, and we take the money. That's all."

It was the smallest of victories in the midst of crushing defeats.

That evening, with the door securely bolted again, Abigail could sing the Prophetess Deborah's song as she bounced the baby on her knee:

> *"Then loud beat the horses' hoofs*
> *with the galloping, galloping of his steeds.*
> *May all Your enemies perish, O LORD!*
> *But Your friends be like the sun*
> *as he rises in his might!"* [7]

If she sang it louder than strictly necessary, it was because the tune and the bouncing made Deborah giggle so . . . and because Abigail wanted Athena to hear.

FIFTH PROPHECY

The Lord Is My Shepherd

The LORD is my shepherd;
I have all that I need.
He lets me rest in green meadows;
He leads me beside peaceful streams.
He renews my strength.
He guides me along right paths,
bringing honor to His name.
Even when I walk
through the darkest valley,
I will not be afraid,
for You are close beside me.
Your rod and Your staff
protect and comfort me.
You prepare a feast for me
in the presence of my enemies.
You honor me by anointing my head with oil.
My cup overflows with blessings.
Surely Your goodness and unfailing love will pursue me
all the days of my life,
and I will live in the house of the LORD
forever.

PSALM 23:1-6 NLT

11

CHAPTER

The knock on Abigail's door early the next morning was completely unexpected. If Komer wanted anything, he stood in the work yard and shouted her name. No one else ever called. Abigail carefully slid back the bolt and opened the door the smallest crack. Peering out, she was confronted by the wizened features of her husband, Zakane.

Hope surged through Abigail. Had he come to offer mercy? He had always been kind while they were married. Did he know how badly she had been abused and come out of pity?

Most likely she would now live in his household as a servant—as a slave—instead of his wife. But it would be a better home for Deborah than this.

Opening the door wider, Abigail said, "Good morning, Zakane."

There was no mercy in his hard eyes, no pity on the stern face. If Zakane's features had been carved from granite, they could not have been colder. "I want to know the name of the man with whom you betrayed me," he said. "I must know it."

Abigail had kept silent through whipping and abuse and vandalism. What could possibly make Zakane think she would betray her lover now?

When Abigail waited without speaking, Zakane continued, "I must know the truth! Do you know what it's like for me now? When I go to synagogue, every man stares at me as if he knows my private shame. And do you know what else? Instead of praying, I watch the expressions of every one of the other nine in the minyan, looking for clues. I think, *Is he the one? Could he be guilty?* I know everyone in the village. All their sons. Which of them betrayed me? How can I go on living here with such a load to bear?"

No expression of regard for what Abigail faced. No concern for her life or the baby's.

Still, Abigail was ashamed of what she had done. Despite everything that had happened, she was sorry for Zakane. She regretted the loss of respect in Zakane's old age.

"I am . . . what happened was wrong," she said. "I make no excuses, and I am very, very sorry. But I cannot give up his name."

Craftiness spread across Zakane's face. His pointed nose and chin suddenly became foxlike. Backing up a pace, he lifted a small leather pouch and dumped its contents into his palm. "Look," he said, extending the coins so they glinted in the morning sun. "Twenty tetradrachmae. Enough for you to move to a new town. Set up a home. Care for your . . . the child. All I ask is the name. I must have his name!"

Abigail was sorely tempted. It was enough money to rent a home or at least a decent room in Shechem. Then she and Deborah would be safe from the persecutors in Sychar. There she could wait until her lover came for her.

At the same moment she realized the utter impossibility of the exchange. If she betrayed Deborah's father, he would never come for them. Abigail would have traded a few months' living for a lifetime of loneliness. Zakane's gold was no answer . . . not on his terms.

She shook her head. "I cannot accept your offer. I'm sorry."

Stepping back and closing the door, she heard him say, "You will be sorry. Oh yes, you will be very sorry. I'll see to that."

Though the whitewashed exterior of Rabbi Tabor's mud-brick home was crumbling, the spring morning glare was troubling to Zakane's gray eyes. His shuffling feet suggested he hoped the rabbi would answer his knock quickly and admit him to the dim interior.

As he waited outside the slatted door, he used his crutch to stab idly at the bottom of the wall, pushing holes through the crusty white outer layer of clay.

A clattering on the wood told Zakane the rabbi was unbolting the door. Before it had even swung aside, Tabor was flattering the old man. "God surely smiles on my house this day that such a wise, honorable man should pay me a visit."

Zakane rolled his eyes. "Don't forget rich, Rabbi. Invite me in, if you love me so much. I am tired from my walk here."

"Have you come without a single servant?" Tabor inquired, leaning to peer around Zakane up both directions of the street.

"Yes." Zakane stepped toward the entry to hurry the rabbi backward. "I have come on a . . . personal matter."

"Of course," Tabor said, allowing him past. "As chief rabbi to the faithful in Sychar—"

Zakane sighed, annoyed. "You're the only rabbi in Sychar, Tabor. Though, for as much as I give the synagogue, we could have a sight more."

"And I am heartily grateful for it," Tabor interjected. "I hope my son might one day . . ."

"Enough," Zakane hissed with a cold stare.

Tabor nodded silently.

The two men stood in the center of the chamber. Neither spoke of sitting.

"I am here about a personal matter, as I said," Zakane continued. "I do not wish to waste the entire day on ridiculous pleasantries before I come to the point."

Tabor did not reply.

The old man exhaled. "Tabor, I am old. All I have I earned by trading years of my life for hard labor and much travel. Now I am too tired to leave, too tired to pack up all my household belongings and *wealth*—" he stressed the word—"and resettle somewhere else."

Tabor sounded panicked when he replied, "Of course not, Zakane. Without question, you should not even consider such a thing."

"And yet, what do I find here, Rabbi? Every day I walk among our townspeople, and I am shamed by the acts of my harlot wife. What good is wealth? It cannot grant respect. In all my years, I worked not for money but for respect. I took her in, rejecting the superstitious mutterings and the gossip of the mob. I shielded her! And now I am made a laughingstock?"

In spite of a halfhearted protest from Tabor, Zakane added, "Don't think I haven't heard what they're saying. 'Poor old Zakane, unable to satisfy the lady, and she strayed.' And, 'Poor old Zakane. I'd kill myself before I allowed such a slight to go unpunished!' This cannot stand, Tabor. Something must be done."

"But what, Zakane?" Tabor spread his hands wide in honest help-lessness. "I was zealous—*zealous* for your honor and for the Law. Before HaShem, I was. You were there when her punishment was interrupted by the centurion. God's very laws have been interrupted by Rome. Not a man among us can change that, unless he wants to find himself on a cross. What more would you have me do?"

Through gritted teeth, Zakane explained, "Why is she allowed to remain in our midst? Why is she not forced out of Sychar? She is known and despised for her deeds, after all."

"But she will not go!" Tabor protested. "She refuses to leave us. Someone—unknown—is paying her expenses, and that infernal Gentile potter lodges her so inexpensively—"

"Rabbi," Zakane interrupted calmly, "you enjoy your post here, do you not?"

Tabor nodded.

"And am I right in thinking you wish to remain?"

Again the rabbi nodded, looking suddenly uneasy.

"Then I suggest you find a reason—anything our law allows—to see that the girl is removed from our town." Zakane pulled a small leather sack from his cloak and handed it to the rabbi. "This may help you accomplish that goal. Whatever portion you do not use is for you to keep." He paused. "But if you are unable to be rid of her, you will find yourself teaching Torah to lepers in Caesarea, with never another drachma to your name!"

The old man spun on his heel and strode through the door, leaving it, and the rabbi's jaw, wide open.

Three days after Zakane's visit to the Tabor home, the rabbi was ready to put his plan into action. "Saul!" Rabbi Tabor bellowed to his son.

"Fetch your cloak." And under his breath he added, "We've a harlot to shame."

"Sir?" Saul asked, emerging from their study chamber.

"Come along, boy. Synagogue business!"

At twenty-five years old, Saul was hardly a boy and hated it when his father called him that. But he did as he was told, laying aside his daily prescribed reading and following the rabbi into the street.

Saul was also studying to be a rabbi. It was his lifelong dream to follow in his father's footsteps. At least, that's what his father always told him. Day and night he studied the ancient scrolls that formed the basis of their religion. Saul did not discuss these things with his father.

"What business do we have in the market square, sir?" Saul asked his father. Rabbi Tabor preferred to be called "sir," instead of "Father" or "Papa." Addressing his elders with respect was a lesson beaten into Saul from a very young age.

Tabor mocked his question with a nasally tone. "What business? Don't ask stupid questions, boy. Follow where I lead and do as I say."

Saul hung his head and trudged along behind his father into the center of the village. As the streets widened, Saul could hear the vendors calling out their wares. The aromas of fresh fish, spring fruit, spices, and more were each paired with a human voice singing their praises.

A cluster of eight men looked up from deep conversation and greeted the rabbi and Saul. So, they were a minyan of ten. Clearly the meeting had been prearranged. But what was their purpose?

Saul glanced sideways at the stall of a fig seller as his father asked the fishmonger, "Any sign of her today?"

"No, Rabbi," the man replied. "Not today."

"Well, she has to eat," Tabor observed. "She'll be along eventually."

"Who, sir?" Saul asked, worried. "Why have we—?"

But the question was interrupted by Abigail as she entered the square. The minyan stirred silently like a pack of jackals preparing for an attack.

Abigail cradled her newborn gently in her arms, walking resolutely through the market from the opposite direction. Her upturned chin seemed poised to deflect the scorn of the citizens of Sychar.

Saul watched her as she approached a man selling berries.

"Disgraceful!" Saul heard Tabor hiss.

The synagogue chazzan sneered. "How can she afford food?"

"She is a kept woman," another returned. "Another name for a high-class harlot."

Saul reacted. "What do you find most disgraceful? That she has money to buy food, or that she lives to eat and feed her baby in the first place?"

"Hold your tongue, boy," Tabor snapped. "You're speaking of a cursed woman. Defense of such a vile sinner is as much as sinning yourself. Ah, here she comes." He instructed his companions, "Say as I do."

Abigail concluded her purchase and started walking through the stalls again but stopped cold when she saw the ten men blocking her way.

"Vile sinner!" proclaimed Tabor.

The chazzan spoke next: "Evil harlot and her putrid spawn."

Tabor elbowed Saul to join in, but his son shrank away, pressing himself against a wall between two carts.

A crowd began to form, so the rabbi continued without the tenth of their minyan.

"Wicked woman!"

"How can you live and disgrace yourself so?"

"That little monster is proof of your unfaithfulness before God."

"Will you deny it?"

"It would be better for the child to have died!"

"Why do you remain in Sychar?"

The crowd became a mob, circling Abigail and the baby. Contempt on the faces of the men alternated with fierce hatred from the women.

"Somebody take the baby," the fig seller's wife suggested as they searched for stones.

"You will not touch my child!" Abigail screamed.

Laughter answered her terror. "Look at her!"

"Let's finish what we started."

"Sir," Abigail pleaded with the rabbi, "you would not let them hurt my child!"

Tabor's face hardened. "The law of Mosheh is clear. . . ."

Saul stepped between his father and Abigail and suggested quietly, "The Law does not condemn the child, Father. Father, put an end to this!"

The clatter of a horse's hooves and hobnailed sandals sounded from the highway, heading toward the outskirts of the souk. A man's stern voice demanded, "Break it up. In the name of Governor Pilate!"

Centurion Romulus was mounted. A dozen foot soldiers

accompanied him. When he sent four of his men into the fracas, the mob scattered, leaving Abigail panting and terrified before the rabbi and the judges. Saul stepped back into the shadows.

Romulus did not speak. There was no need. His rank and air of authority were enough to send a ripple of terror through the citizens of Sychar.

Saul heard the whisper, "So she really is the centurion's woman. Look at him. It must be his child then." He watched as the soldiers brought Abigail to the Roman.

Romulus glared down at her. "You are a fool to enter this city."

"I have no choice, sir."

The centurion stood in his stirrups and scanned the faces of the people. He leveled his gaze on Rabbi Tabor. "Your religion is nothing to me. *I* am the law in Sychar. *I* am Rome. You will answer to me if this woman or her child is harmed."

Hatred for Abigail was suddenly overshadowed by fear of a Roman's authority. So it was clear to all. Abigail was the woman of Romulus; this was his child. She was under his protection.

Romulus commanded her, "Go home. No one will harm you. They understand the penalty too clearly."

12 | CHAPTER

In a sweet voice, as soft as a gentle breeze so as not to offend the potter or his wife, Abigail sang her lullaby to Deborah. The sound swirled around the ranks of pottery, resonating in their emptiness like the stirring of the air before a spring rain.

Deborah breathed deeply and easily, her eyelids fluttering as Abigail sang.

> *"Love to light my darkest night,*
> *to cool the warmest day.*
> *Love, HaShem's most perfect sight,*
> *in all he might survey.*
>
> *Angels fly on silent wing,*
> *sent from heaven above.*
> *With one voice they sweetly sing,*
> *sweet dreams for my Love."*

A loud knock reverberated on the storeroom door. The baby awoke with a start and began crying.

Abigail's heart pounded. Had the townspeople returned in the dark of night to arrest and stone her?

The clatter came again. "Open up! We know you're in there. We can hear that illicit spawn crying."

It was the rabbi. Abigail heard no other voice, but she knew he wasn't alone from the words he spoke.

"What do you want!" she shouted back. "The centurion said I am to be left in peace."

Another voice, dripping enticement, replied, "No harm will come to you. We only wish to talk."

"Who's that?" she asked, holding Deborah closer to quiet her cries.

"It is Jerash the Merchant. Please open the door. We only wish to talk."

Jerash. The one who helped flog her weeks before. Why did he speak to her now as a caring brother?

Reluctantly, Abigail did as they asked, afraid she was falling into a trap. Citing their law, these elders of the town could force the door down with impunity if they chose. She cautiously unlocked the portal, then immediately retreated the few steps to her cot, clutching Deborah in her arms. "It's open," she said simply and held her breath as the men pushed the door inward.

Behind them, Abigail could see Komer the Potter and his wife, Athena, both in nightclothes, watching the scene with irritation. She silently prayed this late-night intrusion would not be enough to convince them to throw her out into the street once again.

The Samaritan men stood in the doorway, neither speaking a word at first.

"What do you want?" Abigail demanded. "You have no right to bother me here. I am a lawful renter of a Gentile's room."

Rabbi Tabor spoke. "And I am the representative of God's law on earth, with every authority that entails. Now you would be wise to stop speaking out of turn and listen to what we have to say."

Jerash was nodding. He wore a thoughtful look, out of place on his unintelligent features. "We only want what's best for you, Abigail." As his eyes wandered over her entire body, a chill coursed up her spine.

His leer and the ridiculousness of the statement made her bold. "Is that what you were thinking when you split my back open?"

The rabbi clenched his fist and stepped toward Abigail as though he might strike her, but Jerash raised his left arm to stay the rabbi.

"We were only doing what our law prescribes in such a case. You must admit that your condition in the absence of . . . a husband . . . is highly suspect."

"I already told you, I was raped."

"And that is why we've come," Jerash continued. "We are prepared to believe you. But you must name the guilty party, so he may be dealt with. We cannot let such a wicked sin go unpunished, but we cannot punish the wicked if we do not know who he is."

"I am no fool," Abigail said. "The only thing keeping Deborah and myself alive is the fact that you do not yet know who her father is, or all three of us would be stoned to death already."

"You are a fool," Tabor exploded, "if you think we will allow such defiance! You are nothing but a common harlot, and we will drive you from our presence one way or another."

He pushed past Jerash's blockading arm and stood face-to-face with Abigail. Deborah began to wail again.

"Do you really think that Roman would care—or even notice—if you were suddenly gone? Do you think even a single person in Sychar would tell the centurion where you were buried?" He raised a finger to poke at the crying baby, and Abigail held her away from him. "Where *this* was buried?"

Abigail peered around him and saw Athena glaring at her, shaking her head.

"It is not safe for you here," said Jerash. "We think it would be best for everyone if you were to leave Sychar and never return."

She looked from the rabbi to Jerash, then back again. "You do not know what you are asking of me. Rabbi, I was one of your faithful. I would be still. . . . Please, you know there is nowhere an unwed mother and her baby can go. You know it."

"Then tell us," Tabor hissed. "Tell us who is the father, so we may dispense justice according to our law."

Abigail was in tears. "I cannot. I won't. Leave now. I don't wish to speak of this anymore. Go. Or I will report to the centurion tomorrow how you've threatened me in my own room." When they did not immediately move for the door, Abigail raised her voice to a shriek. "Go! Get out, Jerash. Leave me alone, Tabor. The centurion has given you orders not to hurt me. Leave me alone!"

The men hurried out then, afraid other neighbors might hear her use their names and the story would reach the ears of the Roman after all. Abigail slammed the door behind them, hefting the bolt roughly into place.

It was quite a while before Deborah could be coaxed back to sleep.

As Saul finished his evening readings by a single dim candle, he heard his father storm into their house with Jerash in tow. He could tell from their angry tone that the evening's errand must not have been successful, and Saul wanted to know what happened. He extinguished the thin ribbon of flame and felt his way to the low door beyond his reading table, pressing his ear to the slats.

"I tell you, Jerash," his father ranted, "she needs to learn her place! We cannot have such open rebellion and denial of authority by even one stupid girl . . . no, *especially* by one stupid girl . . . or our positions will be in question."

Jerash replied, "Of course you are right, Rabbi. But it was foolish to threaten her so openly. By resorting to such drastic measures, we've let at least two other people know where to send the Roman inquiry."

"The potter?" Tabor scoffed. "He'll no more send the Romans after us than he would his own wife. He's comfortable with his position in Sychar. Our merchants may need his trade, but he needs them just as much. If you or I were condemned by his Gentile finger, there's no village in Samaria that would have him."

Saul slipped into the larger room unnoticed and spoke up then. "Why don't you leave the poor girl alone? There is another party to her guilt, after all."

"It is that information we are trying to get from her, Saul," Tabor rebuked. "She knows they would both be stoned if they were found out, and she refuses to name the man for her own safety and that of her illicit child."

"Why should she be punished?" Saul persisted. "She may have had no control over the thing. And now she is merely caring for a child as well as any mother who—"

"You forget yourself, boy!" Tabor bellowed. "She brought her condition on herself. She ought to have lived a life of seclusion while poor old Zakane was away. Instead she flaunted her freedom by frequenting public places alone. She flaunted her enticing looks. It is no wonder she was taken for a common strumpet."

"And taken," Jerash asserted, "like a harlot."

Saul was indignant but ignored the crude joke. "I disagree, sir. The man who did this had evil in his heart that would not be refused, no matter how chaste Abigail—"

"I forbid you to use that name in my house, boy!" said Tabor. He turned to Jerash. "I apologize for my son's churlishness. Is it any wonder he can't be successfully married off? He knows nothing of what strength of character a man's life demands. Speaking up for the harlot, indeed!"

"Stop discussing me as if I'm not here!" Saul yelled. "I'm twenty-five years old. Old enough to understand right from wrong and . . . and . . ." He lost his train of thought.

"Yet not old enough to know when to keep his mouth shut." Rabbi Tabor laughed at Saul's stammering.

Saul persisted. "I was going to say that I know right from wrong, though I do not always do right. Perhaps I am the only one in this room with such a problem?" A sarcastic thought struck him. "I know I am not, because what you're doing to Abigail is wrong. You know it, yet you do it anyway."

"That's enough!" Tabor bellowed. "When you are a rabbi, you may talk to me about following the Law. Until then, you know nothing."

"And if I know nothing of following the Law, Father, simply because I am not yet a rabbi, then I will not be held accountable when I do *not* follow it. Neither can Abigail be."

Tabor lashed out at Saul with a vicious backhand blow that spun him toward his room. "I told you: Never use that harlot's name in this house again!"

Without turning back toward the men, Saul put his hand to his cheek, muttering, "You're lucky, old man, that I know more of the Law than you say I do." He pulled the door open again and shut himself in the dark room.

As Tabor and Jerash resumed discussing Abigail's fate, Saul lay back on his cot and stared toward the ceiling in the pitch black. He was a man. In the eyes of the Law, supposedly so precious to his father, Saul had been a man for twelve years. Yet he was treated as a child, his opinions disregarded and mocked.

Emotion clenched his throat, and hot, angry tears streamed from his eyes.

His father was a terrible man. *Only one who is without sin*, Saul thought, *could bring true justice to Sychar.*

Saul wondered if such a man existed in all the world, or whether every righteous man was merely pretending. "For what purpose?" he mouthed.

What benefit is an outward appearance of righteousness, when the soul remains damned? Can't they see the futility of their lie?

It is better to admit one's faults before the Law and spend every waking moment in atonement than to pretend to have none and spend eternity in torment. With that gloomy thought, Saul drifted into fitful sleep.

It was the day after the rabbi's visit. With a jug of water toted back from Jacob's Well as dawn was breaking, Abigail had washed out Deborah's baby things and hung them over a pottery curing rack to dry. With what remained of the water Abigail gave the infant a bath in the largest of the kneading bowls, borrowed from Komer for the purpose.

While she scrubbed the delighted child Abigail sang Hannah's song, composed after the miraculous birth of the prophet Samuel:

"There is none holy like the LORD;
  there is none besides You."

Abigail's sweet, lilting voice drifted up the hill behind the work yard. It made the men tramping in Komer's clay pit smile. It floated over the eaves of the house and lifted the heart of the charcoal seller.

"There is no Rock like our God.
Talk no more so very proudly,
  let not arrogance come from your mouth." [8]

"Stop that singing," Athena demanded, bustling round the corner of the building like a wine jar rolling downhill. "Stop it, do you hear?"

"I'm sorry if my singing disturbed you," Abigail said. "I'll be quieter after this."

"No, you won't," Athena returned. "You won't sing here at all."

What new persecution was this? How could someone—anyone—keep another person from singing? The truth was, Abigail had little enough to carol about, but since it pleased Deborah, why must she stop?

"What do you mean?"

"I mean, you're leaving. Today. Now. Get your brat's things out of my husband's yard and your filthy belongings out of our storeroom."

"I don't understand," Abigail protested. "Your husband said—"

"Komer!" Athena bellowed. "Komer, come here!"

With shuffling step and bowed head, Komer followed his wife's arc. He appeared around the side of the house like a wayward moon dragged by a brazen sun across the sky.

"Tell her," Athena demanded.

"What does she mean?" Abigail asked softly so as not to frighten the baby, though her own heart was pounding.

"Well, it's this way, see . . . ," Komer began.

"I thought you said you wanted the rent money to continue," Abigail said, her voice trembling a bit.

"That's what I'm trying to tell you," the potter said. "I . . . I got a better offer for the room."

"You—?"

Athena took over the explanation. "Are you deaf as well as wicked? We got a better offer. Twenty tetradrachmae."

Suspicion dawned in Abigail's mind. "Twenty?"

"From your former husband," Athena said, confirming Abigail's thoughts. "Lots more than what your . . . *man* . . . paid us. Besides, that one hasn't come to see you, has he? Bet he's lost interest in you. On to some other filly, no doubt."

Snatching up Deborah, Abigail wrapped the child in a scrap of blanket and hugged her close. "But where are we to go now? Where *can* I go?"

Hands on her ample hips, Athena announced with satisfaction, "Not our concern. None." Then, eyeing the kneading bowl, as if expecting Abigail to try to steal it, she added, "Don't take anything but what belongs to you, either. And don't think I won't check, 'cause I will."

"I'm sure you will," Abigail said wearily. "I'm sure of it."

13 CHAPTER

S ince being forced to leave the potter's house, Abigail and Deborah had again taken temporary shelter in Sychar's sheepfold. Lambs and their mothers were not disturbed by the human infant and her ewe, but the peaceful sense within the animal pens did not calm the swirl of Abigail's thoughts. There was only one way forward that she could see. It was a desperate solution. So was her need. Though she prayed through sunset, fixing her resolution in place, her courage almost failed her at the very beginning of her nighttime journey.

Just as she and Deborah left the security of the sheepfold, she turned a corner and nearly ran headlong into a watchman.

Luckily, he was staring the other way and draining a flask of wine besides. Abigail retreated swiftly into the shadows and waited to see if he gave any sign of having noticed her. Her heart racing, Abigail berated herself for not being more cautious. Just because she had finally made up her mind to confront her *Machama* and ask for his help did not mean there was no reason for caution.

Abigail had seen plenty of evidence to prove his weak, vacillating character. He had never made good on his promise to take her away with him. He had left her to fend for herself against the ravening she-wolves of Sychar and the synagogue's elders. Latest in his string of shortcomings, he must have heard how she was turned out of the potter's shed, yet had made no other provision for her shelter.

He had made no further attempt to contact her at all.

Gone were the days of endearing words whispered in her ear. Vanished were the sighed promises of how they would be together always if only she would be patient.

The last thing Abigail wanted to do was frighten him. Now was not the time for him to deny ever knowing her. What Abigail wanted was practical help. He was the only source possible, so help he must.

Without any lamp on this moonless night, Abigail relied on the lights shining from the windows of houses to guide her. It was a lonely, comfortless feeling. In those homes families gathered to eat supper. Fathers read Torah portions with their sons. Mothers taught the alef-bet to the youngest children. Sisters chorused psalms together. Brothers enacted heroic scenes: Jacob wrestling with the Angel of the Lord.

All these cheerful thoughts were for others . . . not for her. She was outside, wandering the paths of darkness and separation. Recognizing the wide gulf between her and the rest of the world struck Abigail with deepest longing. Where could she build a home for Deborah? Where could Abigail safeguard the life more dear than any other?

While she was absorbed in these morose musings, she trod on something that wriggled and squirmed under her feet. The snake lashed out at her, striking the skirt of Abigail's robe but missing the flesh beneath. As Abigail jumped sideways, the adder slithered the opposite direction.

Abigail stood completely frozen, not knowing whether to remain still or to run. Her resolve shaken, she was ready to abandon her plan and turn back. Now there was something more terrifying than having no home: the vision of Deborah having no mother!

Abigail took a careful step, then another. Darkness shrouded both forward and backward routes. It was no more difficult to press on than to retreat.

She approached the back of the house toward which she had been aiming. Bits of flaking whitewash from crumbling plastered walls crunched under her feet, but Abigail paid it no heed. Creeping up to a window, she stood tiptoe to peer in.

For the first time this night she was in luck; her lover sat at a study table . . . alone. By the light of an oil lamp he was writing on a sheet of parchment. A scroll, partially unrolled, was pushed aside out of his way.

As much as Abigail despised the way he had treated her, and even more his disregard of their child, she softened at the sight of him. If only he would show himself to be a man! Even at this late hour she was still tender toward him, still wholly committed to him, as she had proven over and over.

Her hand on the door latch, Abigail hesitated for the third time that night. What if he rejected her now? What if by coming here she ruined every hope she had? What if he was even now writing her a letter of love and devotion to reward her patience?

Abigail took the moment of indecision to pat Deborah in the sling around her neck. Offered as a gesture of comfort to the child, it became a vow of determination for the mother: *I swear by this life that I hold most precious I will not draw back from getting her the aid we need.*

If her *Machama* was writing her a love letter, then he could share the contents with her in person!

She pushed open the door and advanced into the room.

The rabbi's son looked up with alarm. There was no sign of welcome on his worried face. He did not rise to greet her or embrace her.

"You?" he said bluntly. "What are you doing here? You must leave at once."

"Where am I to go?" Abigail returned. "You know how I was forced from the potter's shed. Deborah—yes, that's your daughter's name—Deborah and I will be sleeping in a sheepfold. We need your help, Saul."

"Not now! Not tonight," he argued, shooting a frantic glance at the door between the study and the rest of the Tabor home. "Please, don't do this. Tomorrow I'll . . . I'll think of something."

"No, Saul," Abigail replied firmly. "Tonight."

"All right, yes." Shoving aside the parchment, he rummaged in the desk. "I was going to find another room for you. I just . . . getting the money from my father is hard. He wants to know why I need it. But here." He thrust a handful of coppers into her hands, spilling them on the floor. "It's enough for a room at an inn for tonight. Go quickly. I have to finish this." He gestured toward the writing. "My father will be back soon for it. He wanted it done hours ago."

Picking up a copper that had rolled beneath a chair, Abigail asked, "What is it?"

"It's the terms of a marriage contract."

Abigail's heart soared. "Marriage? You mean it? Why didn't you—?" She almost leapt toward him, only to be halted midstride by his upraised hand. Cold dread seized her.

"It's . . . it's not for you. Not for us. My father has arranged my marriage to the daughter of the rabbi of Sebaste."

"Your *marriage*?" Abigail heard her own voice as if it were coming from very far away. Her head swam, and she groped for the edge of the study table for support to keep from falling.

"Yes, but I promise I'll still . . . I can still do something. . . ."

The door to the study opened, and Rabbi Tabor strode in. His face was a mask of carved flint . . . a likeness of the pagan god of Tyre: Baal Hadad, the Thunderer. "So," he said.

"Sir," Saul began, "this woman came to us for help. She—"

"Stop," the rabbi said tersely. "Don't lie to me. I heard it all."

"I intended to tell you," Saul whined. "She . . . she used her wiles on me. She enticed me."

"Stop it!" Tabor shouted. Striding across the chamber, he struck Saul on the cheek with the back of his hand. Whirling around, he confronted Abigail. "This must not become known. If you try to make a public accusation, no one will believe you. You will be humiliated. You will be charged with bearing false witness and not even your Roman friend will save you. Your child will be taken away. Do you understand? I can do this. We can do this." Addressing Saul, he ordered, "Stand up! Be a man. Say you renounce her utterly."

"I renounce . . ."

"Louder!"

"I renounce you! She-demon who entrapped me, you no longer have power over me. Be gone!"

Hunching her shoulders and crossing her arms protectively over Deborah, Abigail fled. Outside the room she plunged back into the lonely isolation of the Samaritan night and of the utter aloneness of her soul.

After being turned out of the rabbi's house—out of any shelter and out of all expectations—Abigail wandered aimlessly in the night. Overhead the starry host winked in the warmth still radiating back from sun-baked fields. In the west the reddish wandering light called Ma'Adim, or The Adam, was setting within the grasp of The Water Bearer. Abigail's third husband had been a seafaring man. It was he who taught her to read the signs in the heavens.

She did so now without consciously noticing. Her thoughts were fixed on everything and nothing.

The gloom of utter betrayal dragged her down. Anger, fear, worry, and despair each succeeded the other without boundary, without end. Where was the God of Jacob, who had directed the patriarch's steps? Where was the One who had promised to meet every need?

The dream of Hagar, mother of Ishmael, was likewise proven false. It might be true that the Angel of the Lord met the banished slave girl beside the Well of the Living God Who Sees. But HaShem did not see Abigail. He did not see her need. He did not see her thirst for steadfast love. Jacob's Well would never represent Beer-lahai-roi for her.

Abigail concluded there was no divine assistance for her. Dreams did not feed or clothe her child. She was beyond HaShem's care, and she knew it. Hope would not be born anew with the dawn. The sun might rise, but Abigail's spirits would not.

She might have gone back to Jacob's Well. Blind Leah would speak kindly to her. The cleft in the rock was still there. But the recollection of the viper's attack was fresh in Abigail's mind. The day's heat drove the snakes to seek shade. They hunted by night. Abigail would not take Deborah into that tangle of brush and stones in the dark.

She finally remembered the handful of coins carried in a fold of her robe secured by a loop of belt. Abigail touched them carefully, afraid she might spill them.

She found her way to the alley behind an inn. The establishment just inside Sychar's city gate was called The Stones of Joshua. It was not a caravansary. It served simple meals, wine and barley beer, and provided a handful of rooms. Its proprietors were an elderly Jewish couple named Ezra and Tzippi. They were almost the only members of the Jewish faith in this Samaritan town. Jewish pilgrims wishing to visit Jacob's Well and other scenes from the lives of the patriarchs booked the chambers.

It was a maxim that Jews have no dealings with Samaritans. Ezra and Tzippi provided a refuge and source of provisions for Jews passing between Judea and Galilee.

Abigail knocked softly at first, then driven by the need to protect Deborah, more boldly.

"I hear you. I'm coming," a voice from within proclaimed.

The door opened, and Abigail recognized the owner. Soundlessly he invited her in and gestured for her to approach a lamp gleaming on the serving counter. Ezra did not seem angry at being disturbed in the middle of the night. Jewish travelers who tried and failed to cross Samaritan territory in one day frequently showed up at awkward hours.

Kind, watery blue eyes studied her. Age had drawn his cheeks downward, but Ezra offered a generous smile for the babe in arms. "I know you. Your name is Abigail, I think."

He did not call her "harlot of Sychar."

"Please, sir," she said, unfolding the pouch of her robe and spreading the coins across the wooden planks, "is this enough for a room for tonight? I have no place else to go."

With the tip of a bent and bony forefinger Ezra pushed the coins around, separating them into two piles. His wife, a short, plump, pleasant-faced woman with her hair wound in tight coils on the sides of her head, padded silently to stand beside her husband.

Ezra's lips pushed in and out in rhythm with his tallying. "Plenty."

Tzippi nodded her agreement.

"Comes with a meal, too," Ezra continued. "No pilgrims this time of year. Too hot. Every room empty." He shoved the second heap of coppers back to Abigail. "A second night if you need it. Come along," he offered, lifting the lamp from the counter. "I'll show you the way."

SIXTH PROPHECY

Springs of Life-Giving Water

"They will never again be hungry or thirsty;
they will never be scorched by the heat of the sun.
For the Lamb on the throne
will be their Shepherd.
He will lead them to springs of life-giving water.
And God will wipe every tear from their eyes."

REVELATION 7:16-17 NLT

14

CHAPTER

bigail awoke with a song on her lips:

*"Give thanks to the LORD, for He is good,
    for His steadfast love
    endures forever."* ⁹

It was still true that she had nowhere of her own to go to. It was still true she and her baby had been rejected and abandoned by Saul. It was still true that life in Sychar would not suddenly become easy.

And yet, out of the depths of her despair, she had cried aloud to HaShem, and He had heard her. Being taken in by Ezra and Tzippi without question, without sneering or mocking—to have this safety for even one night made Abigail almost weep with relief.

The room in The Stones of Joshua was simple enough: Pallet stuffed with sweet-smelling straw on the freshly swept floor. Table and stool. Pegs on the wall for clothing.

That was all, but it made for a brighter morning than Abigail had imagined was possible.

She sat in the lone chair, winding up her hair in a braid. When she glanced at the mattress, Abigail was surprised to see Deborah considering her with wide-eyed concentration. Abigail had not known the child was awake.

"No crying?" she asked. Deborah reacted to her mother's voice, waving stumpy fists and wiggling. "Did my singing bother you?" Abigail offered another sample of her praise:

> "*Give thanks to the God of gods*
>   *for His steadfast love endures forever.*
> *Give thanks to the Lord of lords,*
>   *for His steadfast love endures forever.*"[10]

"When you are not very much older, little one," Abigail promised, "I'll teach you to sing the chorus. Then I will begin: '*To Him who alone does great wonders.*' And you will answer: '*For His steadfast love endures forever.*' Do you like it?"

Deborah gurgled her response.

"And we can stay here one more night," Abigail added, speaking her thoughts aloud. "I don't know where we'll go tomorrow." She shivered. Where would they be then? Back among the beggars of Jacob's Well?

She thought of Weasel. There were worse fates than being a beggar.

Abigail thrust the hateful images away. Not today. Today she would not give in to gloom. Today she would sing. "Listen, baby. Do you know this one?

> "*Give ear, O heavens, and I will speak,*
>   *and let the earth hear the words of my mouth.*
> *For I will proclaim the Name of the LORD;*
>   *ascribe greatness to our God!*"[11]

Deborah laughed and signaled her approval.

"Do you know who wrote that, little one? Mosheh, the man of God, sang it to all Israel. Remember, he is the greatest prophet of all, yet he said HaShem would send another like him who would restore all things."

What an enormous task Messiah would have! Was there any part of life on earth that was not broken, damaged, or disappointing in some way? So much needed restoration. How would He know where to begin?

> *"The Rock, His work is perfect,*
>   *for all His ways are justice.*
> *A God of faithfulness . . ."*[12]

There was a gentle tapping at Abigail's door. Once more she felt a wave of panic. Recently every signal for her to answer had meant loss, separation, humiliation, or danger.

"Come in?"

Tzippi slipped through the opening. Her silver hair still had a hint of the golden blond she had been in her youth. Round face beamed as though she had a surprise she was eager to share.

"Good morning, my dears, my very dear dears." She shuffled to the bed and leaned low over Deborah. "Little bee! Little bee!" She tickled Deborah's stomach and the baby burbled with laughter. "Oh, sweet as honey! Little bee! My very bee!"

The baby laughed encouragement. Tzippi scooped Deborah up and held her high over her head. Deborah's tentative giggle turned to an uproarious chuckle as Tzippi nibbled her toes. "Baby bee! Baby bee! Baby bee!"

Abigail and Tzippi cackled at Deborah's hilarity. How long had it been since Abigail had laughed? It was all nonsense. Nonsense! Wonderful glee. Her laughter brought tears of relief.

Tzippi cradled the child against her ample bosom. "Oh, she is a treasure. A treasure! And it's plain to see how much she loves her mother. Well, now. To business."

Abigail reached for her coins. "Oh yes. Another night's lodging."

"Put it away." Tzippi kissed Deborah. "Me and Ezra have talked it over." A long moment passed. "My daughter died in childbirth five years ago. Her husband remarried and moved on to Capernaum. Twice the work now. Me and Ezra, we're not what we used to be. I was saying just yesterday before you came, I could use help. And then here you are with the little one."

"But I'm a Samaritan. You are Jews."

"You're a mother. You've this little one to care for. I've seen what goes on."

"You know my reputation." Abigail hung her head.

"What a beautiful little girl. Deborah. Little Bee. How did you name her?"

"It came to me."

Tzippi nodded. "My daughter's name."

Silence. The two women kept their eyes fixed on the baby.

"Tzippi. Your name is short for Zipporah."

"Sparrow." Tzippi's expression seemed curious.

"I met a woman named Zipporah. She was kind to me."

"Well, then."

"She was a hard worker. Drawing water. I am a hard worker," Abigail stated flatly.

"Servant's room downstairs behind the stable. Nothing fancy. Room for you and Little Bee."

"I will work hard!" Abigail cried. "You won't be sorry."

"Plenty of pilgrims come our way in the season. Everyone wants to visit Jacob's Well on the way to Jerusalem. That means making beds. Hauling water. Laundry. Cooking. Can you cook? Early to rise and late to bed."

Abigail studied Tzippi. The old woman punctuated each sentence by kissing Deborah's toes.

"You would take me . . . us . . . in? After everything—"

"I have seen enough." Tzippi's smile did not waver. "But one more question. Will you sing as you work?"

Abigail remembered how the potter's wife hated her singing. "Have I offended—?"

"You sing like an angel. Such a voice! So. That is part of the bargain. You must sing for us."

Even after many weeks of singing and working at The Stones of Joshua, it remained easier to draw water from Jacob's Well at dawn or at the heat of midday. Walking down Sychar's streets for Abigail was akin to being recognized as a lone spy in an enemy camp. Venom and hatred were still directed at her from every side.

She wondered if the attitudes would change if the women of the town knew about the rabbi's son. Probably not. However horrified they might feel at first, they would quickly coalesce around excusing Saul of any wrongdoing. The women of Sychar might be robbed of an expected prey, but they would have another delicious crime to pin on Abigail.

Within the walls of the inn life was a different story. Abigail waited on tables, did the scrubbing, helped with the cooking, and sang every evening as well. She had never been happier since before her pregnancy became known.

The religious Jews who stayed in the inn were surprised and sometimes concerned that Ezra's serving wench was a Samaritan. The inn was kosher, yet they questioned his good sense. Pharisees mistrusted his religious convictions since he and Tzippi willingly lived among the despised Samaritans as a lone Jewish outpost.

On the night of Saul's wedding, the revelry penetrated the thick walls of the inn. Abigail thought of women who had once been her friends. They were dancing at the wedding of the man who had raped and then abandoned her to disgrace and shame. A strange detachment came over her as she looked at Ezra and Tzippi serving their guests. The elderly couple had become like family to her.

After supper, as the celebration of Saul's wedding became louder, Abigail took her seat beside the fire and began to sing.

> *"The LORD came from Sinai*
> *and dawned from Seir upon us.*
> *Yes, He loved His people,*
> *all His holy ones were in His hand."*[13]

Ezra beamed proudly at Abigail. Tzippi patted her hands together approvingly. She dandled Little Bee on her lap and let the baby tug the ends of her braids.

In Abigail's dream, Zipporah the Shepherdess had told her that a Redeemer was coming. *"The Lord held all His holy ones in His hand."* How long had Abigail wrongly pinned her hopes of rescue on the rabbi's son? That was over now.

When Abigail finished the song of Mosheh, someone in the crowd called out, "Give us a victory song. Give us a triumph."

Abigail understood the motive behind the request. Many Jews, especially those from the Galil, smarted under the whip of Rome and the mismanagement of Tetrarch Antipas. There was widespread but carefully concealed longing to be a great nation again, to experience freedom and have a king of whom they could be proud.

She obliged the appeal.

"I will sing to the Lord,
for He has triumphed gloriously;
Horse and rider
He has thrown into the sea."[14]

Deborah bouncing up and down on Tzippi's knee, Tzippi's cracking alto and Ezra's rumbling baritone led the chorus each time Abigail finished a verse.

As the song progressed, the tempo increased. So did the volume, finally drowning out the shouts and cheers of her lover's wedding. With the final line—*"Horse and rider He has thrown into the sea!"*—the patrons bellowed and stomped their feet as the walls echoed with the enthusiastic shouts.

The pilgrims wandered off to their rooms as the night settled to silence in Sychar. Abigail's thoughts went to Saul and his bride only briefly. There was work to do. All the wooden trenchers were scoured and the floor sanded and swept. When only a single lamp burned in the dining hall, Ezra brought Abigail a handful of coins left by appreciative customers. She had begun to put money aside week by week.

"A good night. You've earned it," Ezra said. "Besides, some of these folks tonight claim they heard about you in Yerushalayim. Said they weren't planning to stop here 'til they heard it. So, you see, you're bringing us more business. Go on, take it."

She held her earnings in her hand. "You are a righteous man."

"Grandmother Tzippi is rocking our Little Bee to sleep," he answered. "The Lord knew what she needed."

"And . . . what we . . ." She faltered.

"The wedding tonight." He shifted his weight uneasily. "The rabbi's son."

Did he see her color rise? "Yes."

"Abigail, I will not ask you."

"There are rumors?"

"Deborah. A resemblance. That's all."

Abigail's chin lifted and fell. "That is all. She is no part of him. Only a resemblance."

The Stones of Joshua was full to capacity with pilgrims en route from Galilee to Jerusalem for Yom Kippur. Such numbers of guests required three trips every day to draw water.

The stone plaza around Jacob's Well was deserted in the early light. It was a long, dusty walk from the inn to the water supply, and Abigail would have been glad for company. The distance was too great for Tzippi's frail limbs. No other female of Sychar would be seen speaking with, much less befriending, Abigail.

Abigail was mostly able to push such unhappy thoughts to the back of her mind. Occasionally a deliberately loud comment uttered in the marketplace still rankled. Small boys, egged on by their mothers, still shied dirt clods her direction before running away, giggling.

Sometimes Abigail had a chance encounter with Saul, from which he turned and fled much quicker than she.

But, for the most part, life was good.

This morning was a perfect example. The seasons of the year were revolving. Rosh Hashanah was past, and they were in the midst of the Ten Days of Awe. The morning was distinctly cooler as autumn approached. The air was full of the sweet, rich scent of drying figs and clusters of dates as the last of the fruit harvest was prepared before the arrival of the early rains.

Taking the water jar carefully down from her shoulder, Abigail lowered the goatskin bag into the depths of the well. When it was full to her satisfaction, Abigail drew it out, pulling hand over hand on the cord with a practiced motion.

She had only half filled the clay jar when she heard soldiers approaching. The tramp of their hobnailed boots raised explosions of dust with each step. The horse ridden by their centurion dragged the toe of each hoof as if the animal thought it too early to be on the march.

Unlacing his helmet, the officer removed his headgear and greeted her. It was Romulus.

"Ah," he said, "Abigail. You look well. And the child? She is growing properly?"

A few ribald comments drifted out of the troop. Abigail blushed.

Romulus whirled in his saddle. "Silence in the ranks!" he demanded. "Guard sergeant, see to it. I'll have no lack of discipline here."

Hanging from a hook beside the well was a dried gourd, cut in half to form a dipper. Abigail filled the ladle from her container and passed it to Romulus.

He drank deeply and thanked her.

"I'll do the same for your men," she said.

"Pour some into their hands as we march past," he said. "That's all they deserve. Guard sergeant, keep them closed up. Forward to Shechem. Quick time or no breakfast."

There was no more commentary as the soldiers filed past, each receiving a double handful of water.

The lack of speech did not take away the hungry desire Abigail saw in their eyes or prevent the knowing glances she saw exchanged.

Somehow word of her encounter managed to reach the inn before she did.

Ezra stopped her in the courtyard. "Not smart," he cautioned. "Not sensible. Being friendly with the Romans. Even those in Sychar who don't despise you already might change their minds."

"Romulus is a good man," Abigail argued. "He saved me . . . more than once."

"Just a warning, then," Ezra returned. "Jewish pilgrims may be down on Samaritans, but they hate Romans. And they hate collaborators worst of all."

SEVENTH PROPHECY

Jesus, the Lamb of God

The next day John saw Jesus coming toward him and said, "Look! The Lamb of God who takes away the sin of the world! He is the one I was talking about when I said, 'A man is coming after me who is far greater than I am, for He existed long before me.' I did not recognize Him as the Messiah, but I have been baptizing with water so that He might be revealed to Israel."

Then John testified, "I saw the Holy Spirit descending like a dove from heaven and resting upon Him. I didn't know He was the one, but when God sent me to baptize with water, He told me, 'The One on whom you see the Spirit descend and rest is the One who will baptize with the Holy Spirit.' I saw this happen to Jesus, so I testify that He is the Chosen One of God."

JOHN 1:29-34 NLT

Peaceful days and months at The Stones of Joshua turned into four years more quickly than Abigail could have imagined. The women of Sychar still despised Abigail for her beauty. Rumors about the identity of Deborah's father remained unanswered. After a while the gossips of Sychar almost forgot to ask the question. Time had dulled the raging hatred against Abigail the harlot. There were always new scandals to occupy the women who gossiped at Jacob's Well. Eventually Abigail and her illegitimate child were tolerated—moved down on the long list of offenders or tragedies or unhappy marriages. Among victims gleefully dissected by the sharp-tongued housewives of the Samaritan city were the rabbi's son and his bitter bride, Mara.

Mara remained childless after four long years of marriage. There was open bickering between man and wife. Saul was a most unhappy man, bonded to an even more unhappy woman. He shared with one or two men in the synagogue that Mara was a frigid shrew who left him cold and disgusted. She confided with one or two trusted friends that he was a bully filled with lust that left her cold and disgusted.

Beginning with the "one or two" who knew the secret misery, everyone in the marketplace soon learned the details. There were rumors that Saul went in disguise to visit the harlots at Weasel's inn. Rabbi Tabor threatened excommunication of anyone who spoke against his son and heir. The turmoil in the most prominent religious family in Sychar was a delicious feast.

Mara needed a child to make her happy, but she hated the act that would make a child possible. Saul had no interest in siring a child by Mara. And so the impasse was a continuing drama, played out like a Greek tragedy.

Abigail held her head high as she swung through the farmers' stalls in Sychar's souk. Four-year-old Deborah followed at Abigail's side. Her right wrist was lovingly secured by a red cord tied around Abigail's waist. Her thick black mop of curls framed a perfect oval face. Wide eyes with long lashes looked every man and woman in the face. Her smile was infectious.

"See! I lost a tooth." Her stubby finger pointed to the empty place where her tooth had been last week.

"And so you have, Little Bee. So you have!" The honey merchant's wife beamed.

"Chewing is . . . difficult," Deborah opined. "It makes me very sorry for old people who have no teeth at all."

Her precocious remark brought laughter from those who heard her. The honey merchant's wife dipped a stick into a honey pot and pulled out a bit of honeycomb. "Then you shall have honey to console your sweet heart."

"*Toda*," Deborah answered her with thanks.

Though the merchants addressed Abigail in businesslike tones, they greeted Deborah with genuine enthusiasm.

No one could deny Abigail's little girl was beautiful and bright. Deborah's smile charmed even the most treacherous females in the city.

Abigail purchased honey for the inn with hardly a word, but inside she was happy. Proud. Perhaps things would not be so difficult for Deborah as they had been for Abigail.

Abigail raised her eyes and met Saul's stormy ones. "You," he said, then stared at Deborah. "The child is beautiful."

Abigail did not speak but only nodded and pressed on as Mara grasped Saul's arm. Abigail stopped at the date seller's. Not far enough away to be spared the next scene in Saul and Mara's drama.

"A pretty thing." Mara raised her nose.

"So polite. Such a polite child," declared the honey merchant's wife to Mara.

"Yes." Mara sighed. "What a shame such a sweet creature is in the care of a vile woman. Don't you think so, Saul?"

He was staring at Abigail's back. He did not answer quickly enough. Mara hissed, "I'm talking to you."

"Yes?" he asked.

Mara turned away. "You're looking at a harlot. Because she can bear a child and I cannot."

Deborah, glancing over her shoulder, pulled at the cord on her wrist and whispered, "Mama, that man is staring at you. And the woman is staring at me. They seem very unhappy."

Abigail put a finger to her lips. "Say no more, Little Bee. It isn't polite to—"

Mara began to weep loudly. "Oh, I am a most unhappy woman! The most unhappy woman in Sychar. A harlot is given a beautiful child, and I am left barren and unloved—"

Saul snapped, "Woman, silence! You shame yourself!"

The outburst was too much. Abigail grasped Deborah's hand and spirited her away. She did not hear the end of the outburst. She did not want to.

There was a clique of five women whom Tzippi said were "sneaking warthogs in all their finery."

Today the warthogs lingered at Jacob's Well. They gossiped over Abigail's head and around her as though she wasn't there.

"He's a phony."

"He's a prophet! I heard it from my sister-in-law in Sebaste."

Abigail dropped the waterskin into the well. She drew it up more slowly than she had to. The news about the prophet from Galilee had spread everywhere along the pilgrim trail. Jews stopping at the inn were buzzing about the conflicts between Rome and Herod Antipas and the Temple authorities. But today's gossip contained new information.

"Maybe the Messiah?"

"His name is Yeshua of Nazareth."

"What good can come out of Nazareth?"

"It was a wedding, see? Ran out of wine—"

"That happened at my cousin's wedding too. They were absolutely—"

"Shut up! Let me tell you this. I heard it with my own ears."

"So tell it already."

"Anyway, a wedding. Cana. Jewish wedding. Out of wine. Disaster. So the steward goes to the mother of Yeshua to ask for help."

"Is she rich?"

"No. But she's the mother of Yeshua, see? So she talks to her son and asks him to help. Yeshua orders the large water jars to be filled at the well of Cana. Then, when they serve the water, it isn't water. It's true. I swear it. That's what I heard. It's turned to wine!"

The women stared at one another in disbelief. "Is this Yeshua married? What a catch. Water into wine. Not just any wine, but the best wine. Such a fellow could be very rich if he used his skills properly."

"I want to know if he's married."

Laughter all around.

Abigail filled her jar and imagined what it would be like to get the water home, taste it, and find that it was no longer water but the finest wine. She blurted, "Is Yeshua a prophet, do you think? Or . . . the Messiah?"

The women stared at her blankly as though she had spoken in a foreign tongue.

Abigail asked again, "Could he be? The Messiah, do you think? The Messiah?"

The leader of the sneaking warthogs, in her eagerness to insult Abigail, spilled her jar. "Stupid woman. We weren't talking to you."

"And what makes you think that a prophet of the Most High would have anything to do with the likes of you!"

Undeterred, Abigail said, "Mosheh gave our fathers water from the rock. Now this Yeshua takes plain water and turns it into wine. Mystical, don't you think?"

The silence was deafening. Faces hardened. Eyelids grew heavy with disgust. Abigail's childish eagerness dissipated. The women at the well ignored her. Turning their backs on her, they continued their chatter as she gathered her water jar and hurried away.

Strange how marginally Mara's outburst in the marketplace affected Abigail. Her past life and love for Saul now seemed nothing more than a vague dream. Long ago his interest in Deborah would have pleased her and given her hope that they might make a life together. Now his smile in Deborah's direction meant no more than that of a pilgrim commenting on the child's beauty or her cheerful disposition. The physical resemblance between Deborah and Saul was unmistakable, yet the connection was only skin-deep. Saul was a stranger to them both. The distance of years and time had severed Abigail from all yearning for him. She had a memory of what he had done to her, but bitterness no longer had a root in her heart.

The evening at The Stones had been quietly satisfying for Abigail. The handful of pilgrims had been wealthy ones. Abigail sang a half-dozen songs, then continued for a half-dozen more when the appreciative audience would not let her quit.

More to the point, a pair of rich Sadducees demonstrated their approval of the entertainment in a practical way. They contributed a handful of silver shekels to Abigail's savings.

Abigail returned to the cozy warmth of their quarters. Deborah was asleep on her cot, a rag doll cuddled in her arms. Abigail stood over her awhile, a sense of deep satisfaction filling her. Where would she be if it had not been for the kindness of Ezra and Tzippi? What would have become of her and Deborah if the couple had not taken her in and offered her a place to stay and honest work to do?

Deborah blinked up at her. "Mama?"

"Yes, Little Bee?"

"Is it time to wake up?"

"No." She touched Deborah's thick black curls. "Time to go to sleep."

Deborah sighed and closed her eyes again.

Abigail let down her thick, waist-length hair and began to brush it.

Deborah climbed from beneath her blanket and sat beside Abigail on a child-sized stool. The seat had been purchased by Tzippi, who doted on the girl. With a serious expression, Deborah duplicated her mother's actions stroke for stroke.

"Thought you were asleep hours ago," Abigail teased.

"Wasn't sleeping," Deborah protested. "Resting my eyes. I let Gramma Tzippi carry me 'cause it makes her happy."

"Uh-huh," Abigail acknowledged.

"Grampa Ezra says you sang better tonight than ever."

"Did he? Why is that, you think?"

"Because you're so happy," Deborah said in a small voice.

"I am. Happy." Abigail spun toward the girl and swept her up in her arms. "Because you are my rainbow, Little Bee! You are sweeter than honey!" Abigail nuzzled her daughter's neck while Deborah giggled and struggled.

Setting the child on her feet, Abigail held her by the shoulders at arm's length. "Now into bed. If you're going to the well with me tomorrow, we have to leave early, so get right to sleep."

"I'm already sleepy, Mama," Deborah acknowledged.

"Time for prayers," Abigail said. "May HaShem bless us and keep us." Deborah repeated the words.

"May HaShem make his face to shine upon us and be gracious to us."

" . . . gracious to us."

"May HaShem lift up his countenance upon us and give us peace."

" . . . count-nance and peace."[15]

As Abigail placed her right hand across her eyes, Deborah mimicked the action. In unison mother and daughter recited:

"Hear, O Israel: The LORD our God; the LORD is one."[16]

Uncovering their eyes, the two leaned toward each other, whispering, "Blessed is the Name of his glorious kingdom for all eternity."[17]

Deborah said in a drowsy voice, "Mama, help me with this part." The child's eyes were nearly shut.

"You shall love the LORD your God with all your heart and with all your soul and with all your might."[18]

" . . . *and might,*" Deborah echoed drowsily.

Abigail completed the rest of the recitation of the Shema, pulling the covers up around Deborah and planting another kiss on her cheek. "You shall teach these words to your children,"[19] she quoted. "Good night, Little Bee."

She was about to blow out the lamp when a tap sounded at her door. Ezra's voice called, "Abigail?" Probably some gratuity Abigail had forgotten to collect. Ezra was so scrupulously honest about passing on the coins. She padded in bare feet to open it. "You could have kept them 'til morning, Ezra," she said, yanking back the bolt. "I trust—"

Instead of Ezra's face, a heavy shoulder forced open the door, knocking Abigail back against the table.

"Help me!" she cried as Ezra's face appeared in the gloom outside.

A guard from the Gerazim shrine pinioned Abigail's arms behind her back while another shoved a gag in her mouth. Roughly she was pulled out into the courtyard.

Rabbi Tabor confronted her there. The other elders, Jerash and Abel, who had presided over her public flogging years earlier, flanked him.

So did Saul.

She struggled against her bonds. Ezra and Tzippi stood to the side, heads down. Tzippi wept openly. "My lamb! My Little Bee," the old woman moaned.

Saul's wife, Mara, bustled into the bedchamber. Her ruddy face was set in a victorious smirk. The dumpy woman carried something wrapped in a purple shawl.

Abigail shrieked into the cloth in her mouth, but only a muffled groan was audible. What was happening? How could this be? What were they doing?

Ignoring Abigail completely, Tabor addressed the Jewish couple. "We know this child is Samaritan by birth. She may be illegitimate, but she is still of our race and our faith. It is wrong for her to be raised in the household of Jews, who do not know our ways. And by a mother who is a known harlot. We will see this child is properly reared and instructed."

Ezra clenched his fists. "You are stealing her."

"You would do well to not interfere," Tabor warned.

From the courtyard Abigail heard Mara inside the room, coaxing Deborah awake: "Little girl? Wake up. We have a surprise for you. You get to go to a big, nice house."

Abigail's eyes widened, and she struggled against her captors.

A sleepy voice asked, "But where's my mama?"

"Don't worry about her. Let me wrap you in this nice, new shawl. And look what's in it—a doll. Would you like it?"

"For my very own?"

Abigail kicked the guard, managed to free one hand, and tried to rip the gag from her mouth. Before she could call out a warning to Deborah, she was seized again and the cloth jammed deeper in her throat.

"Interfering with our faith will not be tolerated," Tabor warned Ezra. "The prefect would certainly make you leave our territory if you tried."

"Let me carry you, child," Mara crooned to Deborah. "Just sleep, and when you awaken, you will have everything . . . everything." Mara emerged, toting Deborah in her arms.

"Mama?" Deborah asked, eyeing her mother in the shadows. "Will you come too?"

"It's a game," Mara said soothingly, striding quickly through the group. "Did you know there's even another doll at the big house? Would you like to have it too? Come, Saul."

Then they were gone.

Abigail was thrust back into her room and the door bolted on the outside. Spitting out the gag, she slammed her fists against the panels and shouted, "Don't do this! Please, don't do this. Don't take my baby! Please . . ."

Over her own anguished cries she heard Tabor declare with satisfaction, "I'll leave a guard here tonight, so you won't be tempted to release her. It's for her own good . . . and yours."

Then Tzippi began to keen as if death had entered the house. "Let me go to her. Poor Abigail! Lock me away with her. Please, I implore you!"

Abigail sank to the stone floor. The cries continued. The door crashed open, and Tzippi was thrust into the space.

Tzippi caught Abigail and held her. Abigail tore free and threw herself at the door. "Let me go to her. Please, don't do this!" She clawed at the rough planks, tearing her nails.

Her cries grew hoarse, and she sank to her knees. Her forehead rested against the barrier. "Please," she repeated in a barely audible voice. Then plaintively: "Deborah. Oh, Deborah."

Tzippi knelt beside her, clasping her by the shoulders. "Don't torment yourself, child. They won't hurt Little Bee. You must be patient."

"They've taken her," Abigail returned bitterly. "All I had to live for was her! All that mattered to me in the world was her. Why am I still breathing?"

"Don't say that," Tzippi urged. "You don't mean that. Don't tempt the Lord your God."

"Where is HaShem now? Where was he tonight?" Abigail demanded. "Why didn't he stop this?" she shrieked, then collapsed into sobs.

"Shh, my dear." Tzippi stroked Abigail's hair as if she were a child. "Shh. Don't give up hope. HaShem is keeping watch. You'll see."

Though quieter, Abigail would not be comforted. She sat on the floor, clutching Deborah's blanket to herself, rocking and rocking.

At dawn the latch popped, and the door was opened. Abigail jumped to her feet, her hair a tangled mess and her eyes bleary and red.

The guard blocked her exit. "Ain't you a sight?" he mocked. "Not such a fancy harlot now, are you?"

"Please let me out."

"Not without a warning first," the guard said, menacing her with a staff. "You go anywhere near the rabbi's place or come within a hundred cubits of the child, and you will be beaten. And you will be arrested." Then he spoke the most dire threat of all. "But what you won't do is see that brat ever again. Understand? There's guards watching all the time, see? Don't even try."

Abigail nodded, stunned at how thoroughly her life had been destroyed in the midst of what she believed was happiness. What had she just said to Deborah at bedtime? She had never been happier?

Abigail nodded her understanding of the order.

The guard turned on his heel and left.

The door was open. The sunshine was bright.

There was nothing but darkness all around Abigail. She felt herself inside a well—trapped in its depths without escape.

"Come into the house, child," Tzippi urged. "Let me fix you something to eat. Ezra will know what to do, you'll see. Come into the house."

Shoeless and still in her nightgown, Abigail stepped into the courtyard and bolted. Though Tzippi called after her, she neither turned nor slowed.

Out the gates she ran, to the amazed looks of passersby and the shouted derision of the sentries.

Where could she go? Who could help her? This was worse than being shunned, worse than being homeless. This was drowning on dry land—each breath more painful than the last and no rescue anywhere.

Without realizing where she ran, Abigail found herself atop the hill looming over Sychar's quarry. The precipice was sheer . . . a drop ten times the height of a man, onto a pile of jagged stones and rubble.

"Why not?" a voice whispered in Abigail's head. *"It's hopeless. You're useless. You can't change it. You can't fix it. There is no help for one like you. You're finally getting what you deserve, and you know it."*

Abigail looked around wildly. What difference would it make to anyone if she stepped forward two paces? The rocks would rush up to meet her, and then all this agony would be over.

She moved up to the very edge. It would not be difficult—not nearly so hard as living without Deborah. Never being allowed to hold her daughter, love her, sing with her.

If all that was gone, then life was already gone. Why not finish it?

Only one thing held her back. What if Tzippi was right? What if there was the least chance, the faintest gleam of a chance, that Abigail might get Deborah and run away with her? Even slaves escaped their masters. Sometimes they reached freedom. Sometimes there was life after despair.

Romulus, she thought. *What if Romulus can help me?*

To take the tiniest step forward was to deny there was any hope left. One pace would seal her separation from Deborah, who would grow up without her mother.

Abigail backed up a stride, then another. The quarry would still be here on another morning. The plunge to embrace the rocks would be possible another day. For today she would continue to live.

The city of Sebaste was a half-day's walk from Sychar, toward the northwest. In an earlier age of the world it had been the town of Samaria, from which the province drew its name. From being the royal city of King Ahab and Queen Jezebel hundreds of years before, it had declined in status until it was little more than a country village.

Then Herod the Butcher King decided to refurbish it and rename it in honor of his patron, Caesar Augustus. *Sebaste* was Greek for "Augustus." In its current form the principal buildings were less than fifty years of age. It was home to a garrison of Roman troops.

It was also where Centurion Romulus was on duty, though his home was in Sychar.

The day Abigail decided to make the trip to Sebaste she did not tell Ezra and Tzippi where she was going. Connecting them with any plea to a Roman against the citizens of Sychar would only do them harm.

Besides, they liked Roman rule even less than the Samaritans did. They might try to talk her out of the attempt.

Over two sleepless nights Abigail convinced herself that she had no other option. Tzippi might speak of having patience, of trusting in HaShem, but Abigail could not wait to recover her daughter. Romulus had always been kind to her. Surely he would help her now once she explained.

So she did not tell her Jewish family where she was going—only that she would be away all of the following day. "I'll be back before dark," she told Tzippi cheerfully.

The old woman studied Abigail's face and shook her head. "Be very careful. And may HaShem guide your steps."

Abigail was cautious. It was unusual for a woman to travel alone. So, for safety, she walked close behind a party of Jews, without imposing on them, on their way to Nazareth in Galilee.

"Have you heard what they said in Yerushalayim about Yeshua of Nazareth?" she overheard one of the group ask another. "That he's going to be another fiery preacher like his cousin, Yochanan the Baptizer."

"Then 'Good-bye, Yeshua,'" his companion returned. "Yochanan makes so many enemies—Pharisees, high priest, Herod Antipas, too. The only question is which of them will kill him first. Then they'll turn on Yeshua."

"What business does a carpenter have turning preacher, I ask you," the first questioner ventured. "And besides, wasn't there some scandal about his birth? Involving his mother, Mary?"

Abigail's ears perked up despite her aversion to gossip. So some other woman's reputation was also being slandered?

"Before I lived there. Something about Yosef bar Jacob, HaShem rest his soul, not being the boy's real father. And some wild tales about angels and shepherds. Mind you, this was when the Butcher King was still alive, so no one but his mother knows the truth of it now, and she's not talking, is she?"

Abigail didn't know who Mary of Nazareth might be, but she

offered up a prayer to HaShem for her. Abigail hoped whatever scandal had plagued the Galilean woman in the past was no longer an ache in her heart.

The conversation drifted into other gossip. Abigail might still have followed and listened, but the party opted to stop for rest at Weasel's inn in Shechem.

Abigail hastened past that, turning with a shudder and a sign against the evil eye.

It was not until she was less than a mile from the Sebaste garrison that she began to have doubts about the journey. There had been no opportunity to send a message to Romulus. It would have felt presumptuous in any case, and whom could she have trusted to deliver it?

What if he was not in Sebaste at all? What if he was off in the Galil, fighting rebels? Or had been reassigned altogether?

She had come this far. It made no sense to turn back without an answer.

Abigail breathed a sigh of relief when the sentry at the gate confirmed that Centurion Romulus was indeed on the base. The guard added, "Is he expecting you?"

From the way the soldier ran his interested gaze all over her, Abigail gathered that Romulus did have women call for him. That observation was not reassuring.

"No, no," she said. "I'm from Sychar. I have a question about some business there."

The sentry appeared dubious, but summoned his guard sergeant anyway and explained.

"I know you," the grizzled sergeant said. "The woman at the well. Come in. I'll take you to Master Romulus."

"I . . . I'd rather wait here," Abigail responded.

The sergeant was not offended. He nodded and went to fetch Romulus, who returned almost immediately.

"Abigail of Sychar," Romulus said with a big grin. "But where's the girl? Not ill, I hope," he added quickly.

Abigail shook her head but bit her lip. This was going to be harder than she imagined. Every thought of Deborah made her want to cry. It would not do to sob in front of a Roman officer.

"Here," Romulus suggested. "Come into the shade, and tell me what the trouble is."

Controlling her emotions with difficulty, Abigail explained what had happened, concluding with, "And I could think of no one else I could turn to for help. You've been very kind to me . . . to Deborah and me, I mean. I thought perhaps—"

The centurion scratched his beard and grimaced. "Not so easy as you might think. You know about the rebels in Galilee? Well, Governor Pilate says everything that's wrong with this province is about religion. We keep the peace—make no mistake about that! But when it comes to religion, we're supposed to bend over backwards to keep from offending. So you see my problem. If the Sychar elders claim this is a religious matter and I'm interfering, and if they report me to the governor . . ."

Tears welled up in Abigail's eyes. "Yes, I see. I'm sorry I bothered you." She turned to leave. "I shouldn't have come."

Romulus put his hand on her arm. "Not so fast. I didn't say I wouldn't help. It'll simply require some thought, that's all. Give me time, and I'll see what's to be done. Now, won't you come in and take a meal with me?"

Abigail saw both sentry and guard sergeant staring at her with raised eyebrows. "No, thank you. I must head back. But thank you. From the bottom of my heart, thank you."

EIGHTH PROPHECY

Waters Continuously Flowing

*On that day the sources of light will no longer shine,
yet there will be continuous day! Only the LORD knows
how this could happen. There will be no normal day and
night, for at evening time it will still be light.*

*On that day life-giving waters will flow out from
Jerusalem, half toward the Dead Sea and half toward
the Mediterranean, flowing continuously in both summer and winter.*

*And the LORD will be king over all the earth. On
that day there will be one LORD—His name alone will
be worshiped.*

ZECHARIAH 14:6-9 NLT

16 CHAPTER

Two weeks had passed since Abigail's journey to Sebaste. She greeted each day eagerly, but each sunset saw her less hopeful than the day before. No message came from Romulus. Either he was unable to help or he had promised without ever intending to assist. Either way, Abigail was plunged back into despair. She went through the everyday motions of life, but she was not living. She went to Jacob's Well once, twice, three times a day, as the needs of the inn required, but she found no refreshment there.

The growls and nips of Sychar's human vermin no longer troubled her. The women of the village noticed her haunted mask of desperation and were afraid of her.

"She has seen death," Jerash's wife said.

"She has the look of death," Abel's wife returned.

Abigail did not sing.

Today was a market day. Tzippi drew the grieving mother with her, forced her out into air and sunlight, but doubted anything would make a difference.

Abigail wandered, unseeing, from stall to stall. The wicker basket

135

on her arm somehow acquired lemons and honey and butter and cheese, but Abigail recalled making none of these purchases.

When Mara appeared at the far end of the square with Deborah in tow, every other sight and sound in the world vanished. A tunnel of light connected mother and daughter. All else faded into a gloomy, out-of-focus haze.

Abigail's breath caught in her throat. Why couldn't she move? Why could she not run to her daughter, grab her, sweep her away? If they had to flee to the ends of the earth, couldn't escape start in this moment?

Then the moment passed. A Gerazim guard loomed beside Abigail. "Just so you know," he said, "you're being watched."

Abigail nodded, but her entire being was focused on Deborah's face. Though the little girl was still extraordinarily beautiful, there was no radiance in her features now. The animation that had enlivened and cheered everyone she met was absent. She stared, silent, at the ground, not even acknowledging the cheerful welcome from the date seller, or the offer of a sweet bit of comb from the honey seller's wife.

Gone was the thin scarlet cord of protection by which Abigail had extended love to her daughter.

In its place was a horse's lead rope. Coarse and heavy, it was knotted around Deborah's waist. The slack of the bonds lay coiled at her feet like a length of chain.

When Mara, who held the end of the restraint in her hand, moved toward the table of olive oil, Deborah did not follow. When the rope grew taut and the child still did not walk, Mara yanked viciously on the end, jerking the child forward.

The savage demand awakened both Abigail and Deborah. The child saw her mother and cried out, "Mama! Mama, help me. Please, help me! Come get me, Mama. Save me."

Another cruel tug on the rope pulled Deborah to her knees in the dirt. When she tried to resist, to pull away, Mara dragged her across the gravel.

Abigail leapt forward, only to be yanked back by the rough hands of the guard. "No you don't," he said. "Leave them alone. She's no longer your concern, see?"

"Mama," Deborah cried. "Why don't you help me? Don't let them take me again, Mama. Please!"

Abigail struggled against her restraint. She had to go to her daughter.

She must! How could she let Deborah think her mother stood by and let her be carried away? Better to die trying to save her!

Indignant, angry, frustrated, and embarrassed, Mara hauled Deborah from the square like a recalcitrant lamb or an unruly colt. Even after they disappeared, Abigail still heard Deborah's gulping cries: "Mama, please help me. Please! Why don't you help me?"

The charcoal seller shook his head, muttering, "This isn't right."

The honey seller's wife remarked loudly, "That's wrong, that is! What cause do they have to take away her child? Wasn't the babe happy before? Wasn't she sweet and bright, I ask you? Before HaShem, how is this right?"

But Abigail heard none of the comments. Stumbling as if blinded by her grief, she allowed herself to be led by Tzippi back to the inn.

She did not speak or acknowledge being spoken to for the rest of the day and night.

Afraid for Abigail's life, Tzippi sat by her bed, stroking her hand and murmuring, "Poor lamb. Poor, poor lamb."

Abigail left the lamps unlit. The fire on the hearth was cold, gray ash. What did it matter?

She did not get up to eat. She turned her head away from the spoon when Tzippi brought soup and clucked her tongue for sorrow and for shame.

"You must eat, my dove, my delight."

"No." Abigail resisted.

"You'll die."

"Oh?"

Tzippi sternly told Abigail as she held the spoon before her stubborn mouth, "You must live. Fight this thing. The baby is yours. She needs her mother strong and waiting."

For Little Bee, she ate the soup. Only for Little Bee, Abigail lived on. Not living, really. Her heart beat. She breathed and moved. But she was somewhere else, and she longed to be done. She did not sing again.

The spring rains came, hard and unrelenting. Thunder rolled. Dry branches rattled against the stone walls of the little house. Abigail could think only of how Little Bee was afraid of the thunder and the rain. She used to cry and come and crawl in bed next to Abigail. "Mama, keep me safe! Mama, hold me!"

Only then, in Abigail's arms, did she sleep. Only then . . . lightning flashed. Thunder rolled. Little Bee slept. Then. Only then.

Tzippi left her to her grief. It was like death, after all. Time, she said. Abigail needed time to heal. Her heart was like the gash in the earth after an oak tree topples. Her wound too great to fill or heal. It simply was what it was. Puny words could not define the loss. Deborah had been everything. No, Deborah was the *only* thing that ever mattered to Abigail.

Outside Abigail's cottage Tzippi sobbed into Ezra's chest. "How can she live?"

In the night Abigail peered up as tattered clouds passed across the moon. Did Deborah look out the window of the big house and see the same moon now?

Each night with Abigail the child had awakened and said, "I'm thirsty, Mama."

Abigail had sat on her bedside and offered her a drink. But Deborah had wanted more than water. "Sing to me, Mama."

Who would sing to her now?

Deborah would not understand where Abigail had gone. She would not know why her mother was not with her.

The winepress where adulterers were stoned was an ill-omened place. Abigail shuddered as she approached it in the twilight. How close had she come that day, years ago, to being killed? And then Deborah would never have been born, never have lived to sing and give joy to her mother and to others.

However, neither would mother and daughter have been cruelly separated. If they had died that day in this very pit, would they not have flown off to *olam haba* hand in hand?

There was no comfort in that dark thought. Deborah was not an imagined child, a mere pretense. Hers was a life worthy of living—to succeed, to be nurtured, and to nurture. Deborah must live to find the happiness that so eluded her mother.

It was the search for that happiness that brought Abigail to the stone circle in the advancing gloom. A thrush sang in the bushes on the hillside, caroling away the daylight.

Abigail had no such song.

She was out in this desolate spot because a boy had delivered a message to her, directing her to this time and place. It was unsigned, except for the letter *R* in the bottom corner.

Romulus, of course. His anonymous summons meant he was looking out for her reputation.

The notion made Abigail wince. She had no shreds of reputation left, not in Sychar.

What if the note had not really come from the centurion? What if this supposed meeting was a ruse by the elders to draw her away from the town and kill her?

Then if her body was discovered and an explanation demanded by Rome, they would pretend ignorance. Why was she out here alone? No one knew. Killed by wild beasts, perhaps. No concern of Rome's.

Even as the fear of treachery crept into her mind, Abigail knew she could not stay away. If there was the least chance Romulus could help her recover Deborah—the slightest vestige of that hope—any risk was worth taking.

Any risk.

Abigail heard movement in the bushes. Whatever stalked there was much bigger than a thrush. "Who's there?" she demanded. "I have a knife."

Romulus replied, "And well I believe it. If I come out slowly, will you promise not to use it on me?"

The Roman emerged from the undergrowth. He was not wearing armor—not even in uniform. His short sword was strapped to his side, but in appearance he was a man, not the might of the Empire.

"You really came," Abigail said, advancing toward him. "You will help me?"

Reaching out, Romulus grabbed Abigail's arms and pulled her against him. Crushing her to his chest, he kissed her. His beard was rough against her skin. His breath hot. His clinch insistent.

Abigail struggled, turning her face away from his kisses, saying, "No. No! Please, don't."

The officer held her at arm's length, but Abigail refused to meet his eyes. He released his grip and stepped back.

His voice was husky. "They still have your child?"

Abigail nodded.

"I know how to free her . . . and you," he said. "You and the girl will be free of these wretched people. You must come and live with me."

For a minute Abigail's thoughts raced in time with her heart. Reunited with Deborah! The two of them safe forever!

Romulus took her silence for consent. "If I claim the child for my household, they won't be able to refuse me. An illegitimate girl? If they went to the governor with a complaint, they'd be laughed out of court."

"Claim Deborah as your own?"

The Roman laughed. "As part of my household, I said."

"As your slave," Abigail ventured, her voice trailing away.

"And reuniting the two of you," Romulus added. "What do you say?"

"And my part? What role do I play in your household?"

He pulled her against him. His breath was hot against her cheek. "You know what I have always felt for you. From the first time I laid eyes on you . . . what I wanted."

"Love?" she asked like a child, longing for someone to care for her.

His lips curved in an amused smile. "Call it what you want. I'm asking you to share my bed. My protection . . . and your child in return."

Abigail was glad the encroaching darkness hid her shame and disappointment. Even this man, whom she had believed honorable and upright, had the same view of her as the elders. The harlot of Sychar, exchanging one illicit lover for another.

"We call her Little Bee. Deborah. That's her name."

"I will be good to you. You will find I am not a harsh master."

"How will you . . . how can you do this? Bring Deborah back to me?"

"A petition to Governor Pilate. Explain the circumstance. That your child was stolen from you by these . . . Samaritans . . . and that you are my bond servant. You are mine, and therefore the child is mine."

"Your property."

"Technicalities. The child is yours, and you are mine. Roman law prevails."

"How long until she is with me?"

"As long as it takes to submit the petition and obtain judgment."

Abigail was silent for a time as Romulus gazed into her face and stroked her cheek. He knew what her answer would be. He regarded her like a starving man at a feast.

She answered quietly, "I must say good-bye to those I love."

"The Jews at The Stones of Joshua?"

"Ezra and Tzippi. They have been good to me. To us. When I go into your house—share your bed—they will never acknowledge me again."

Romulus snorted. "Surely they will understand."

She replied dully, "Yes. Surely."

"I am glad for it."

"I don't love you."

He shrugged. "Love is not required."

"The price I demand for my soul is my child . . . restored to me."

"Done. When can I expect you?" His eyes swept over her body as if she were undressed.

She held her chin up. "Tomorrow. This time."

"I will count the hours." Romulus regarded her for a long moment. "It's getting late. Get on the road, quickly now. I'll follow from a distance, so you can call for me if there's trouble. Good-bye, Abigail."

"Good-bye, sir," she said, her heart sinking. Freeing Deborah from Saul and Mara . . . but at such a cost? Was her reasoning wrong or right? Or was the dilemma so great as to have no solution but this?

Supper was over when Abigail returned to the common room of the inn. A dozen guests traveling to Jerusalem were at the table. Tzippi had cooked and served them alone. The old woman's face split with a grin when Abigail entered. Seeing Abigail's expression, however, Tzippi's smile faded quickly.

"Here she is." Ezra poured wine for the diners.

A plump, wealthy merchant in a silk turban wiped his fat lips. "The singer?"

"Abigail by name." Ezra gave a curt bow toward her.

"Your honors," she greeted them weakly.

The curious stares of the guests made her uneasy.

Ezra said eagerly, "Abigail, they have come to stay with us just for the purpose of your entertainment."

The merchant's son, a slender young man dressed in the newest fashion from Alexandria, applauded. "The fame of Abigail, singer at The Stones of Joshua, has reached us even in Egypt."

The father proclaimed, "Three different members of our guild who traveled through the territory spoke highly of you upon their return to Alexandria. For your sake, my son and our companions planned our journey to Jerusalem. We journeyed through Samaria so we could hear your songs."

Abigail looked from Ezra to Tzippi. Couldn't they see the brokenness on her face?

At the back of the room, Tzippi turned away and put her hand to her head. Ezra glanced from one woman to the other. "What? Are you unwell, Abigail?"

"No. No, everything is . . . will be fine." She shook her head and took her usual place by the fire. "What should I sing?" she asked Tzippi.

The old woman raised a hand and dabbed her eyes. She could not speak. Somehow she knew this would be Abigail's last night of song for them.

CHAPTER 17

It was indeed Abigail's last night at The Stones of Joshua. She let her
gaze caress rafters and stone walls as she memorized every detail of
the place where she had found happiness for the first time in her life.

In gratitude for the performance the guests left coins for Abigail.
They staggered up the stairs to their bedchambers, well fed and humming the tunes Abigail had taught them.

"Has there ever been a better night?" Ezra asked as he shook the
coins out into Abigail's hand.

The embers of the fire were banked. Ezra and Tzippi, exhausted
from the long day of work, went up to bed shortly after the guests
retired.

Abigail remained on hands and knees, scrubbing the stone pavers.
Scouring pots and trenchers until they were as clean as new, she lingered over every task.

How she loved this place. Memories flooded her thoughts. Ordinary
moments that had passed within these walls were holy in her heart.

She held her clay lamp high and took one last look around. For an
instant she saw Little Bee and Grandma Tzippi reading in the corner
while Ezra worked on his accounts.

Ezra's eyes crinkled at the corners as he smiled at his wife and the little girl. "A gift. A gift from HaShem," he had said. "An angel from heaven."

How different the old man's heart was from the townspeople's response toward Deborah. The acceptance and love of Tzippi and Ezra had been a shield raised against every unkind remark Abigail had endured.

Tonight Abigail whispered, "You are cool water to my thirst."

What would the elderly couple say when they knew what Abigail had done? Was her struggle to save Deborah a betrayal of the two who had treated her like their own daughter?

Abigail put the lamp on the table. Her hands hung limp at her sides as she surveyed the space for even one more final task.

On the stair, Tzippi's sleepy voice spoke her name. "Are you still awake, darling girl?" A pool of light preceded her as she descended.

"Oh, Tzippi," Abigail said, hoping her anguish did not spill over into her voice.

Tzippi squinted into the light of Abigail's lamp. "Still working? What is it, my dove?"

Abigail did not reply. How could she speak of the bargain she had made? The truth would break Tzippi's heart. "Just cleaning up."

Tzippi's bare feet touched the still-damp stones of the floor. "You should have been in bed hours ago."

"Couldn't sleep." Abigail's voice trembled.

"I know. I know, my darling girl." Tzippi came toward her with her arms out. "I miss her too. But we have one another." The old woman enfolded Abigail in an embrace.

"Please don't speak kindly to me. You don't know. Don't speak to me with such love. I will break. Break!"

Still Tzippi patted her and crooned, "My dove. My Abigail. I am praying. Praying. You will see. Our merciful Lord will not let this injustice stand. He will make a way. We must only trust!"

If she told Tzippi what she was about to do, what would Tzippi say to her?

Abigail knew: Tzippi would tell her that going to live with Romulus was not trusting God.

"I have to go on," Abigail said through her tears. "I have to try. Do what I can. Please understand."

"Of course. Of course." Tzippi rubbed her back. "I know. I know."

"I can't just wait and do nothing. I can't—" Abigail's tears soaked the old woman's nightshirt.

"Pray. We'll pray together. Mara is a bitter, selfish woman. She will grow tired of Deborah. Little Bee will sting her vanity one last time, and Mara will send her packing back to you. You'll see. I pray it. Our stubborn little one. You'll see."

"If only I could believe," Abigail choked. "The well of my faith is so dry. Oh, Tzippi, if only I could believe. . . ."

"Ask the Lord to give you faith. Meanwhile, I will believe for both of us." She cupped Abigail's face in her hands. "Can I ever doubt? Look what the Lord did for me. And for Ezra. We were so alone. And then he brought you and Little Bee into our lives." Tzippi kissed her cheek. "What would I do without you? My dove."

Abigail could no longer reply. "For everything . . . thank you. Thank you."

Abigail went off to bed. She dozed and then awakened a half-dozen times. At last, as the rooster crowed, Abigail wrote a hasty note.

Dear ones,

When you find this, I will be in the home of Romulus the centurion. Romulus promises if I go to him, he will bring Deborah back safely to me. You saved my life. You gave me and Little Bee all your love. I will never forget you. I know you must forever turn away from me for what I am doing. I pray you will forgive me.

shalom, Abigail

Beside her letter, she left the coins she had been saving.

The sun was not up as she hurried from the inn. She did not look back as she made her way through the city gates.

After a journey as far again beyond Jacob's Well as the water source lay from Sychar, Abigail approached the turning leading to Romulus' villa. At the sight of the Roman's estate, Abigail's courage almost failed her.

What if he was not pleased with her? Could Romulus change his mind and send her away, leaving Deborah lost forever?

Abigail was a Samaritan woman of Sychar who had never been more than twenty miles from the place of her birth.

Romulus was a Roman centurion, trained to take and give orders. He was a man of physical strength and courage. She knew little about him, but he was not from Judea. Where else had he served? In what campaigns had he been tested?

What other women had he known?

Abigail looked down at her plain, homespun gown. Tan in color with a dark blue hood pulled back to reveal her lustrous hair, the robe was the best clothing she owned. The rest of her belongings traveled in a small bundle toted at her side.

The centurion's lands included a vineyard and an olive orchard, but the house took pride of place. Set on a knoll above the valley, the two-story structure gleamed. From its red-tiled roof to its white-columned entry, it was the picture of Roman architecture adapted to Judean climate.

Romulus waved to her from the front steps, then came forward to meet her.

Had he been waiting for her arrival? watching for her?

His handsome, chiseled features wore a brilliant smile of welcome. The muscles rippled in his arms and shoulders as he took Abigail's baggage and clasped her about the waist. "You really came," he said eagerly. "I wasn't sure you would."

He had doubted *her*?

"I want my daughter back," she said quietly. "We made a bargain. I'm here to keep my part."

Behind the tall front, the house was built around a central courtyard paved with dark red tiles. A male servant approached and took Abigail's parcel.

"My servant, Cicero," the centurion said. "Those are clothes?"

Abigail nodded.

"Throw them away," Romulus instructed.

"Wait!" Abigail pleaded, seizing the bag again.

"As of today, you'll have all new things," Romulus promised as Abigail unbound the pack and rummaged inside it.

Abigail held aloft a doll with a crudely painted face and strands of yarn for hair. "It's Deborah's," she said.

Romulus nodded and waved the servant away. "Let me show you around. Besides Cicero and my stable hand, there is my cook, Amitai. You'll like her. She's from Cappadocia."

"I can cook . . . a little," Abigail said. "Will I be assisting her?"

Romulus shook his head. "You're my property, but not my slave. Someday you may take charge of the household, but for now let me get to know you."

The centurion's frankly appraising gaze left no doubt what he meant, but as he escorted her around the villa, he still spoke as if she were a guest and not a courtesan.

Abigail was surprised to find herself warming to him. He spoke with personal delight of his home; clearly, he enjoyed sharing it. "The dining hall is painted plaster. The same artist who did a room for Governor Pilate in Caesarea did this for me. Now, come see the bedchamber."

Abigail stiffened and flinched away from his touch.

"I want you to see your new clothing," he said.

Hanging from a rack in the upstairs room was what appeared to be the entire contents of a clothing shop. "From Sebaste," he explained, smiling. "Pick out what you like, and we'll send the rest away."

Abigail considered. "I like the forest green tunic," she said, then stopped to see if her choice was approved.

Laughing and slapping his thigh, Romulus retorted, "They are all for you! I meant, send back any you don't like, and we'll try again. Of course, you must see if they fit."

"When?"

"Now," Romulus said. "Through that tiled hallway you'll find water and those magic potions I'm told women favor. Spend as much time as you like trying things on. I have to see to the harvest of early figs. I'll be back for supper at sunset . . . if that suits you." Stepping close, he stroked her cheek with his fingertips, then cupped her chin in one hand. Without force or haste, he kissed her. "Until later."

"Yes, of course," she said.

The goblet Romulus pressed into Abigail's hand as she entered the dining room smelled sweet, with a hint of orange blossoms. "Mead," Romulus explained. "Made from honey."

He circled her slowly. From her new gowns she had chosen the one on which she had first commented—the one in forest green. "You were so right," he said. "Your tawny skin fairly glows in this color. It sets off your hair and eyes well too."

Stopping behind her, he touched the back of her neck with his lips. "I approve the scent you chose. Like a garden after a spring rain." He ran his fingers down her spine.

A tingle went up Abigail's back to her hair, and she shivered. How long had it been since anyone had touched her like this? Five years?

Romulus laughed, but it was an appreciative sound and not mockery. "Come, sit," he said, pulling a low chair away from the table. "Amitai offered to wait on us, but I said I prefer to serve you myself. We could recline at table, but I like the style of my homeland."

Lifting the cover from a clay cook pot, Romulus displayed the contents for her inspection. "Lamb with rice and pine nuts, flavored with peppercorns. Amitai asked what you liked and I said I didn't know, so she fixed one of my favorites. I hope you approve."

As they ate, Abigail asked the centurion to tell her about himself. "You mentioned your homeland?"

"I'm from Tarshish," he said. "About as far from here as you can go to the west on the Great Sea of Middle Earth. Iberia, it's called. My family is all merchants. The ships of the House of Gades—my grandfather's name—are famous."

"So you're rich?" Abigail asked.

He refilled her goblet with honey wine. "Not me. I'm the fourth son." Romulus shook his head. "I don't think much of taking orders from my older brothers. Never did."

Abigail smiled. "And with this dislike for taking orders, you joined the army?"

The centurion laughed. "Strange, I admit."

Reaching across the table, Abigail touched a jagged scar on Romulus' forearm. "Tell me about this."

"Idistaviso," he said. "In Gaul . . . Germania we call it now. I was wounded and captured that day."

"You escaped?" Abigail asked, intrigued.

"I could make up a story about how heroic I was that day, but I won't lie to you." Pausing in his narrative, he picked up her fingers and kissed them. "I'll never lie to you. Not about anything. So I'm not a hero. Battle was lost that day, and my head might have been on a spike outside some Teutons' encampment except for the real hero of Idistaviso. A young man named Longinus. Won a crown of glory for himself that day, he did."

Romulus drained his cup and poured himself another. "So instead of being slaughtered, I was ransomed. Since then I've been all over this part of the world. Up on the Parthian frontier. Putting down revolts in Egypt. Catching smugglers in Crete." He shrugged. "But I tell you this: In all the places I've been, I've never met a woman as beautiful as you. The moment I laid eyes on you, I was lost. I knew I had to have you or die."

From a side table inlaid with mother-of-pearl and rosewood Romulus produced another platter. This one contained dates and raisins and dried figs. "Try one of these," he said, holding a milky white date for her to nibble.

"Wonderful," she commented, surprised by the flavor.

"From the old Herod's special grove near Jericho," Romulus said. "Back in the days of Caesar Augustus part of the annual tribute sent from Judea to Rome was cases of these. Fit for an emperor."

Abigail thought how incredibly handsome Romulus was. He was also being so attentive. It was not an experience that existed in Abigail's memory.

"Almost forgot," he said, reaching beneath the cushion of his chair and producing a cloth bag. He passed it to Abigail. "Open it," he invited.

The sack contained a solid gold bracelet formed as spirals of ocean waves.

Abigail slipped it on her arm and held it aloft to the lamplight.

"Do you like it?" The centurion sounded genuinely concerned that she be pleased with the gift.

"I've never owned anything as fine. It's beautiful."

"Exactly my thought," he said, drinking her in. "Never in all the world."

18

In the blue light before dawn, Romulus stirred. Abigail awakened as he reached out to draw her near.

"You're awake early." She kissed his chin. "What is it?"

"Nothing. Really."

"Really?"

"Politics. Lunatics."

"Galilee again?"

"There is another prophet preaching in the Galil," Romulus told her as she lay against his chest in the tangled sheets.

"Are you worried?" she asked, combing his beard with her fingers.

"The Jewish leaders are afraid of him. So is Herod Antipas."

"Afraid? Of a prophet? They come and go."

"This one may be here to stay," Romulus remarked. "I heard him on the last patrol."

"What's different?"

"He gives the people hope," the centurion said.

"They always give the people hope. Always false hope."

"There is truth in what he says. A great orator, perhaps. Reaches the heart of the common man."

"Like the man called the Baptizer?"

Romulus grimaced. "They may both end up with their heads on spikes. Or spiked to a gate like a butterfly. I never said that what the common man appreciates is approved by Rome or Herod Antipas."

Abigail propped her chin on her elbow and studied Romulus. His dark gaze stared into the rafters, but he was seeing something else. Hearing another voice.

She kissed his lips and toyed with his ear. He did not respond.

"This one, this prophet, really troubles you."

"There's trouble brewing." Romulus sighed and pulled her close. "It affects . . . everything."

"Everything?" She smiled as his desire for her awakened.

"The governor is concerned the riots of Jerusalem will spread. To Galilee. To Samaria."

"But you're not afraid of a prophet?"

"I have my sword, but hard steel is not enough to stop his words." He ran his fingers along her back. His voice was husky as he said, "You are dangerous, Abigail."

"Dangerous?" she teased. "How can a woman be dangerous to mighty Rome?"

"You make me forget I am Rome."

She answered, "And I could almost forget myself . . . for the first time in my life. When I remember you."

His mouth pressed against her lips, igniting a raging fire in her. "Abigail. Abigail. Can you love me?"

"No," she teased, pleased that he wanted love from her at last.

"But are you happy with me?"

"Romulus." She sighed, suddenly made tender by his vulnerability. "Only in your arms . . . only then . . . I forget my life, and I am happy."

She still wore the gold bracelet.

Romulus was gone when Abigail awakened. The sheets were cold where he had been. She gazed at his pillow and imagined his face. His hunger for her.

Was this what it felt like to be loved? She did not love him, yet he had stirred some long-dormant life in her. Like the new tendrils of a grapevine reaching for the sun, her body awakened, arched, and climbed, reaching for his warmth.

Romulus did not love her. She was his property, his chattel. Like his horse or his dog or the cattle in his field. Abigail would give him pleasure. And Romulus would bring Deborah back to her. That was the bargain.

What was love? Abigail had never really experienced it. Only old men and then the pain of Saul as he had forced himself on her. In contrast, Romulus had wooed her gently. He had coaxed her to move with him. As the long, slow melody of passion played on the wind, his hands had played her like the strings of a harp. They danced and swayed.

Abigail slid her hand across the smooth bed linens where he had been. She inhaled and closed her eyes. The aroma of his skin lingered. His scent, almond oil and cloves, was on her hands.

She leaned her cheek upon her hand and replayed the night. His strong fingers had started at her shoulder and traced the curve of her hip. Had she ever felt such fire?

Where had he gone? she wondered. And why had he gone? This morning of all mornings she wished he was there with her. She had awakened hungry and filled with hope.

No, she did not love him. She told herself she would not let herself love any man ever again. The pain of love's betrayal was too great. But Abigail knew she would take pleasure in giving him pleasure.

She got up. She was alone when she entered the bathing room. Her bath had been prepared at the first sign of her awakening. Rose petals floated on the surface. Hypocaust heat radiated from the floor and warmed the water. Abigail had heard of such miraculous inventions, in the great Roman villas and gymnasiums of the Empire, but she had never experienced anything like it.

She lay back in the marble tub and let the warmth wash over her entire body. The thought came to her briefly that Romulus must have other women he preferred as much as her. She would have no say in who he was with. She had no right to be jealous. He would keep his end of the bargain, and she would enjoy the luxury for as long as it was offered.

The steady stream of Passover pilgrims through Sychar dried to a trickle, yet Romulus did not come home. Abigail guessed he would remain on duty in Jerusalem until the last threats of unrest and rebellion vanished with the holiday crowds.

In the daylight, she remained within the confines of the high-walled estate. Her thoughts were focused on Deborah and the promise of her return. Abigail tended the flower garden beneath her window, training sweet pea vines to climb the trellis as she and Deborah had done at The Stones of Joshua. Perhaps they would be reunited before the flowers bloomed. Surely Romulus would set to work on regaining custody of the child when he returned.

At night she dreamed of Romulus. Abigail fought the hunger he had awakened in her, the desire to be held. The longing to feel his lips on hers. The ache for his eyes to consume her with a glance.

She awakened reaching for him, hoping he would return to her soon.

Romulus was awed by the sea of people packed inside the Jerusalem Temple walls. He and twenty Roman troopers stood in a semicircle in the southeast corner of the Court of the Gentiles, lances pointed skyward. One such group was posted in each of the four corners of the plaza, allowing them to keep watch over all the activity within.

At the Passover holiday in the holy city of the Jews there was much to oversee. Pilgrims were wedged so tightly there was hardly room to move. Between Romulus' detachment and the next Roman detachment in the northeast corner, all kinds of merchants conducted business. Some sold sacrificial animals, others peddled souvenirs and trinkets, and still more exchanged foreign currency for the Temple shekels for newly arrived travelers.

It was monetary activity Romulus was most concerned about. If some desperate thief was brave or foolish enough, the bankers would make excellent targets. Moreover, the press of bodies would make escape difficult. Simple robbery could deteriorate quickly into bloodshed if the security forces were not constantly vigilant.

Countless doves, destined for sacrifice, flitted nervously in slatted crates, panicked by the movement and noise of the crowd. Young lambs tied to the tables also sought cover from the chaos, winding their ropes around the legs of angry vendors. Those tied closely enough to prevent such movement shook in terror and fouled the paving stones of the courtyard. Oxen likewise stood tethered together, chewing their cuds and soiling the air and ground, unknowingly waiting for their turn under a priest's ceremonial blade.

Myriad foreign accents speaking threescore languages haggled over the prices of their intended treasures, as well as the rate of exchange for their particular money.

The worst treated by far were the religious travelers from distant, tiny towns who had to rely on a merchant's good character. Who would truthfully quote a fair price for a sack of almonds, a basket of figs, or a good laying hen—anything they had brought for barter in place of the money they did not possess?

Romulus watched in disgust as a fresh-faced young Jewish man surrendered a beautifully carved wooden box, lined with woven cloth, to a coinage changer. The pilgrim turned with a frown, pushing scant pennies around his palm, trying to make sense of the transaction. Even though unable to hear, the centurion interpreted why the banker celebrated the deal behind the poor man's back: The man gleefully held the box out for a colleague to examine.

"That'll make a nice profit," Romulus mumbled under his breath. "Pious frauds. Hypocrites."

A shofar sounded from the parapets of the inner courtyard, signaling the start of some ritual mysterious to Romulus. He told himself he didn't really care. The fact remained that there were few places in the Empire where a Roman soldier was forbidden entry. But the prohibition against non-Jews passing the Soreg Wall into the Court of Israel was absolute, reconfirmed by Imperial decree.

Romulus admitted to himself that he did not understand the intricate workings of governance. If he were emperor and had conquered a people, he'd have destroyed what remained of their identity so they wouldn't re-form their opposition. A soldier certainly would never allow a defeated enemy to keep revenues that rightly belonged to the winner. Politics! The old Herod had managed to make himself an ally of Rome and a friend of Caesar. That explained why he had enough wealth to build such elaborate temples and palaces and even whole cities.

Such special treatment also led to arrogance amongst those who should have been subservient to Rome, making a soldier's duty that much harder.

Romulus' reverie was interrupted by a louder-than-usual commotion within the ranks of the merchants. When he looked up the row of tables again, he saw one suddenly turned over toward the man standing behind it, then another. The crowd was not panicking, yet. They were merely trying to move away from the disturbance.

Goats, now freed from restraint, darted through the confused throngs.

Lambs, bawling in fright, wandered underfoot.

The humans unconsciously mimicked the animal uproar.

In a wordless command, the centurion gestured for four of his men to fall in behind him. As they began pushing their way against the tide of people, the remaining sixteen soldiers closed rank behind them, forming a smaller but equally impervious semicircle. Pilgrims who found themselves backed that far turned away again without hesitation. *Whatever is the cause of this unrest*, Romulus thought, *it's obviously preferable to a Roman lance.*

Even brandishing his sword and cursing the crowd to part, it took too long for Romulus to reach the place where the tables had been upset. Several bewildered-looking merchants were nervously righting their displays.

"What has happened here?" Romulus demanded in his deepest, gruffest voice. "Who is responsible for this commotion?"

By then a small clearing had opened for the soldiers to stand, ringed by people who either hadn't seen or wouldn't say. Romulus couldn't tell which.

"I say, who is responsible for this?" he repeated.

One of the merchants spoke up. "He was a madman!" A couple others echoed the sentiment. "He called us a den of thieves!"

Romulus snorted a laugh in spite of himself. So far this event was an echo of the centurion's own conviction.

"He was no madman," another money changer corrected. "He was a rebel! He ought to be arrested and crucified." When a majority of the pilgrims groaned, the merchant tried to convince them. "He might have started a riot. People could have been killed!"

More groans.

Romulus rolled his eyes. "Will no one tell me who this man was?"

"I will," responded a clear, calm voice. Romulus turned to recognize the young man from earlier, the one who'd been so taken advantage of by the vendor.

Romulus was pleased. The centurion had no wish to punish anyone who stood against such knavery as these merchants peddled. If there was one witness who could be relied on to portray the accused fairly, it would be this one. "Go on, then."

"He is a rabbi . . . from the Galil. His name is Yeshua. He used this." The young Jew held up a braided whip in awe but did not hand it over to Romulus. The boy spoke as though he had seen something miraculous—more than just a brawl in the marketplace. "He made it himself. I watched him make it. He was very deliberate. Took the time to plait this flail before using it. I'd say he knew exactly what he was doing . . . almost as if he had come here to fulfill this purpose."

The young man's voice trailed off as other incredulous voices interrupted:

"Nonsense!"

"Lunatic!"

"Revolutionary!"

Romulus couldn't understand the discussion. Ordering the onlookers to be quiet, he addressed the young man. "What do you mean about fulfilling a purpose? If it wasn't robbery and wasn't rebellion, what was his purpose?"

The young man responded, "He said his father's house should not be a place of commerce . . . or something like that. He meant this Temple."

Romulus suddenly didn't want to hear more. If this was some Zealot's trick to validate a new leader, then the Galilean rabbi really was a rebel, and they would have to hunt him, capture him, and crucify him.

The Roman had no desire to take such actions against someone who spoke the truth about this den of thieves. He shouted at the crowd, "All over with now. Move about your business. No one hurt, nothing broken. Move along. . . . And what about you, boy?" he asked, with his back to the pilgrim as he nudged others to leave. "You seem wise beyond your years. But I saw what happened with your carved box. How is it you allowed yourself to be so cheated?"

There was no reply. When he turned around, the young man was gone.

Romulus felt compelled to get a better understanding of what had happened here. There was one name that came to mind, one who would tell him the unvarnished truth: Nakdimon the Pharisee. The centurion would seek him out at the first opportunity.

NINTH PROPHECY

Born of Water and the Spirit

There was a man named Nicodemus, a Jewish religious leader who was a Pharisee. After dark one evening, he came to speak with Jesus. "Rabbi," he said, "we all know that God has sent You to teach us. Your miraculous signs are evidence that God is with You."

Jesus replied, "I tell you the truth, unless you are born again, you cannot see the Kingdom of God."

"What do you mean?" exclaimed Nicodemus. "How can an old man go back into his mother's womb and be born again?"

Jesus replied, "I assure you, no one can enter the Kingdom of God without being born of water and the Spirit."

JOHN 3:1-5 NLT

he animated conversation between Amitai and Cicero echoed in
the courtyard and brought Abigail to the balcony.

"Let her in," said Amitai.

"It's a Jew," Cicero exclaimed to his wife. "Jews won't come into
the house of a Roman."

"If she wishes a word with Abigail, she'll have to come in."

"I tell you, it's a Jew. An old Jew at that. It knows the rules, and it
won't enter under the roof of a Roman soldier in order to speak to a
Samaritan courtesan."

"Foolish. If she wants to speak with Abigail, she'll come in."

"You know what they all say about Romulus and his woman."

"Abigail's not a common strumpet to stand in the street and con-
verse with a Jew," Amitai insisted. "Abigail is the property of our lord
and master and at least deserves respect on that account."

Cicero rubbed the stubble on his chin and raised his eyes heaven-
ward in thought. "These folk would not insult the horse of our master
or spit on his cattle, but the Jews have nothing to do with Romans or
Samaritans."

Amitai agreed. "No doubt this Jewess has come because she

despises Abigail as a traitor and a harlot. She will insult her at the gates of our master."

"I'll send it away," Cicero concluded.

Abigail called out from the balcony. "Who is it?"

Startled, the two aged servants looked up guiltily. Cicero replied, "It's nothing. Nothing."

Abigail pulled her robe around the low-cut gown. "What are you talking about?"

Amitai confessed. "An old Jewess is outside the gate."

Cicero confirmed, "Says it has come to see you."

Abigail knew who it was before she asked. "It is Tzippi, wife of Ezra?"

"That's its name." Cicero tugged his ear. "Do you know it?"

Amitai blinked up at Abigail. "Cicero asked her inside. All very proper and polite, but she says she can't enter our master's house. So I say send her away."

Abigail hurried down the stairs into the courtyard. Brushing past the servants, she rushed to the pedestrian gate and threw it open.

Tzippi was there. Traffic passed behind her. Pedestrians on the road stared curiously at the sight of a Jewess standing outside the residence of the Roman centurion.

Abigail's hands trembled. "Tzippi!"

The old woman's expression was at first worried, then sad, and then relieved. Tzippi tottered for a moment as though she might fall. With a cry, she flung herself into Abigail's arms and would not let go. Both women began to weep. "Oh, my angel! My dove. My Abigail!"

"You shouldn't have come here," Abigail protested quietly.

"How could I not come?"

"Please, come in, then."

"I can't. You know I can't."

"Away from their prying stares."

"Let them look! You are a daughter to me."

Abigail whispered through her tears, "There will be gossip, Tzippi."

"What else is new? Let them talk."

"Then let them say how Tzippi entered my gates." Abigail pulled the old woman through the portal and slammed the door shut. "Tell me what you want now. In private."

Panting, Tzippi whirled around, raised her fist to the closed gate, and cried, "You hear me? You viper tongues of Sychar! This is my daughter. My child! Say what you will!" She collapsed again in Abigail's arms. "Where is this Roman swine who seduced you?"

"Called to duty in Jerusalem. Passover. They fear riots."

"There's a riot here. In my heart. He has stolen you from me!"

"My own dear Tzippi, mother to me when there was no one. Why did you come?"

"You ran away from me. From me!" Tzippi wiped her tears on her sleeve. "All these years I have loved you until I could not tell the difference between you and my own child. When they stole our darling girl, our Little Bee, my heart broke with yours. And now you've gone!"

Abigail was aware of Amitai and Cicero at her back. She guided Tzippi into the garden, where the two sat on a stone bench beside the pond. It was a long time before Abigail could speak. Tzippi wept as though her heart would break, and Abigail let her.

"Passover? Difficult without me?" Abigail asked.

"Abominable." Tzippi sniffed.

"I'm sorry."

"We've hired a woman to take your place. An imbecile. She works at quarter speed. Slovenly and indolent."

"I should have waited to leave," Abigail said.

"Waited? Waited? For who? For what?"

"'Til after the pilgrim travels were over. After Passover."

Tzippi babbled, "Do you think I mourn because you aren't there to help me cook or scrub the pots or wait on guests? Your songs? Oh, Abigail! I mourn the loss of your company. First Deborah snatched away from us . . . and now this!" She patted her heart. "Breaking. Breaking. And Ezra. His heart! Oh!"

Abigail took Tzippi's hands in her own. "Does Ezra know you've come to me?"

"No."

"He will soon enough."

"How could he think I'd stay away from you forever?"

"You're in violation of . . . Jewish law."

"Violation? God is love, so I hear. Violation? Because I speak to my beloved girl? Never mind. Never mind!"

"For Deborah's sake," Abigail insisted.

"Of course. My dove." She fingered the fine fabric of Abigail's gown. "I knew it was not for this . . . finery. Or for love of a Roman. What has the Roman promised you? What vows did he make that you would leave your home and those who love you so well?"

"He promised me . . . Deborah. Home with me again."

Tzippi drew a deep breath. "What mother would resist such a bargain? Who can judge you for this after everything . . . everything."

Abigail bowed her head. "If Romulus can free her . . ." Hot tears coursed down her cheeks. Like a small child in need of comfort, she leaned against Tzippi. The old woman encircled her with her plump arms.

"I saw our Little Bee in the marketplace. She called out to me. She asked where you have gone. Asked me if you were alive."

"Yes?" Abigail couldn't help herself. She had to know details of the encounter. "How does she look?"

Tzippi's faded violet eyes considered her for a long moment. "You know. You know it all. That woman who leads her about like a dog on a leash. Abigail, everyone in Sychar sees it. They remember our Little Bee buzzing and happy with her mother."

Abigail whispered, "Her mother. The harlot of Sychar."

Tzippi threw her head back in a moan. "My dove, they had almost forgotten. Almost given up hating you. Hating your beauty and your song. But now you are with the Roman. Saul and his father, and the shrew Mara, say they will never allow you to claim Deborah as your own. Mara has the spirit of Jezebel in her. They will fight, they say, if Romulus tries to use his power to claim her."

Abigail stared at a bee on a red rose petal. "Romulus is . . . a good man . . . a just man. Kind to me, Tzippi. He will keep his promise."

Tzippi patted her hand. "Then what else can you do, I ask you? What mother would leave her child in the hands of someone like Mara?"

"Even so, I am the Roman's harlot. Is that it?" Abigail said gently. "You shouldn't come back here, Tzippi. Mustn't speak to me if you see me in public. Associating with me will destroy your business. I am a Samaritan. Bad enough you took me in as a servant. This is . . . it must be beyond what the Jews can ever tolerate."

"Abigail!" Tzippi moaned.

"Tell them you came to try to coax me away from my transgression. Tell them that. Tell them you were fulfilling a mitzvah to save my soul."

"My darling girl, my Abigail. To see you and not speak!"

"I will understand. I do understand. Now listen: This is the last I will acknowledge you. Only pray. Pray that my master will find a way to free our girl from Mara."

"The Lord must hear my prayers, Abigail. He who is always merciful will not shut his ears to the cries of one who carries such sorrow."

The women embraced one last time. Tzippi caressed Abigail's cheek, then left her alone in the garden.

Romulus sent word ahead that he would arrive back in Sychar the next night. All that day Abigail prepared for his arrival. Consulting with Amitai, the two women devised a menu certain to please the centurion.

"Melons," the cook said. "The master is fond of melons. It's very unusual to find them this early, but I heard of some. With your permission, I'll send my husband to the market."

Abigail was still not used to being deferred to, but Romulus had instructed his servants to obey her in everything. "Yes, please," she agreed.

With a last check of the dinner arrangements—roasted partridge, stuffed with wild rice and raisins—Abigail went away to prepare herself.

After bathing in scented, oiled water, she perfumed her skin and hair. She chose a pale blue tunic trimmed in magenta. Her arms were bare, and the shoulders of the gown held in place by a pair of golden clasps.

On her left arm she wore the bracelet Romulus had given her.

She was, she admitted to herself, impatient to see him again. Though she did not love him, she found herself missing him. It surprised her. This was a business transaction, after all. Her presence in his home was about getting her daughter back.

She heard the clatter of hooves in the courtyard and Cicero welcoming his master home. Back to the looking glass she went for one last inspection. She approved what she saw there, was certain he would approve as well. Every facet of her appearance was selected to drive Romulus crazy.

It was a goal for her to reach. The centurion must not think he was the only one who could exercise control over another.

Abigail deliberately delayed going down the stairs. Let him come to her, or let him be impatient.

"Abigail," he called.

"Be down in a moment," she replied.

She took him a basin of warm water and a towel, bending low to present them to him. "Or perhaps you'd prefer to bathe before supper," she offered.

When Romulus swallowed hard, Abigail knew she had captured him. "No," he said quickly. "I've been thinking . . . wishing I was home . . . to speak with you. Jerusalem. I have much I want to talk with you about."

"As my master pleases," she said. "Come into the dining room."

Abigail served him and then herself, but Romulus seemed distracted. "What is it about Jerusalem?" she asked.

"I've been trying to think how to explain it," he said. "I met a man. . . . No, that's not exactly right. I heard about a man. . . . Let me start from the beginning."

Romulus recounted for her what he knew of how the man named Yeshua of Nazareth had overturned the tables of the money changers and whipped the animal sellers out of the Temple courts.

Abigail was horrified at where this story seemed to be leading. "Was he arrested? Was he . . . crucified?"

"No," Romulus said, dismissing the notion with a wave of his hands. "Though I daresay the merchants and their priestly partners would have been happy to stone him. No, nothing like that."

"Is he a madman, then?"

Romulus took a bite of melon and chewed it thoughtfully without seeming to taste it. "Perhaps, in the sense that all Jewish prophets are mad. You see, I've witnessed the hypocrisy of turning religion into profits. I think he was right to do what he did. The Temple of the Jews is a cesspool of corruption. But it's not merely what he did. It's what he said."

The centurion's faraway expression suggested he was revisiting the Temple Mount in his mind.

"And what did he say?"

"Eh? Oh, he said, 'Take these things away; do not make my Father's house a house of trade.'"[20]

"Madness, again? His father's house? What else did he say?"

"A Pharisee who witnessed it all reported to me that he said, 'Destroy this temple, and in three days I will raise it up.'"[21]

"The Temple built by the Butcher King? Hasn't it been forty or more years in the building and not done yet? Is he a giant? a Hercules?"

"Not at all. Very ordinary appearing, I would say. Except for whatever fire is driving him."

"So he must be crazy." Noticing the centurion's empty plate, Abigail offered him more melon.

"What? No, thank you. I'm not certain who . . . or what . . . he is. Because of the concern about rebels, the governor assigned me to ask around about this Yeshua, but the more I listened, the more confused I became. You see, I talked with another Pharisee, a man I respect, named Nakdimon. He said this rabbi from Galilee can work miracles. Said he can heal the sick, make cripples walk, open the eyes of the blind. Perhaps he is truly a prophet. Perhaps he is the one you Samaritans call the Restorer."

"The prophet promised by Mosheh? If he turns out to be a Jew and not a Samaritan, that will make Rabbi Tabor very angry."

It took a moment for the comment to register with Romulus, but when her words sunk in, he threw back his head and howled. "Well, it doesn't appear to make the Jewish high priest any happier!"

Abigail slipped out of her chair and slid her arms around Romulus' neck. "And what has this man to do with us? Madman or prophet?"

"It's just . . . Abigail, from your own life you must see that much needs to be restored and put right. Yes?"

"Some things can't be put right," she said sadly. "And to me, the only one who matters is Deborah."

The welcome meal had not turned out as Abigail planned. Not at all.

⚘

Abigail stood on the balcony staring up into the night sky. The waning half-moon was only just rising. Its beams shone on her hair, infusing it with sparkles of silver.

In the trees below the house a nightingale sang.

A gentle breeze out of the east rose with the moon. The scent of roses and night-blooming jasmine spiraled up from the garden. The wafting wind caressed Abigail's face and made the sheer gown she wore ripple against her body.

Abigail glanced over her shoulder. Romulus slept on his side, facing her. His breathing was deep and even. The flame of a single oil lamp burning in a sconce on the wall illuminated his features. One of his brawny, sun-bronzed arms—the one with the scar—rested across the imprint left by Abigail's departure, as if seeking her.

She studied his face: strong jaw; straight nose; full, sensuous lips, all combined to make the centurion an extraordinarily handsome man. Abigail shivered and hugged herself.

What was happening to her? Was she falling in love with the Roman?

If true, would that be such a terrible thing?

Abigail gazed into her future and, for the first time in many years, was not anxious about what she saw written there. She and Deborah, living here together, under the centurion's protection and care? Abigail sighed.

Did Romulus love her? Could the desire he felt for her grow into love? It was delicious to consider.

An owl hooted in the olive tree atop the ridge. The moon, freed of the hazy horizon, leapt into sharper focus. A ribbon of light stretched across the pond, connecting Abigail and the orb of night.

Heavy footsteps padded behind her.

Romulus' beard was scratchy as he kissed her shoulders. First one. Then the other. Then he swept aside her hair and kissed her neck. "Your skin," he said. "Magic. You glow."

"It's the moon," she murmured without turning.

He wrapped his arms about her and tightened his grip. "Not true. The moon will be envious. Come back inside with me. Come back now."

20 CHAPTER

enturion Romulus' mount strode smartly between the massive round towers of the Western Gate of Sebaste, the seat of power for Governor Pilate's assistant prefect Aurus Titinius.

Romulus knew Titinius from their younger days in Rome, before they were both sent to the Eastern Provinces. Titinius had been a rising star then, destined for a consulship. *But*, thought Romulus, *Judea has a way of swallowing up good men's careers.*

Sebaste was mostly Gentile in population and had no need of a large garrison of Roman soldiers. There were fewer than fifty legionaries at any one time. The Samaritans of the surrounding countryside didn't seem to mind the presence of the Romans. The Imperial troops kept some order and peace between them and the Jews to the south and north.

The centurion glanced over his shoulder at a carved relief above the gate, depicting a mother wolf nursing Romulus' namesake and his twin brother, Remus, the mythical founders of Rome.

Ahead of him and to the left, above tidy rows of olive trees, the Sebaste Acropolis loomed, with columned porticos and ornately carved pediments. The white gravel road leading into the city center from the gate was a half-mile long and lined with colonnades. They provided an obvious track for the horse, who plodded steadily with barely a touch on the reins, as if he knew their destination.

Romulus passed through a block of shops that interrupted the colonnades halfway to the main town. The pace slowed as a throng of shoppers browsed the stalls that fronted the homes of the vendors. One man sold carved wooden models of the acropolis, and Romulus decided he would buy one on his return trip. *A toy for the little girl, perhaps.*

After Romulus passed the shops and the crowd, the pillars resumed along the road, backed by more orchards. The lower roof of the forum and basilica—his final destination—could be seen above them now.

The road looped around at the eastern end of the city and turned him back northwest toward the offices of government. Aside from the unpleasant business he must deal with, Romulus was quite happy with the excursion and eager to see his old acquaintance again.

Romulus dismounted. Tying the horse at a post along one wall of the forum, he stretched his legs. He saw his opponents in today's upcoming proceedings across the courtyard in front of the basilica: Rabbi Tabor and two business leaders of Sychar—Jerash the Merchant and Abel the Cloth Dyer.

Romulus suddenly forgot all the pleasant aspects of his journey and felt like smashing the trio's heads against the stone columns. He busied himself with the horse's saddle to give the men opportunity to ascend the stairs and find their way to Titinius' chambers. Romulus did not want to walk next to them or talk to them until it was necessary.

When enough time had passed, Romulus mounted the steps himself and crossed the marbled porch to the smallest of three entries on the massive face of the basilica. It took his eyes a moment to adjust to the shadows. The antechamber was lit only by what filtered through the doorway from outside.

On a low marble bench along the left wall, the three men sat huddled and speaking in low tones, which were muted abruptly when Romulus strode through the door. He sat on an identical bench on the opposite wall and stared openly at them. A uniformed Roman officer had the power to intimidate.

The bronze door swung open, held by an attendant. Romulus leapt to his feet and hurried through. "Aurus!" he exclaimed. "How have you been, you old dog?" The prefect had the reputation for scrupulous honesty, but shaking the confidence of opponents in battle was a time-tested tactic.

Titinius managed a tired smile, but he certainly looked older, even by the orange glow of the four torches lining the walls and a fat round candle on his desk. He rose to take Romulus' hand. "My friend, how are things with your posting?"

"Well, apart from this poor business, all is well."

"Any family yet?"

"None. You?"

The corners of the magistrate's mouth flicked upward in a brief smile, then fell again. "I was married. She died last year, leaving me with a newborn son. He died shortly after."

"I'm sorry to hear it, Aurus."

The prefect shrugged. "That's life . . . and death . . . in this backwater province."

A throat cleared behind them.

Titinius leaned one palm on his desk to peer past Romulus' massive hulk. "These must be our defendants?" Titinius gestured to them. "Come in, come in. You'll be heard as equals before this seat."

Romulus moved to one side to allow the rabbi to approach the desk as well. Titinius unfolded a letter that had been sealed with red wax. Smoothing it flat in the ring of light cast by the candle, he said, "You kidnapped a little girl from her mother. Is that correct?"

Romulus smiled. Things were going his way already.

"Rescued," Tabor said simply.

Titinius turned to Romulus again and, in an official tone, said, "State your case, Centurion."

Romulus understood. Titinius would conduct the proceedings according to exact rules. "The girl's mother is indentured to me by legal contract. Her property is therefore my property, and all rights to the girl are mine. These men did not just steal from a poor unwed mother. They stole from me."

The prefect turned to the rabbi. "You said you did not kidnap the girl but rather rescued her. What do you mean?"

"The girl is a Samaritan, like us. She is blood kin to us. She must be brought up in our ways, in our religion."

"And you do not believe the mother is capable of this?"

"Forgive me." Tabor inclined his head and spread his hands as a supplicant. "The centurion has taken the mother as a concubine. The good centurion is not of our faith, and since the child is illegitimate, she should properly be a ward of the city of Sychar."

"Mother and child are both my property," Romulus repeated. "Neither is the concern of the elders of Sychar."

"With respect," Rabbi Tabor said evenly, "by long-established practice, as reconfirmed by Governor Pilate this year, the Empire does not interfere with the internal religious beliefs of a people or province. Samaria is a peaceful region. We have neither the political intrigues of Yerushalayim nor the dagger-men of Galilee, and we want it to remain free of both."

There was the barely veiled threat. If the decision went against them, the elders of Sychar would appeal the matter to Pilate. Romulus could have happily strangled the rabbi at that exact moment.

"Very well," Titinius said. "I will consider your case and render my verdict by this afternoon." As the rabbi and his cohorts began filing from the room, Titinius asked Romulus, "Will you lodge overnight in the city?" Then his face brightened for the first time since the gathering convened. "Perhaps you can take in the noonday play tomorrow in the market square?"

Romulus smiled. "Are you still writing plays, old friend? You always did have a passion for the arts."

The assistant prefect smiled and nodded. "A tragedy in four acts. I call it *Night in Sebaste*."

"Sounds interesting," Romulus said. "But I'm afraid I must be away again before dark. Thank you for the offer, though."

Titinius' smile faded, though he seemed to understand. "You've other duties to tend to. I myself have yet to see the thing entirely through in one viewing. Such is life in the service of Rome, eh?"

"It was good to see you, Titinius. I await your good judgment in this trivial affair."

The men shook hands, and Romulus strode back into the sunlight.

Abigail's heart fluttered as she awaited Romulus' return from the hearing in Sebaste. Would he have Little Bee with him? Would they arrive together on horseback? Abigail's arms ached with longing to hold her daughter. She wanted to soothe away Deborah's hurts and fears. Abigail would promise over and over that they would never again be parted.

Before leaving for the meeting, Romulus had warned her not to expect an immediately joyful conclusion. "For appearance's sake," he said, "the magistrate will have to take the matter under advisement for a few days before delivering the claim to me. Deborah won't be at the hearing, so even if the judge gives me ownership today, I won't be able to bring her home tonight."

Despite the cautionary words, Abigail was able to think of nothing else.

She and Little Bee would sing together of the terrace on the centurion's villa. Abigail would tuck Deborah in with prayers and reciting the Shema: *"Hear, O Israel . . ."*

Abigail bit her lip as she pictured her prayers ascending to the throne room of the Most High. Having betrayed her husband with Saul and now living openly with a man—not her husband, and a pagan at that—would HaShem ever hear her prayers again?

Abigail raised her chin. So long as Little Bee came home to her, she did not regret her choice. Compared to saving her daughter from the clutches of that bitter, evil woman, nothing else mattered.

Romulus was a gruff man but a considerate one. Since the day Abigail had moved into his home, he had lavished gifts on her: fine linen from Antioch and perfumes from Arabia Felix and unguents from Egypt. Such things were beyond a centurion's standard pay.

Abigail wondered if Romulus had taken bribes or if he had extorted such finery from Samaritan merchants. Compared to the bargain he had exacted from Abigail, the rest seemed of little consequence.

She wore one of his gifts now: cream-colored linen, belted at the waist with a cloth-of-gold sash. Her arms and throat were bare, and her hair tied up at the nape of her neck. She was, she recognized, the portrait of a courtesan, but this was a victory celebration and a thank-you. She would do her best to make Romulus happy.

Below the house was a pond. A pair of ducks glided lazily on the water, carving loops and whorls in the surface with seemingly no effort. Their movements perfectly framed an olive tree reflected in the pool.

Abigail watched until the setting sun turned the surface of the water pink, then violet and then cobalt . . . and still Romulus did not return.

The lateness of the hour must mean that the best of all possible results was about to happen. The Roman must have gone directly to retrieve Deborah and was even now returning her to her mother.

Abigail was already planning how they would spend their day together tomorrow. With Deborah's return, everything for Abigail was changed! She would take Little Bee to visit Ezra and Tzippi. The Jewish couple adored the child. In every way they could not have loved or cared more for her if she was their own granddaughter.

When Deborah had been dragged away in the middle of the night, they had been devastated. When they saw how Mara mistreated her, they were appalled.

The centurion's body servant went out to light the torches at the front of the house. Their wavering flames set up an orange glow that linked the white steps to the gathering dark under the trees.

Abigail knew Ezra and Tzippi did not approve of her living with Romulus. Still, perhaps seeing Deborah restored to her mother would in some way balance the scales.

Hooves clattered in the darkness of the highway. Breath quickening, Abigail looked out from the balcony. She wanted Deborah to see her immediately, to know instantly she was safe.

Romulus was in full uniform, helmeted with his transverse plume of office and wearing a red cape. He looked magnificent as he rode into the torchlight in front of the house . . . alone.

His groom went out to assist with the mount.

Abigail could not help crying out, "Where is she? What happened?"

The centurion looked up at her. His brows were furrowed.

Throwing the reins to the groom, he strode into the portico. Moments later, Abigail heard his boots clumping up the stairs. She hurried into their bedchamber.

Abigail reminded herself not to act too let down. She should not have expected Deborah's return tonight. She had let herself anticipate something that had never been likely. She had only herself to blame if she was disappointed.

Besides, Romulus had ridden all the way to Sebaste and back today. He had used his influence to help her, just as he promised. Abigail must be grateful for his efforts and show it.

"Welcome home," she said bravely as he swept into the chamber. "Romulus, I should not have spoken—"

She quailed before the black mask of his emotion. His face was hard as flint and unreadable. "Romulus? What?"

"I . . . I'm sorry," he said.

"Why? What's happened?"

"The magistrate," he said slowly. "I never thought . . . I should have guessed. . . ." Drawing himself up and taking Abigail's hands in his, he said, "He turned us down. Deborah must stay with Mara and Saul for now."

"Must . . . stay?" Abigail's senses dulled. This could not be happening. How was it possible? "But the judge? He's a Roman. He can't possibly be afraid of Samaritans."

"Not of Samaritans," Romulus corrected, shaking his head. "Of Governor Pilate. The assistant prefect has strict orders to keep the peace in Samaria. No riots, like in Jerusalem. No rebels, like in the Galil. The magistrate was prepared to be . . . very accommodating . . . when they made it a matter of religion."

"Oh no, Romulus! Oh no!" Abigail sat down heavily in the chair beside the window. "Is that final?"

"No," the centurion said. "But it means I can't bring her home. It means I . . . I failed you, Abigail."

21 CHAPTER

ime passed but the dull ache in Abigail's heart did not. Exotic scents, expensive gowns, sumptuous meals—none of these alluring attractions made life worth living. To go on existing without Deborah was to have no life at all. For what purpose had Abigail sold her soul?

She retreated from thoughts of being in love with Romulus, preferring to think of herself as his servant, his slave. When Amitai was ill, Abigail took over household duties, even going to Jacob's Well to draw water. There was no need. The Roman's estate had a spring of its own. Within the very mindlessness of the task lay its appeal.

Then the day came when Abigail waited too long to draw water.

The women gathered at Jacob's Well past midday fell silent when Abigail approached. Obviously she was the topic of conversation. They stepped back, forming a lane for her to pass through.

She did not look up. She could not speak. The well of her tears was dry. They turned to stare openly—some with pity and others with cool curiosity.

She belonged to the household of the Roman centurion. She was the woman of Romulus. She had sold herself for the sake of Little Bee, yet the promises of the Roman had come up empty.

Abigail's motions were mechanical as she placed her water jar beside the stone wall.

The honey seller's wife whispered, "I gave Little Bee a honeycomb."

Abigail's gaze flitted up to the ruddy face of the woman in thanks. Sad brown eyes gazed back at her with compassion. Abigail was grateful for this small kindness shown to Deborah, but she could not make words form on her lips.

Abigail nodded once and let the waterskin down over the wall.

The date seller's wife covered her mouth with her hand and said in a very quiet voice, "So sorry. Know what you must feel."

Abigail's emotions flashed with resentment. How could anyone know what she felt? These women who had hated her for so long? Had they not encouraged this cruelty by their judgment? Love had been ripped from Abigail's heart as agonizingly as if her heart had been torn from her chest. And what of Little Bee? Another woman had stolen her away, and there was nothing Abigail could do to save her. The governor had yielded to the threats of Rabbi Tabor. Deborah would not be relinquished to the care of Romulus.

The waterskin splashed down and filled. The clique remained rooted, watching . . . waiting for what would happen next.

Hand over hand, Abigail pulled up the heavy container. On the road beyond the well a troop of twelve Romans rode toward the gates. Romulus' cavalry back from patrol.

Abigail felt Deborah's presence before she saw her or heard her cry. She tried to resist looking up but could not. Following the Roman horses was a cart driven by Saul. Mara and Deborah perched on sacks of provisions. Heavy iron-clad wheels churned up the dust.

Abigail moaned softly.

The women turned to stare. "It's Little Bee with Mara."

"Now we're going to see something."

"Poor little one."

Heads swiveled to stare. Color drained from Abigail's face. The waterskin fell back into the depths as Deborah spotted her from the wagon and wailed, "Mama! Oh, it's my mama. Look!" The child struggled against the rope holding her captive.

Mara jerked her hard. "Stop this now!" she shouted.

Deborah screamed and lashed out at Mara as the woman tried to restrain her. "Let me go! I hate you. I hate you!"

A battle ensued as the cart lurched forward. Mara slapped the child across the mouth.

Abigail ran forward from the well. Fists clenched, she roared, "Stop!"

Mara's wild face jerked up defiantly. With great deliberation she slapped Deborah again, harder.

At her mother's voice, Deborah fought back. "Mama! Mama, it's me!"

Abigail charged down the road toward her child as Mara fought to restrain Deborah.

Abigail shouted, "Stop! Mara, don't hurt her!" Four deep and four abreast, the cavalry horses blocked Abigail's progress. "Saul, help me!" she cried desperately.

Saul, as if awakened by Abigail's plea, snatched Deborah's leash from Mara's hands. "Enough!"

Still blocked by the cavalry formation, Abigail dashed forward through the ranks of prancing horses in an attempt to reach Deborah. Iron-shod hooves sparked against the paving stones of the highway. "Let me by!" Abigail wailed.

"Mama!" Sprawled on the cargo, Deborah seized an instant of freedom and leapt to her feet, balancing on the edge of the cart. Saul scrambled for the rope, but Deborah yanked free. The side of the narrow road fell away in a steep precipice into a wash twenty feet below. Deborah crouched to jump.

"No!" Abigail shouted. "Stay where you are. Deborah, don't!"

A soldier spun in his saddle and bellowed, "Little girl, don't jump!"

But the warnings were too late. Frantic to reach her mother, Little Bee spread her arms as if to fly away as she plunged from the cart. The wheel struck, tossing her like a rag doll, high into the air. Abigail screamed as Deborah tumbled over and over, like a stone, down the rocky embankment.

Mara's voice was the screech of a bird of prey. "It's not my fault! You saw her. Disobedient, wretched child. You saw it. She wouldn't obey me."

The woman made no move to clamber down the precipitous slope toward where Deborah lay crumpled, facedown, in the ravine. Mara did not even leave the oxcart.

Saul did get down from his place beside his wife but went only as far as the edge of the cliff.

Sliding, tearing her hands on the boulders, Abigail tumbled down the incline after her baby. She never stopped calling out, "Deborah! Oh, Little Bee, I'm coming!"

Don't let her be dead, she thought. *She can't be dead. She was trying to get to me. Oh, God, save her!*

A trio of soldiers converged on the motionless form. As Abigail reached for Deborah, the guard sergeant of the troop caught her by the shoulders and held her back. "Wait," he said. "Don't move her yet."

With tenderness surprising in one so coarse and gruff, the Roman soldier placed two fingers on Deborah's neck. Abigail held her breath.

Mara continued to wail, "It wasn't my fault!"

"Shut her up!" the sergeant demanded.

Saul, who had barely moved from the edge of the precipice, motioned for Mara to be silent.

"She's alive," the sergeant said.

"Thanks be to God," Abigail cried, breathing again.

"Gently, now. Carefully," the sergeant instructed. Running his hands over the child's neck and head he said, "Neck's not broken. Help me turn her over."

Cautiously, as though holding a vase of fragile porcelain, Abigail and the Roman lifted Deborah and revolved her in the air before laying her down again on her side. The child's face was smeared with gore. She had a gash over one eye and her nose streamed scarlet. A tiny bubble of blood appeared and disappeared at one nostril.

Why doesn't she wake up? She must have hit her head. But thank you, HaShem, she's not dead. She's not dead.

The sergeant ran his hands over Deborah's limbs. "Nothing broken in arms or legs. Can't tell about her head, though. Too much blood."

"Come on, baby, Little Bee," Abigail implored. "Wake up, baby."

"Nobody can control that child," Mara said loudly. "She causes nothing but trouble. Uncontrollable. Incorrigible."

Ignoring the outburst, the sergeant said to Abigail, "Don't try to wake her just now. Let's get her up from here and somewhere to clean her wounds." Calling up to the remaining troopers, he shouted, "Dump the contents of that wagon. We're using it to take the child to the centurion's home. Lively now! Move it!"

The Romans leapt to obey, heaping Saul's cargo beside the road.

Indignant, Mara protested until a pair of soldiers grasped her arms and tossed her aside like another sack of grain. When Saul tried to intervene, another Roman put the point of his javelin on Saul's chest. "Stop there," he said.

"You two," the sergeant commanded the troopers beside him in the canyon, "link arms under her. On three, now. One. Two. Three . . . lift!"

Fighting for balance every step of the way, they made their way gently back up the precipice. The sergeant remained ready to catch Deborah if they stumbled. Abigail, praying and beseeching HaShem, came last.

The soldiers laid Deborah in the wagon bed and made room for Abigail alongside her.

The sergeant took the ox goad himself.

Abigail looked at Mara, who remained rooted on the heap of barley bags. The woman's face betrayed anger and fear but no sorrow or concern. "I don't want her back," she said to Saul, pushing him away. "She's never been any good. Now this! More trouble. Useless, stupid, disobedient. Let someone else take her and keep her. I don't care. Take her!"

Clucking to the beast, the sergeant prodded the ox into motion. "To the centurion's."

TENTH PROPHECY

The River of Healing

In my vision, the man brought me back to the entrance of the Temple. There I saw a stream flowing east from beneath the door of the Temple and passing to the right of the altar on its south side. The man brought me outside the wall through the north gateway and led me around to the eastern entrance. There I could see the water flowing out through the south side of the east gateway.

He asked me, "Have you been watching, son of man?" Then he led me back along the riverbank. When I returned, I was surprised by the sight of many trees growing on both sides of the river. Then he said to me, "This river flows east through the desert into the valley of the Dead Sea. The waters of this stream will make the salty waters of the Dead Sea fresh and pure. There will be swarms of living things wherever the water of this river flows. Fish will abound in the Dead Sea, for its waters will become fresh. Life will flourish wherever this water flows.

"Fruit trees of all kinds will grow along both sides of the river. The leaves of these trees will never turn brown and fall, and there will always be fruit on their

branches. There will be a new crop every month, for they are watered by the river flowing from the Temple. The fruit will be for food and the leaves for healing."

EZEKIEL 47:1-2, 6-9, 12 NLT

22 CHAPTER

bigail knelt beside the bed. Deborah's face, sponged clean of blood, was fearfully pale, ashen in its coloration.

All the color had drained from Abigail's countenance as well. Tenderly holding one of Little Bee's hands, she stroked it gently and willed the child to live.

For every breath I take, she silently offered, *you take one. Every time your sweet heart beats, mine will also. Stay here, Little Bee. I can't have found you again and then lose you the same day. HaShem would never be so cruel. Come back to me. Come back.*

Since being placed in the master's chamber, Deborah had not stirred. Her breathing, ragged and thin, came so faintly at times that Abigail panicked, leaning closer and squeezing her daughter's hand as if to pump life back into her veins.

Amitai stood by. After sponging Deborah's face with a rag dipped in cool water, she tried to do the same for Abigail but was pushed away. "If she doesn't live, I don't want to either," Abigail said.

"What can I do for you, then?" the cook asked.

Abigail could think of only one thing. "Would you please send Cicero into the village? Ask him to go to The Stones of Joshua. Tell Ezra and Tzippi what has happened. Ask them to pray for Little Bee."

"You are a Samaritan, and they are Jews," Amitai said bluntly. "Do you not want me to send a message to your own people?"

Abigail nodded toward Deborah's slight, still form. "Here is my people. But please. Pray to whatever god you serve, Amitai, please."

"I am a God-fearer," the Cappadocian responded. "I will speak to Yahweh for your child." Amitai left the room on her errand.

Several minutes later Abigail became aware that someone had entered the chamber and stood behind her. Did Amitai have a question? What had she forgotten?

A pair of strong hands gripped her shoulders, and the scent of almond oil and cloves reached her.

Romulus!

The centurion knelt beside her. "I heard. I came back as quickly as I could. Is she better? How is she?"

Shaking her head in misery, Abigail responded, "No change. She won't wake up. She doesn't even try. Oh, Romulus, why won't she wake up? I'll die if she dies, Romulus. Or, if HaShem demands it, my life for hers." Raising her face toward the ceiling, she bargained, "Do you hear? My life for hers."

"Shhh, stop now," Romulus said. "Here, drink this." He handed her a flask of wine. "Go on, take a swallow," he urged.

Taking a drink, Abigail wiped her lips but did not rise from the floor. "My sergeant told me everything," Romulus said. "All my men witnessed it. In front of witnesses Mara renounced her claim to the child. There is no way the judge will force you to give her back. Not now. She's yours."

"If she lives," Abigail said fearfully.

"If she lives," Romulus agreed.

There was no holding back Tzippi and Ezra. On the second day they came to the Roman centurion's villa. Cicero answered the pounding at the gate. Tzippi plunged in with Ezra panting at her heels.

Ezra asked Cicero, "Where is she?"

"Sir?"

"Our grandchild. Our daughter."

Tzippi's heavy cheeks and kindly eyes turned upward toward the balcony, where she somehow sensed the presence of Abigail and Little Bee. She launched herself up the steps. "Abigail?"

Abigail threw open the bedchamber door as Tzippi pulled herself up onto the landing by the banister. "Tzippi! You've come!" Abigail cried and flung herself into the old woman's embrace.

Puffing and wordless, Ezra hung back, observing the women.

"Of course, dear, my dove. Where . . . ?" Tzippi stepped around Abigail, then froze at the sight of Deborah, unconscious, bruised, and battered on the bed. So still. So tiny. "Little Bee." Tzippi tottered as though she might fall.

Abigail slipped her arm around Tzippi's waist and guided her to the chair beside the child. "She hasn't moved," Abigail said, resigned. "Two days. Her head."

Tzippi lifted Deborah's fingers to her lips. "Little Bee?"

"She jumped. Trying to escape from them." Abigail's voice turned husky.

"I heard about it." Tzippi's gaze was fixed on the pallid face. Chalky, as if death had already claimed her, Deborah did not stir. "Everyone in town is talking. Everyone. Mara cared nothing about her. Now she's only eager that she not be blamed."

"I blame myself." Abigail sank down on the bed. "My fault, all of this."

Tzippi gasped. "What are you talking about, girl? Your fault? Deborah leapt from the wagon to escape Mara. Everyone saw it."

"Trying to reach me," Abigail countered.

"You are her mother. Of course she—"

"She is innocent. She doesn't know what kind of woman I am."

"That you surrendered your freedom trying to free her?"

"It's more than that. You know it. I know it. I'm . . . I'm everything they accused me of, Tzippi. I sold myself to Rome. Can never belong anywhere. Not to anyone."

"You belong to Deborah. She loves you."

"And look what loving me has brought upon her. I am cursed. Of all women. The one person in this world I loved more than my own life and look . . . look." She twirled Deborah's dark curls around her fingers. "Like the death of the firstborn . . . God has taken her away from me because of my sin."

Tzippi straightened the linen around Deborah's chin. "I've known you both since she was a tiny thing. I've never known a better mother. Pure love. Always laughter. Song. She loved you with a perfect love."

"But now. What good has love been?" Abigail pressed her palm against her brow. "If I wasn't . . . alive . . . you would take care of her for me? You and Ezra?"

At the mention of his name Ezra cleared his throat. He stepped forward and put his calloused hand on Abigail's shoulder. "Don't talk nonsense," he said gruffly. "She'll live, and you must live for her."

Abigail searched his face. "If she lives—if—I must ask you and Tzippi to raise her for me."

"What foolishness is this? You'll both come back to The Stones of Joshua. Everything will be as it was."

Abigail slowly shook her head. "It can never be. I've made a bargain. My life for hers. I'm in exile . . . from what might have been. If she lives, if she flies away, I still belong here now. Belong to Romulus."

Tzippi and Ezra exchanged grim looks. Tzippi said, "Grief has made you crazy. You need sleep, not a grave. How long has it been since you slept?"

Abigail stared at the floor. "I don't know."

Behind her, Romulus replied, "Barely more than a few minutes at a time since the judgment in Sebaste. You see she grows thin. Barely eating. She never sings. Now this. She won't close her eyes. She's afraid the child will fly away if she rests even a moment."

Tzippi drew herself up. "Sir, it is good of you to bring my daughter and granddaughter into your home. Abigail told me how you protected her and provided at the beginning of our Deborah's life. I am certain you have a good heart."

"If there is a true God, perhaps he will have mercy on me." Romulus bowed slightly. "My home is their home. And yours, if a Jewess will stoop to take shelter beneath the roof of a Gentile."

Tzippi rolled up her sleeves. "I'm here. I'll stay as long as I am needed. And I am needed. Abigail, you will eat." With a flick of her wrist she ordered the centurion, "You. Go to the kitchen. Command your cook to kill a chicken and make soup." Then to Abigail, "You, my dove, will sleep. I'll stand watch." To Ezra she commanded, "Go home, Ezra. You're worthless here. Mind the inn, so business does not fall apart. I will be staying here to care for my girls."

For six days the women stayed at Deborah's bedside in shifts. The child remained in a semi-comatose state. It took the effort of both Abigail and Tzippi to nourish her. Drop by drop, oxtail broth and chicken soup were spooned down her throat.

Tzippi sent to Ezra for her clothes. Her presence was a comfort to Abigail. She did not judge. She did not seem to mind Romulus and even remarked how handsome he was, and how good to give up his room and his bed for Deborah.

"He almost seems like a Jew, this Roman. If I did not know the truth, I would say he was almost human," Tzippi remarked.

Little Bee hung on to life by a thread, but she did not awaken. Her eyes, half open, did not focus on her mother's face or acknowledge movement or light. She was, Amitai reported in the market square, breathing but not truly alive.

The slow dying of Little Bee, the indifference of Mara, and the grief of her true mother became the focus of conversation in Sychar.

At the well these startling words could be heard: "You have to pity poor Abigail. Selling herself to the Roman for the sake of her child."

"What mother wouldn't give her life for her child?"

"We know Mara wouldn't."

"I said *mother* and child. Mara's not a mother."

"She's a slaveholder, that's what."

"If it hadn't been for Mara . . ."

"Poor Abigail. How she loves Little Bee."

In Romulus' villa the fight for Deborah's life went on. This morning the shutters of the window were thrown wide. A lark sang on a budding branch of a pomegranate tree. Abigail, weary from the long night, washed Deborah and dressed her in a clean nightdress.

Romulus stepped into the room as Abigail tucked Little Bee in. He wore his cavalry uniform and held his helmet. "How is she?" He towered over the child and gazed down into her face.

Abigail turned from the window. "No change." Her tone was weary.

He glanced at Abigail. "As you see, I'm called away."

"Again?"

"Patrol duty." He shrugged. "Herod Antipas has grown irritated at the wild Jewish prophet baptizing at the Jordan. Yochanan the Baptizer. Preaching against the illicit marriage of Herod and his brother's former wife. Religion and politics. Herod's informed Pilate that if there is a rebellion, it will all be the fault of Rome's leniency toward crazy Jewish fanatics."

"What will you do?"

"I'll get my orders in Tiberias. I am guessing that Herod's guards will arrest the fellow. We will be there in reserve. The might of Rome to intimidate the folk who have come to hear the Baptizer preach."

"He's a criminal because he has offended Herod and his woman?"

"He should have kept his mouth shut. Religion and politics are a sure way for the faithful to end up slaughtered. Herod will have his pleasure with that woman Herodias, and what business is it of the prophet?"

Romulus reached for Abigail. She was cool in her response.

"There was a queen named Jezebel married to King Ahab," Abigail said quietly. "They lived not far from here. In Sebaste. Some say the demon of Jezebel lives now inside the body of Herodias."

"I've seen her. Demon. Yes. Her eyes." Romulus seemed troubled.

"The talk in the inn among the pilgrims was about that. Same Jezebel demon, only a different body," Abigail said. "Be careful, Romulus. It is an ancient evil inhabiting those who worship earthly power. They persecute and crush the innocent for no reason."

"I have wondered if the demon of this ancient queen whispers to the cruel women of Samaria." Romulus toyed with her sleeve.

She knew he was speaking of the cruelty that had been aimed at her. "There's no changing what was."

"I think . . . you are a woman with a good heart," Romulus said.

"I've paid for my mistakes. I just don't want my child to pay for my sin."

"Surely the God of Israel is not so cruel as that. Cruelty comes from a creature like Jezebel's demon, not Israel's God."

"What do you know of Israel's God?"

"I've lived here many years. He seems to be everywhere."

"There are some who believe what has happened to Deborah is because God is punishing me. The same ones who will say that what is coming upon the Baptizer is what he deserves. Stay silent?"

Romulus returned, "What I mean . . . silence is safe. I pity the prophet who crosses Herodias."

Abigail realized how long she had been out of touch with events in the land. Only Deborah really mattered to her. "How long will you be gone?"

"I think you won't notice."

"I can't. Can't think of anything but . . ."

He raised his chin and narrowed his eyes. "You know you are mine. I don't need to ask permission."

"You wouldn't like me that way." She turned away from him, stepping beyond his touch.

"I'm patient. When I return, perhaps she'll be awake."

"What if . . . what if she doesn't wake up?"

Both were silent at the possibility that Deborah would never wake up, never recognize her mother. Romulus stepped to the window and inhaled the scent of jasmine blossoms.

"The blossoms. Smell like my home. Reminds me of home," he said. "Tarshish. Jasmine beneath my window, the humming of bees . . ." He snapped his fingers as a thought struck him. "Abigail! I've got the answer!"

"Answer?"

"For Deborah. Little Bee. You must take her home!"

"What? What do you mean?"

"Scent is the most powerful evoker of memory. In men. In animals. In children, I am certain. This room is filled with aromas and voices. You are here, but it is not home to her. She dreams. Dreams of her home in The Stones of Joshua. Do you understand me?"

"Home," Abigail murmured. "You will let me go with her? leave your house?"

He grasped her arms. "You will come back to me. But you must take her to the place she has known since she was a baby. And then you must sing again, Abigail. To her. Like you used to. Make everything as it was. Surround her with everything familiar."

"You would do this for me? Let me go back to The Stones of Joshua? For her?"

He pulled her tight against him. "While I'm away. For a while. Just promise me you'll come back when I return. Then, maybe . . . maybe she will awaken for you. And you will awaken to me again."

23

It was beside Jacob's Well that the roads diverged. The centurion's track headed toward the east, toward the Jordan River and the prophet. Accompanied by a quartet of soldiers, the cart bearing Deborah, her mother, and Tzippi continued north to Sychar.

As they parted, both Abigail and Romulus gazed at each other. The officer raised his hand in a gesture of farewell. Abigail nodded gravely in reply, grateful for the allowance he had made.

A group of Sychar's women was gathered around the water supply. At the approach of the soldiers they hitched the skirts of their robes and drew aside.

But what Abigail overheard did not match their gestures.

"Looks like a funeral procession," one said.

"Is the child dead?"

"We would have heard," the charcoal seller's wife returned. "Poor thing! Sorrow heaped on sorrow for her mother."

Suddenly the faces and the voices displayed something Abigail had not witnessed from Sychar before: compassion.

"You know the little one's the same age as my Susanna," the wife of the tanner replied. "HaShem help her and all our babies."

"Amen. Amen," the other mothers echoed fervently.

The consolation she might have drawn from the change barely registered with Abigail. Mindful of Romulus' notion of immersing Deborah in pleasant memories, Abigail kept up a running commentary for the unconscious child.

"Look, Little Bee," she said, "there's the well. You remember going to the well with me, don't you? Remember how cool and delicious the water is on a hot summer day? Remember how heavy the jar is when we carry it home to Tzippi? Don't you want to help me with it? What do you say, Deborah? Shall we get the water for Gramma?"

"Poor Abigail," the tanner's wife remarked. "About out of her head with grief."

"See the gates?" Abigail asked. "We're nearly there now. Look—there's Grampa Ezra coming out to meet us. Can you smell the horses and the camels? How sharp the smell is today. In the corral across the road from the inn? I see four camels there."

As the cart arrived in front of The Stones of Joshua, the soldiers stepped aside. Raising the limp body of her daughter, Abigail passed her to a pair of the troopers who toted her ever so carefully, following Ezra back to the servants' quarters and their old room.

When Deborah was placed on the bed, the soldiers departed. The last one out of the courtyard, a grizzled old campaigner, tugged his forelock respectfully. "Lady," he said, "I hope—we all hope—the child recovers soon. She's a sweet one, and no mistake."

Abigail tucked the rag doll close beside Deborah's face. How gray she looked, less color than the plastered wall. Bravely Abigail said, "Here we are, Little Bee. All tucked in. Just like coming home at night. On the table are some lemons. Can you smell them, Little Bee? You always like the smell of lemons. You say it tickles your nose."

Raising both hands toward heaven, Tzippi prayed for the deliverance of the child from the bondage of this deathlike sleep. "Oh, mighty and merciful Lord, free our granddaughter from this evil. Heal and restore her, Lord."

"Heal and restore her," Ezra echoed. "Your word says You are *our refuge and strength, a very present help in trouble.*'22 Reach out and touch our dear granddaughter, O Lord."

"Listen, Little Bee," Abigail continued. "Can you hear the hammering of the blacksmith at his forge? Listen to how it rings! Like music, yes? Would you like me to sing for you, Little Bee? You always did like that.

> *"Love to light my darkest night*
> *To cool the warmest day.*
> *Love, HaShem's most perfect sight,*
> *In all He might survey."*

Abigail did not notice the speed with which Ezra left the room, muttering about guests to attend to. Nor did she see the tears that hung, trembling, from Tzippi's eyelashes.

Abigail never wanted to leave Deborah's bedside. She took all her meals—a swallow of soup, a couple bites of bread—in a chair next to Little Bee.

When she dozed, which was seldom, she started awake, roused with any change in Deborah's breathing, whether real or imagined.

"You need to get out," Tzippi urged.

"I can't leave her," Abigail argued. "I have to be here when she wakes up. What if I was gone and she—?"

Looking at Abigail's wan complexion and bedraggled hair, Tzippi finally insisted. "Dear one, I need your help. We need water. Ezra has too many guests to leave just now and my old bones are too brittle to walk so far."

When Abigail protested, Tzippi replied, "I'll keep watch. You know I will. Go. It'll help me and do you good."

Jar on her shoulder, Abigail approached the well with trepidation. The plaza was not empty. A half dozen of Sychar's wives were there, gossiping.

She could turn around and go back at once, but that would leave the chore to be done later or by another. Raising her chin, Abigail parted the Red Sea of Samaritan women and approached the well.

"Let me help you with that," the honey seller's wife declared, letting down the waterskin. "How's the baby? How's Deborah?"

"She . . . she still hasn't moved or spoken."

The charcoal seller's wife said, "We all pray for her . . . Abigail."

"I think about her every time I look at my girls," the tanner's wife added.

"If there's anything you need," the honey seller's spouse volunteered. "Anything at all."

Unnoticed 'til that moment, Mara approached the well. Staring coldly at Abigail, she said loudly, "What's she doing here? What gives you the right to show up here with decent women? Contaminating the—"

"Mara," the tanner's wife said, "be so good as to close your mouth before I close it for you."

"Exactly," agreed the honey seller's wife. "If you weren't so selfish—"

"And so cruel," the charcoal seller's wife noted.

"If you weren't so selfish and so cruel, none of this would have happened," the honey seller's wife concluded. "Is the jar full, Abigail? Come on, let's walk Abigail home. No, no, my dear. We'll carry it for you. We hear you singing to Little Bee. Such a beautiful voice. What are the words to that lullaby? How does it go?"

It was nearly dawn. The light gathering outside the windows of Abigail's room at the inn climbed over the sills and overpowered the flickering oil lamps. Abigail rubbed her eyes and stretched. Deborah slept on.

Abigail straightened the covers, kissed the girl on the cheek, and patted her rumpled hair.

What good had it done to bring the child back to this place? It was an enormous comfort for Abigail to be near Ezra and Tzippi. It was wonderful to return to the spot where mother and daughter had shared happy hours. But had it made any difference? Romulus' idea that familiar sounds would touch Little Bee in some way had not proven true. His plan that comfortable, familiar aromas would lead her back from whatever forest she was trapped within had not worked out.

Abigail closed her eyes and tried to imagine being Deborah. What chords were struck that required no view of the dawn?

A dog barked in the distance. Was it the same mangy animal Abigail had encountered by the ash heap?

Camels bawled in the corral. From two streets away came the sounds of digging and scraping as the potter's workmen got an early start on their work for the day.

Abigail heard a voice asking her to sing. *I have nothing else to bring,* she thought, *so this is my offering, HaShem.* Softly she began the lyrics without consciously recognizing the song.

> *"Hear, O kings; give ear, O princes;*
> > *to the LORD I will sing;*
> *I will make melody to the*
> > *LORD, the God of Israel.*

> *The sound of musicians at*
> > *the watering places,*
> *there they repeat the*
> > *righteous triumphs of the LORD."*[23]

"*Musicians at the watering places,*" Abigail mused. *What is that song? Oh, HaShem, how I will sing your praise by the Well of Jacob if you give my daughter back to me. I will compose a song for you, and I will sing it every day. What a righteous triumph that will be!*

She suddenly recalled the title of the piece of music: It was Deborah's Song of Victory. Deborah, who was recorded among the judges of Israel.

> *"Awake, awake, Deborah!*
> > *Awake, awake, break out in a song!"*[24]

The aroma of baking bread insisted on being recognized. So Tzippi was up early, tending to the round loaves in the beehive-shaped brick oven in the courtyard. Abigail noticed with some surprise that she was hungry. Thirsty too.

"Mama," Deborah said, "can I have a drink of water? I'm thirsty, Mama."

Abigail's eyes snapped open.

Little Bee was sitting upright in bed, yawning, clutching her doll, and sniffing the air. "Bread smells good, Mama."

Abigail gathered Deborah in her arms, but carefully, carefully, afraid to hug too tightly.

Little Bee more than made up for the lack of intensity, squeezing her mother around the neck with all her might. "I had the funniest dream, Mama. I want to tell you all about it. But first, I need a drink of water."

It was a celebration of miracles. Abigail could not wait to share the joyous news and to thank Romulus for his suggestion.

Abigail arrived back at Romulus' villa just as the centurion galloped up, returning from his mission to the Jordan. When he saw Abigail walking alone, his eyes were troubled and his expression anxious. "Little Bee?" he asked. "How—?"

"Awake!" Abigail exulted. "Awake. Hungry. Chattering a mile a minute. Singing."

Jumping from his horse and grabbing her in his arms, Romulus lifted Abigail off her feet and swung her around. "That's wonderful! Wonderful news. When I saw you, I feared . . . did you hire a physician?"

Abigail gushed, "You were right about taking her home! The familiar surroundings. The sounds!" She paused to reflect. "Romulus, she talked about angels she saw, who told her not to be afraid. Angels who led her by the hand. It's a miracle."

Abigail waited for his response. The Romans, especially soldiers, were a cynical lot, dismissive of any superstitions except their own personal talismans.

"I believe you," Romulus said. "Listen: Something is happening in Judea greater than anything anywhere in all the Empire . . . perhaps than in all the world."

"The Baptizer?"

Romulus gnawed his mustache. "No." He shook his head. "But the other man—the one from the Temple in Jerusalem?"

"The madman?" Abigail prompted.

"Him," Romulus agreed. "Only he's not crazy. Or if he is, then I am too. I met him at the river. He was teaching. His *talmidim* were baptizing. People came from all over to hear him preach. I met Jews from Caesarea Philippi and from Joppa and from Capernaum. I think the whole country's going out to see him."

Now it was Abigail's turn to wait while Romulus marshaled his thoughts.

"I never heard anyone speak like this man speaks," he said. "I heard him say that just as there are earthly kingdoms, so too there is a heavenly kingdom. He said, 'God did not send his Son into the world to condemn the world, but in order that the world might be saved through him.'"[25]

"So he claims to be the Son of God?"

Romulus took both Abigail's hands in his. "Feel how I shake? I saw a man—a stonemason, I think—whose hand had been crushed in an accident and was withered. Abigail, I saw Yeshua heal that man! It was no trick. I saw it myself. The withered hand restored to be as powerful as the other. If ever there was a man who could be the Son of God, Yeshua is he!"

"And what will happen next? He's a Jew, yes? Will the Jews proclaim him to be their Messiah, their King?"

"I hope not," Romulus said with a worried frown. "If he allows such things to be spoken of him, then Herod and the priests and Rome will combine to crush him utterly. I hope he will stay far away from Jerusalem. I hope I am never the one Rome calls to arrest him." The centurion shook his head, pondering.

"Romulus, I have something to ask you. I am your property. We made a bargain. You have kept your part, and I intend to keep mine. But I want Deborah to grow up where HaShem is honored every day. I want her to learn from truly righteous people. I want her to live with Ezra and Tzippi."

"After all you suffered?" Romulus appeared confused. "After all you went through to get her back?"

"Yes, I think it's for the best. So that's the first part of my request. The second is this: I want to see her often. I promise to come back to you every time, for as long as you want me to keep returning. But I need to see my daughter growing up happy, raised by better people than I can ever be."

ELEVENTH PROPHECY

King David's Well

Once during the harvest, when David was at the cave of Adullam, the Philistine army was camped in the valley of Rephaim. The Three (who were among the Thirty—an elite group among David's fighting men) went down to meet him there. David was staying in the stronghold at the time, and a Philistine detachment had occupied the town of Bethlehem.

David remarked longingly to his men, "Oh, how I would love some of that good water from the well by the gate in Bethlehem." So the Three broke through the Philistine lines, drew some water from the well by the gate in Bethlehem, and brought it back to David. But he refused to drink it. Instead, he poured it out as an offering to the LORD. "The LORD forbid that I should drink this!" he exclaimed. "This water is as precious as the blood of these men who risked their lives to bring it to me." So David did not drink it.

2 SAMUEL 23:13-17 NLT

Deborah was propped up beside the table. Tzippi worked the stiff dough in her kneading trough while Deborah, with a small lump of dough, imitated her movements. Weak from the weeks of inactivity, Little Bee's muscles required exercise. Tzippi knew just how to deal with the need, making work into a game.

"See here now, Little Bee." The old woman's hands were strong from years of bread-making, her arms accustomed to the chore. "Harder now. You've got to pound your dough. That's it. Harder now! Work in the leaven. See? A pinch of salt. See how I do it. That's right. Right!"

Deborah's oval face was covered with flour. Her expression was intense and serious in the effort. She turned to her doll. "See, baby. Look how Gramma Tzippi makes bread. Do what she does. And what I do." Little Bee thrust her hands into the white paste.

Tzippi exclaimed, "That's the way. Strong and good as new in no time."

Every day, with the permission of Romulus, Abigail spent a few hours at The Stones of Joshua. When Romulus' travels took him away more than a day, then Abigail stayed overnight with Tzippi, Ezra, and Deborah. Each afternoon, when the sun was at its zenith, the city of Sychar shut down for a rest. That was when Abigail ventured out, carrying her water jug to Jacob's Well to draw and sing to the Lord in fulfillment of her vow.

Today was especially hot. Abigail spread a blanket beneath the apricot tree near the inn and carried Little Bee outside for a nap.

"Will you stay with me, Mama?" Deborah asked.

"For a while."

"I mean, will you stay here with us all tonight? Like you used to?"

"I have work to do, Little Bee. My life is not my own to order."

The child gazed solemnly through the branches at the blue sky. "I wish everything was like it used to be."

Abigail lay down beside her. "I have you back with me. You are alive. That is better than anything in the world."

Little Bee stuck out her lip. "When you can stay here all night again, all the time. And when I can run and play. Then I will think everything is better than before."

"Then you and I will ask HaShem for that to come true." She stroked Deborah's face lightly with her fingers. "Pretty girl."

Within minutes the child drifted to sleep.

Tzippi emerged from the door of the inn and murmured, "Too hot to fetch water now, my dove. Wait till it cools off a bit. Stay awhile, and I'll fix you a bite to eat."

Abigail put a finger to her lips and shook her head. "I need to go now for the water." She rose quietly and strapped on her sandals. The aroma of bread recently out of the oven made her mouth water.

Tzippi half scolded, "You choose the hottest time of the day to draw water, my lamb, my dove."

"While everyone else is asleep, I offer my thanks to the Lord. Deborah's song . . . for the life of my Deborah."

Tzippi crouched before the oven to check the bread. "Hot. So hot. Even the Lord will be sleeping on a day like today."

"Then I'll sing him a lullaby. I'll be back soon."

"Then gone again. Such a life." The elderly woman sighed.

Abigail shouldered the water jar and stepped out onto the nearly deserted street. At the gate she heard the babble of male voices.

A group of twelve male Jewish pilgrims was haranguing the gate sentry. "Twelve of you." The sentry tugged his ear. "Like Jacob's sons, come to Jacob's Well?"

They were too hot and weary for his banter.

All their conversation was grumpy:

"What do you mean the baker shop is closed?"

"We've been traveling all day."

"Where can we get provisions?"

The guard offered directions.

"No. Not a Samaritan shop! Must be kosher."

"Are there no Jews in Sychar?"

"Where do Jewish pilgrims usually stop for provisions?"

Abigail considered directing the tribe toward The Stones of Joshua, but the sentry beat her to it. "There's one Jewish inn here in Sychar. Just up the street. Ezra and Tzippi. Jews. Stones of Joshua, it's called. A clean establishment, designed to serve Jewish pilgrims. It's where all your kind stop for rest and meals."

Satisfied with this information, the dozen pilgrims set out, shielding their eyes and turning dusty faces away from Abigail as she passed.

No wives or children in the group, Abigail observed. They must be students of some itinerant rabbi.

The sun beat down on the valley. Harsh light glared from the stones, intensifying the sense of being too near an oppressively hot oven. The hike to the well was arduous, but Abigail rewarded herself with thoughts of how refreshing the water would be on such a day.

The heat rising from the roadway made the air shimmer. She began to sing the song of Deborah as she walked.

> "To the LORD I will sing;
> I will make melody to the
>   LORD, the God of Israel!
> Awake, awake, Deborah!
>   Awake, awake, break out in a song!
> Tell of it, you who ride on white donkeys . . .
>   and you who walk by the way!
> To the sound of musicians at
>   the watering places,
>   there they repeat the
>   righteous triumphs of the LORD."[26]

As Abigail neared the well, her voice fell away. She saw the image of a man, blurred by the ripples in the air. Abigail had expected the site to be deserted. She was vaguely disappointed and wary.

As she drew nearer, she saw the man was resting, sitting on the rock rim of the well. He held a prayer shawl over his head for shade. From the fringes of his tallith, which were white instead of Samaritan blue, Abigail recognized that he was a Jew.

There would be no need for any conversation then. Besides the barrier between Jews and Samaritans, it was also understood that an unaccompanied female would never speak to a strange male. To do so would bring accusations of harlotry.

He glanced up at her. His eyes seemed familiar somehow. She looked down quickly, not wanting to be caught by his direct gaze. The memory of her dream about Mosheh and Zipporah came to her mind. What was it Zipporah had said to her? *"Water means salvation. No one has the right to deny water to another."* Would this Jew drive her from Jacob's Well?

Nodding politely, Abigail approached the opposite side. She felt his eyes follow her movements. Setting aside the jar, she grasped the end of the rope used in drawing water. The goatskin bag was missing. It was nowhere to be seen. Abigail sighed. In her thoughts she replayed the song as an offering to the Lord: *". . . musicians at the watering places."* She ignored the stranger and pretended she was alone. Tying the cord to a handle of the clay jar, she carefully let it into the depths.

As she drew it out again the man lifted his head and looked directly at her. Before she could drop her gaze, he gently asked, "Give me a drink?"[27]

This was so unexpected, so improper, that Abigail blinked dumbly at him. He held out his hand, palm up. She nodded, carried the jar, and poured him a double handful. She stammered, "How is it that you, a Jew, ask for a drink from me, a woman of Samaria?" Was he ignorant about what was polite? Or was he merely thirsty enough that conventions didn't matter?

Swallowing gratefully, the man's full lips curved in a smile of thanks. He accepted a second offering, then wiped his face with the cool drops that remained. Lifting brown eyes lively with golden flecks, he said, "If you knew the gift of God, and who is saying to you, 'Give me a drink,' you would have asked him, and he would have given you living water."

Living water? Abigail was nonplussed. Was the Jew ill from the heat? Hadn't he just received liquid hauled from the depths with Abigail's jar, when there was no other means at hand?

"Sir," she said, politely pointing out the physical impossibility of his suggestion, "you have nothing to draw water with, and the well is deep. Where do you get that living water?"

Besides the stranger's inability to plumb the depths of the well without a skin or jar, there was another objection to his statement. Water was not called "living" unless it was freely flowing. There was no stream nearby. Not even a spring bubbled up from the Samaritan hills. The patriarch Jacob had dug this well for this very reason.

"Are you greater than our father Jacob?" she asked. "He gave us the well and drank from it himself, as did his sons and his livestock."

The image of the twelve strangers who had tramped into Sychar came to her mind. Twelve sons of Jacob indeed!

The man gestured toward her water jar. "Everyone who drinks of this water—" he glanced over his shoulder at the mouth of the well— "will be thirsty again. But whoever drinks of the water that I will give will never be thirsty again. Forever."

Abigail appraised him with open curiosity and doubt.

He continued, sure of himself. "The water that I will give will become a spring of water welling up to eternal life."

Abigail recognized he was a rabbi or a philosopher. What was he saying? Almost everyone had to come to the well every day in order to get only one day's supply of life-giving fluid. What was a spring of eternal life?

"Sir, give me this water, so that I won't be thirsty or have to come here to draw water."

The man nodded as if agreeing to her request, then said, "Go, call your husband, and come here."

A swallow darted rapidly past overhead. Abigail's thoughts raced every bit as rapidly and almost as chaotically. She admitted, "I have . . . no husband."

Abigail's heartbeat quickened as the stranger leveled his gaze at her. He seemed to see deep into her soul. The knowledge in his eyes made her uncomfortable.

"You're right in saying, 'I have no husband.' You've had five husbands." She gasped. How could he know this?

He continued, "And the one you now have is not your husband." Drily he added, "What you've said is true."

Not again! When life in Sychar had just gotten bearable, how could it be that her reputation was known to a total stranger? "Sir, I perceive that you're a prophet."

How could she get this conversation to go somewhere else? To what subject could she jump to get off of painfully personal topics? History and geography seemed like good choices.

Lifting her arm, Abigail waved toward Mount Gerazim. "Our fathers worshipped on this mountain, but you Jews say that in Jerusalem is the place where people ought to worship."

That should redirect things into safer realms.

The man stood and brushed fine white dust from his robe. "Woman, believe me. The hour is coming when neither on this mountain, nor in Yerushalayim, will you worship the Father."

What did that mean? With a snap of his fingers could the Jew eliminate one of the chief arguments between Jews and Samaritans? What was the proper place to worship? It was a dispute that had existed for hundreds of years.

The brown-haired man continued, "Salvation is of the Jews, but the hour is coming, and is now here, when the true worshippers will worship the Father in spirit and truth. For the Father is seeking true-hearted people to worship him."

Truth? Abigail was flooded with confused emotions. She had long believed that HaShem was through with her. She felt forever separated from God and unwelcome in His courts. Her thirsty soul had been driven from the well by righteous people. Yet now this stranger seemed to be saying that God was actively seeking her, and that what He valued was not expensive gifts or scholarly achievement but her honesty.

The stranger appeared to confirm Abigail's surmise when he continued, "God is spirit. Those who worship him must worship in spirit and in truth."

The truth of Abigail's life was stark and hopeless. Her choices had led to misery. What if everything that had gone wrong could be washed clean? What if there really could be forgiveness—complete, total forgiveness—for her? And what if Abigail could have the assurance of that forgiveness and acceptance?

It would be like having a fountain of refreshing water within her life!

Suddenly Abigail understood what the stranger meant about "living water." But when? Who would make this triumphant transformation true for her? How could all the damaged parts of her life get restored?

Abigail had another flash of insight. Romulus had told her something mighty was afoot in the ancient land of Israel. He had witnessed miracles and told her about them. If a Roman could believe, why should she doubt?

"I know Messiah is coming," Abigail said, expressing her belief in the Restorer sent by God. The greatest expectation for Samaritans was the coming of the Prophet promised by Mosheh who would succeed the Lawgiver in authority. "When he comes, he'll tell us all things." She thought, but did not say, *Just the way you already told me my innermost heartaches.*

With quiet intensity, leaving no doubt or room for misunderstanding, the stranger confirmed, "I who speak to you am he."

When had Abigail's heart leapt with such complete, unquestioning joy? Only twice she could recall: when Deborah was born, and when she received Deborah back to life from the sleep of death. *"Awake! Awake, O Deborah!"*

And now! This was the third occasion in her life when unbridled, unfettered, expectant joy bubbled up in her heart. She was indeed awake! Could this be the Messiah? The One she had heard about! Had the One whom Romulus had said turned water into wine asked her for water? What could this mean? Was He the Good Shepherd she had longed to meet?

Their feet trailing in the dust, their arms laden with provisions, the twelve sons of Jacob, scowling with disapproval, returned to the well from the inn. So Abigail had been right: This was a group of *talmidim*, and she had been speaking to their rabbi.

The disciples gathered in a semicircle, their expressions conveying varying degrees of weariness and even hostility, but none of them spoke to her.

Then she heard the students address the teacher as Reb Yeshua.

Yeshua. Salvation! He had said it clearly, straight out, and she had almost missed the significance. His name was Yeshua. Salvation! *"Salvation is of the Jews,"* he said. *Yeshua . . . Salvation . . . is of the Jews.*

This was the man. The one Romulus had told her about: Yeshua of Nazareth! Like Mosheh driving cruel shepherds away from the well of Midian, Yeshua had driven out the money changers from the Temple. The expected Prophet, like Mosheh, was here at Jacob's Well!

Forgetting her water jar and the errand on which she had come to the well, Abigail backed away, turned, and dashed off toward Sychar. She had to tell Ezra and Tzippi about the stranger at the well. And the honey seller's wife. And the charcoal seller's wife. And . . . and . . . everyone who had ears to hear.

Awake! Awake! Deborah! Break out in a song! Messiah has come at last to Jacob's Well!

As Abigail hurried back into Sychar, she was singing. Every verse was praise to God:

"O God, You are my God;
earnestly I seek You;
my soul thirsts for You;
my flesh faints for You,
as in a dry and weary land
where there is no water.
Because Your steadfast love is
better than life
my lips will praise You."[28]

There it was again! Steadfast love! What Yeshua of Nazareth offered was as refreshing as cool water in the desert. He taught—no, more than that—He *showed* that the love of God was reliable and always available.

Like a well that never runs dry!

Even before she reached the inn, Abigail began sharing her

experience with the people of the town. "Come with me! You must come back to Jacob's Well to meet a man."

"What is it? What's all the excitement about?" the charcoal seller's wife demanded.

The honey seller's wife jumped into the hubbub. "Is it Little Bee? She's not ill, is she? Ah! Praise HaShem, there she is."

Deborah appeared at the door of The Stones of Joshua with Tzippi. "Mama," the child said. "We could hear you clear inside the inn. What's going on?"

"Come with me," Abigail said. "You too, Tzippi. And call Ezra. You must! Come, see a man who told me all that I ever did."[29]

"What do you mean, my dear, my dove?" Tzippi asked.

"A prophet," Abigail said. "But not one who shuns me or turns me away from the well."

The townspeople gathered around her as Abigail described her encounter with Yeshua of Nazareth. "He knows everything there is to know about me," she said openly. "Everything I wanted all of you to forget. But here's what he says: 'God's love is steadfast, like living water. Like a spring that gives eternal life.'"

"What else did he say?" Tzippi asked.

"He said HaShem is seeking true-hearted people to worship him."

"Not hypocrites," the honey seller's wife declared emphatically. "Not greedy priests or cruel rabbis."

"What HaShem wants," Abigail said, "is people honest enough to admit their faults and ask him for forgiveness."

An excited murmur swept round the group.

"Do you think . . . ?" Abigail said. "Can this be the Christ?"[30]

"Let's go and find out," Ezra urged.

"Wait a moment while I get my cart," the charcoal seller offered. "It's too far for Tzippi to walk. She can ride in my cart."

On the way back to the well, Deborah urged Abigail to sing.

"Only if you sing with me, Little Bee."

"Of course, Mama. You start."

And so all the way back to Jacob's Well the land around Sychar resounded in praise:

"With joy you will draw water
from the wells of salvation. . . .

Give thanks to the LORD,
    call upon His name,
make known His deeds among the peoples,
    proclaim that His Name is exalted.
Shout, and sing for joy . . .
    for great in your midst is the Holy One of Israel."[31]

The Stones of Joshua had never seen such a diverse gathering. Besides its Jewish host and hostess, the space was packed with Samaritans, a Roman centurion, and the pagan potter, Komer, and his wife, Athena.

All had come in response to Abigail's invitation to "come and see a man who told me everything I ever did."

At first Yeshua's *talmidim* held themselves apart from the Samaritans, as if fearful of some contagion. But as they witnessed how the people of Sychar were captivated by their Rabbi's teaching, old barriers began to topple.

This breaking down of suspicion and distrust began when Yeshua asked Abigail to sing.

With Deborah at her side, Abigail launched into Mosheh's song after the waters of the Red Sea had covered the Egyptians:

"The LORD is my strength and my song,
    and He has become my salvation;
this is my God, and I will praise Him,
    my father's God, and I will exalt Him."[32]

Her hands resting on her daughter's curls, Abigail beamed as she sang. This hymn was all about not giving in to despair and how rejoicing follows trust.

"The enemy said, 'I will pursue,
    I will overtake,
I will divide the spoil. . . .'
You blew with Your wind;
    the sea covered them;

> *they sank like lead in the*
> *mighty waters.*"[33]

It was all about not giving up on trusting HaShem. What if the Israelites had turned back and surrendered to slavery when they thought they were trapped against the sea?

What if Abigail had given in to depression and taken her own life?

What if too much sorrow and too much shame had kept Abigail away from Jacob's Well?

> *"You have led in Your steadfast love*
> *the people whom You have redeemed;*
> *You have guided them by Your strength*
> *to Your holy abode.*"[34]

The steadfast love of God for His people overcame all struggles . . . so long as they continued to trust Him.

Abigail saw a smile dancing in Yeshua's gold-flecked eyes. Apparently Deborah saw it too, for she pulled free of her mother and ran to Him, climbing onto His lap as if she had every right to be there.

When the song was completed, the crowd quieted to hear what the teacher had to say.

Yeshua began by quoting from Mosheh: "*'The LORD your God will raise up for you a Prophet like Me from among you, from your brothers—it is to Him you shall listen.'*"[35]

He continued, "Mosheh did not promise this out of his own authority, for HaShem had said of this prophet who was to come, *'I will put My words in His mouth, and He shall speak all that I command Him.'*"[36]

How clever Yeshua was, Abigail thought. There was no argument here about worshipping in Jerusalem or on Mount Gerazim. Yeshua's words took Jews and Samaritans back to a common belief in the promised Messiah, to the words of Mosheh with which both groups agreed.

Instead of addressing the things that divided them, Yeshua reminded them of their common heritage. He taught at length about how Abraham had waited so very, very long to have a son. The Rabbi talked about how much Abraham loved his son, how every promise of God to Abraham was bound up in the boy.

Then Yeshua reminded them how Abraham was called upon by God to offer his son, Isaac, on an altar.

Abigail looked at Deborah and shivered. *I love her so much*, she thought. *I could die for her, but I could never ask her to die for me. What enormous faith Abraham had!*

"And you remember how HaShem stopped the sacrifice?" Yeshua said. "Not only stopped it but provided a substitute life for the sacrifice?"

Everyone nodded. This was a famous story. Even Romulus and Komer expressed recognition of the tale.

"Listen carefully to what Abraham prophesied," Yeshua continued. "He said to Isaac, '*God will provide Himself the lamb for a burnt offering, my son.*'[37]

"The hour is coming," Yeshua said, "and is now here, when true worshippers will worship the Father in spirit and truth."[38]

Abigail thrilled at His words. This was an echo of what Yeshua had spoken to her, personally, at the well.

"Unless one is born of water and the Spirit, he cannot enter the Kingdom of God."[39]

Romulus murmured to Abigail, "This is what the Pharisee Nakdimon reported to me. Yeshua said the same thing to him."

"For God so loved the world, that he gave his only Son, that whoever believes in him should not perish but have eternal life."[40]

Abigail did not understand all of what Yeshua taught that day. She did not comprehend all of what lay behind God providing a Lamb of sacrifice and God giving His only Son.

But she understood what it was to love when she gazed at Deborah. And she understood the promise that God loved her with a steadfast love, despite her past, her sins, her failures.

And she understood that Yeshua had come not only to express that love or explain that love but to *demonstrate* that love.

Scanning the room she saw from the faces of Jews, Samaritans, and pagans that they understood as well.

Not everyone in Sychar experienced the cool waters of steadfast love that day. Rabbi Tabor, Saul, and Mara stayed away. So did Jerash the Merchant.

But Abel the Cloth Dyer broke ranks with his fellow elders. He was present, and at the close of the lesson he was the first to beg Yeshua to stay another day and preach again.

Which Yeshua agreed to do.

And, at Yeshua's encouragement, Deborah sang from her name-sake's verses:

> *"To the sound of musicians at*
> *the watering places,*
> *there they repeat the*
> *righteous triumphs of the LORD. . . .*
> *Awake, awake, Deborah!*
> *Awake, awake, break out in a song!*
> *I will make melody to the*
> *LORD, the God of Israel."*[41]

As they filed out of the inn, the honey seller's wife stopped and took both Abigail's hands in hers. "It is no longer because of what you said that we believe," she said, "for we have heard for ourselves, and we know that this is indeed the Savior of the world."[42]

From: Peniel of Jerusalem
To: Romanus Melodus
Constantinople, A.D. 551

Jesus, a weary traveler in this dusty world, asked her, "Give me something to drink."

But it was her thirst He had come from heaven to satisfy. In that ordinary moment He reached without condemnation to the thirsty heart of every woman and man who longs for mercy and love.

Abigail Photini continued to tell the story of the Living Water she received at Jacob's Well. Throughout the villages of Samaria many of her kindred believed, including the great man who was first her master and then her husband.

WITH MY OWN EYES I witnessed Abigail Photini in Jerusalem on that most terrible and awesome day when our crucified Redeemer gave His life as the atonement for the sins of all the world. On the Via Dolorosa, when Jesus stumbled and fell, while others fearfully shrank back, Abigail rushed past the Roman executioners and knelt in the street at His side to hold a cup of water to His bleeding lips. For her great courage, the whip that tore our Savior's flesh also struck her.

WITH MY OWN EYES I saw her as she boldly stood beside the mother of our Lord at the foot of the cross. She held out her hands as spikes tore those beautiful hands into which she had poured water.

She whose thirst He had satisfied with Living Water was at His feet when He cried in agony, "I thirst."

WITH MY OWN EYES I witnessed as Abigail shed tears beside the mother of the Lord. How Abigail grieved for the torment of His thirst and for the sorrow of Mary. She could not save the One who had saved her. Cruel men prevented her from offering one drop of kindness to Jesus.

Abigail grieved among us during the three dark days when Jesus lay in the tomb. And with the righteous women, she believed before the apostles when her sisters returned, proclaiming they had seen the Lord alive and risen from the grave. She was among the five hundred disciples to whom the Lord appeared alive. On Pentecost she was beside me when tongues of fire appeared above our heads, and we were filled with the Holy Spirit.

WITH MY OWN EYES I witnessed her baptism. She took the new name Photini, which means "the enlightened one."

Many years passed before I met Abigail Photini again, with her husband, Romulus, two sons, and five daughters. They preached the Gospel with great boldness in Carthage.

For safekeeping Abigail gave me this document, which I now entrust to you. It is her own story, written in Samaritan dialect. She promised there was more to be written in her life and that it must be written in Rome.

During the persecution under Emperor Nero, the Lord came to her in a dream and told her she must go to Rome. There she was arrested and brought before the emperor. She declared she would worship only the true King of Heaven and of Earth.

She proclaimed to Nero, "God is my help. No matter what anyone does to me I shall not be afraid."

Her preaching converted Domnina, the daughter of the madman Nero, and also the slave girls of the palace. For this, Abigail Photini and her family were condemned to death. All but Abigail were beheaded. She who had met Jesus at a well and had drunk deeply of His Living Water was lowered into a deep, dry well. The citizens of Rome were commanded to pass by and, with cursing and insults, pour their filth upon her. For many days from this dark abyss Abigail Photini preached on twelve prophecies that foretold His first coming and the establishment of His eternal Kingdom. She joyfully sang to her tormentors of Jesus, the Living Water.

"To satisfy your thirsty soul, Jesus the Living Water came down from heaven! Come receive the waters he pours out freely to you! Drink deeply of God's love and forgiveness! Taking your sins upon himself, Jesus has died for you! Come receive the living waters and drink deeply of God's love and forgiveness! Because of Almighty God's love for you, the Savior who died for your sake is risen from death! He has conquered death forever!

Come to the waters and drink of God's love and forgiveness, and you will never taste death! Jesus Christ is seated at the right hand of the Father now! Come to the waters and drink deeply from the well of Salvation! Jesus is our Eternal King, and he will come again to judge the living and the dead, and his kingdom will have no end! Call out to Jesus in your sorrow! He will not reject you! Receive the waters of eternal life! With open hand he will quench your thirst."

After many weeks of her sweet voice rising from the well, she called up to the crowd and told them the Lord had appeared to her. Her story in this world, she said, had come to an end. Her eternal life was just beginning. That night she offered her soul up to God.

Many pagans were converted by her last song. The accounts of those who heard her sing are recorded in the writings of the church among the martyrs of that time.

She met our Lord beside Jacob's Well, and there received Living Water.

I have kept her manuscript with me many years.

In her song perhaps your spirit, my brother, will hear

and compose a new praise to the One who freely gives the
Living Water.

Perhaps there may be one woman, forsaken by all others,
who will hear and drink deeply of the free gift of eternal
life and unending joy offered by Jesus at the well of salvation
because of Abigail's story.

May the grace and peace of our Lord Jesus Christ be yours.

Peniel of Jerusalem
Once I was blind. Now I see.

Epilogue

It was one minute to midnight on New Year's Eve when Eben finished translating the manuscript of Abigail Photini's early life. The ancient Aramaic script written in Samaritan dialect had been difficult to decipher and time intensive.

Eben completed the last paragraph of Peniel's letter to Romanus Melodus into English, then placed the original back in the temperature- and humidity-controlled storage container.

The grandfather clock in the foyer downstairs struck twelve times. Eben knew the end of something important was at hand. Something new was beginning. The beginning of the end.

Outside Eben's window the London sky erupted with a fireworks display.

Loralei came up the stairs and stood framed in the doorway. Jeans and lambskin UGG boots were topped by a long, red wool, cable-knit sweater. Light from the hall behind her made a golden halo around her head. "Done?"

He nodded slowly. "Done."

"The world is celebrating." She smiled. "If only they knew."

"The passing of a single year." He came to her and wrapped his arms around her slender waist. "A breath. Their lives less than a breath. They strive and bicker and seek ways to destroy those they envy. They believe they know God, yet they deny the truth about themselves. Jesus loved Abigail. Loved her honesty. I've seen men and women forget about truth because they only want to win. They forget how Jesus comes quietly, to comfort the outcasts they persecute and despise." Eben swayed and closed his eyes as the thunder of revelry shook the house. "If only they knew."

"A thousand years is as a day unto the Lord."[43] Loralei rested her cheek against his chest. "They won't know . . . until."

"They're celebrating the passing of minutes. Mere hours have gone by since Jesus asked Abigail for water at Jacob's Well. And since she heard him say, 'I thirst.'" Eben kissed the top of Loralei 's head.

Pyrotechnics blossomed over the Thames. Light reflected from the buildings of Church Row and streamed through the window, pooling colors onto the manuscript. The delayed boom rattled the windows in their frames.

Loralei held him tight. "So few left now, Eben, who remember."

He led her to his desk where the complete, translated manuscript lay in a cardboard stationery box. "Abigail was sad and beautiful before Jesus came. Alone. Hoping for something to change even when there was no hope. Nothing has changed. Millions are like her. I see her face every time I step onto the street. The longing lives from generation to generation. Only Jesus can satisfy such thirst."

"And who was she after the story you translated?"

"A willow planted beside a clear river. Graceful. Sparkling eyes. Quick wit. Funny. She could make you laugh. Her laughter was like a brook. 'Til the very end of her life, her gaze could reach right into an aching heart and touch a soul. She had suffered at the hands of hypocrites, so she understood the suffering of women especially. She used to say, 'Every woman . . . we are all Eve, longing to taste the waters of Eden again.' Jesus is the living water. Some refuse to drink, and they remain in exile, bitter and cruel. Some know the truth about themselves and reach out to him and are changed."

"Her death?"

"Nero's court. I think they were afraid of her eyes. That's why they put her down a well. So she couldn't look into their hearts. Even then she sang."

"So, her story's told now. What will you do with it?"

"The original. Shimon will carry it back to Jerusalem. Israel is the only safe place for such hidden treasures now. The translation must be published. Soon. Soon it will no longer be merely fireworks exploding over London. Or Paris. Or Washington. Or New York and Los Angeles. Chicago. Other places. I have seen the vision of what is coming, Loralei. This is the last turning of the year. That's why there has been so much opposition to all true things."

"They don't know what they are doing. Father, forgive them."

"We've traveled far to arrive at this moment, but it seems like hours to me, Loralei. What we know and have written by the commandment of the Holy Spirit is recorded in *The Book of Hours*. The clock strikes. The whole world forgets to look up. One by one those who traveled with me have prayed to be taken home. It is a prayer that is always answered."

"But you . . . you never have asked."

"I've seen heaven. He called me back. I remain in this desert place because I long to show many the way. If I reach even one soul in every generation, heaven will rejoice. Eternity changed forever. There is no other reason to stay behind." He smiled. "All the dear ones we knew in the beginning, the cloud of witnesses—Abigail Photini, her husband, her children—they will return in glory with the King. And I want to greet them when they come."

"Is this the year, Eben? Do you think?"

A giant blossom of light illuminated the horizon. "You are the final gift of my life. Sent by my Lord to comfort me these last, lonely moments. I am glad you are here with me 'til the end of our journey."

TWELFTH PROPHECY

Rivers of Living Water

"Whoever believes in Me, as the Scripture has said,
'Out of his heart will flow rivers of living water.'"

JOHN 7:38 ESV

Digging Deeper into
TWELFTH PROPHECY

Dear Reader,

Have you ever felt like the odds of life are stacked against you? Do you wonder if the one poor choice you made in the past will overshadow your entire life? Or if another's evil against you or someone you love will haunt you to the end of your days? Are you burdened by the gossip of others and their judgmental attitudes, but you feel powerless to change your situation?

Abigail, of all people, would understand, because she experienced all of those situations and emotions. At a young age, she was forced into marriage, then married five times as her first three husbands died, another left her, and then she was married off to an old man. After being raped by a rabbi's son, she began an affair with him, and became pregnant.

Now, in *Twelfth Prophecy*, the townspeople are out for her blood because she has "sinned." Abigail can't go anywhere without vicious gossip chasing her. Yet she longs for love, mercy, and grace—and a place for her heart to call home. Then she discovers Yeshua, graciously awaiting her at the well. . . .

Do you wish for love, mercy, and grace in your life, as well?

Following are six studies. You may wish to delve into

them on your own or share them with a friend or a discussion group. They are designed to take you deeper into the answers to questions such as:

- What can I do when I'm unfairly judged and condemned by others?
- Who, and what, is "family"?
- In the midst of difficult circumstances, how can I hold on to hope?
- Is it possible for people to change—*really* change?
- Does God really care about the "little things" in my life? How can I be sure of that?
- What does lasting love look like? Where can I find it?

Can lives, bodies, and hearts truly be transformed? With Yeshua, *anything* is possible! Through *Twelfth Prophecy*, may the promised Messiah come alive to you . . . in more brilliance than ever before.

1 OUTCASTS OF MERCY?!

> "Abigail. I've seen you many times in the town."
> "Why do you help me? I'm an outcast."
> —ROMULUS AND ABIGAIL, P. 38

Have you ever felt like you were on the outside, looking in, of any group? If so, how did that make you feel?

_____

_____

_____

Why was belonging to that particular group important to you? If you did eventually get in, were their acceptance and your belonging what you thought they would be? Why or why not?

_____

_____

_____

Take a look at any group of people, and there will always be some on the inside of the group, some on the fringes, and some on the outside. Abigail was definitely on the outside—for some reasons she could help, and some she couldn't.

READ

Zakane had taken in Abigail when no one else would, becoming the last of her five husbands.

It seemed ages, but had only been a handful of years, since Abigail was a cheerful young woman, beautiful in face and form, with many suitors. When her first husband was killed in the rock quarry in an accident, there had been no shortage of those vying for the widow's hand.

Even after husband number two died of a fever their first winter together, no blame attached to the sorrowing young woman.

But when Abigail's third husband was drowned at sea, all the pent-up superstition and need to fix blame crashed in on her. . . . Either Abigail was a sorceress, or she brought a curse with her to the marriage bed.

When Reen married her, becoming husband number four, Abigail did not know if it was during one of his sober moments or in his usual drunken state. Within a month, the distinction did not matter. He was never sober, and he beat her every night.

Then he had divorced her and left. It was the only kind thing Reen had ever done for her.

—PP. 11–12

Abigail, alone in her home, had not suspected she could be in danger from one of the most respectable young men in Sychar. How could she know he was watching her every move? that he was consumed by thoughts of her?

She had awakened in the middle of the night with a man in her bed. His hand was clamped hard across her mouth, preventing her scream. She fought hard, but he overpowered her and forced her to yield to him. Fleeing in the darkness, he kept his secret well. She did not know who her assailant was. Fear and shame kept her silent.

A month later he approached her as she walked home from the marketplace. Confessing his love for her, he said she had bewitched him with her beauty. . . .

Weeks passed. He slipped unsigned love letters beneath her door. He begged her to forgive him. Begged her to love him as he loved her. He said his heart was broken because he had ruined her life.

Then one night he returned, climbing the balcony as she slept. He had called her name and told her he could no longer live without her. She discovered a terrible truth. She loved him as much as he wanted her. Night after night he crept into her bedchamber. She fell ever more deeply and hopelessly in love.

When she told him she had conceived a child, his midnight visits came to an end.

—PP. 32–33

ASK

List the events that happened in Abigail's life before *Twelfth Prophecy* started.

_____

_____

_____

How would any one of these events have affected you emotionally, had it happened to you?

_____

_____

_____

In what way(s) do these circumstances cause Abigail to make the choice she did—to continue an affair with the rabbi's son, after he raped her?

_____

_____

_____

Have you ever made choices that deeply influenced your life at a time when you were confused? How did those choices turn out?

_____

_____

_____

READ

Though the square was ringed many ranks deep with spectators, the only merchandise on offer was misery; the only hunger to be satisfied was vengeance.

On every side Abigail saw hatred. The menfolk might behold and turn away, but the women's eyes challenged her. There was no pity there, no sympathy.

There must be one on whose face concern glowed. After all, there was one in the crowd who truly did share her guilt. Where was he? Why did he not intervene?

—P. II

ASK

Why do you think the townspeople hate Abigail so much?

_____

_____

_____

Is it easier to be part of the crowd or to stand up for someone who is being maligned? Explain your reasoning.

_____

_____

_____

READ

"Stop this instant!" a commanding voice bellowed. . . . "I said, stop! And I'll crucify any man who disobeys. Cut that woman down."

When the knife hacked through Abigail's bonds, no one tried to catch her as she fell.

"Centurion Romulus," Rabbi Tabor said, "this is a religious matter. We have authority—"

"I don't care if your religion demands that you cut your own throat," the centurion responded angrily. "You'll not flog a pregnant woman."

"She is a transgressor of our law," the rabbi argued. "An adulteress."

"And she was not guilty of this crime alone. Where is the other party?"

"That's what we are going to determine."

"Not this way," the Roman officer ordered. "Let her go!"

—P. 13

Rabbi Tabor moved to Zakane's side at once. "Honored Zakane, let me help you." Dropping their rods in the dirt, Jerash and Abel joined them. "Let us assist you to your home."

Zakane shook his head violently, his entire upper body swaying with emotion. "Not until I do something here. Help me," he demanded. "Support me."

Aided by the trio of Abigail's judges, Zakane released his crutch and bent to unlace his sandal.

In the entire crowd no one moved. All were transfixed by what they were witnessing.

Shoe in hand, Zakane slapped the ground violently. "I divorce thee," he said, striking. His voice rising in both inflection and volume, he repeated, "I divorce thee! I divorce thee! I utterly cast thee out!"

His faltering energy completely spent by his outburst, Zakane sagged into the arms of his friends.

"Come, sir," the rabbi said. "Let us help you home now. The rest of you, disperse. Leave her. She is dead . . . the same as dead."

—PP. 14–15

ASK

How does Rabbi Tabor treat Abigail? How does his hatred make him bold enough to even argue with a despised Roman centurion?

_____

_____

_____

How does the rabbi treat the "honorable Zakane"? Why the difference, do you think?

_____

_____

_____

If your friends, relatives, or community considered you dead, how would you feel? How would you respond?

_____

_____

_____

READ

By the time Abigail reached Jacob's Well, she knew she could go no farther. Her back stiffened; her feet stumbled. Each step gave birth to a groan through clenched teeth.

The well, located on the main trading route, was home to beggars. A few homeless souls huddled beside the stone wall flanking the water supply. The well drew travelers, and such pilgrims gave alms.

Suspicious faces peered out of palm-frond shelters and lean-tos formed of broken roof slates and discarded timber. The outcasts of Sychar built their meager existence from the cast-off bits of others.

"Go away, then," one legless indigent demanded as Abigail approached.

She swayed where she stood and would have fallen had she not sat down abruptly on the lip of the well.

A blind woman, eyes wrapped in a band of black cloth, emerged from a hut. "Who are we to drive anyone off?" she demanded.

"You don't know who this is, Leah," the cripple retorted. "It's the harlot of Sychar. Her as was beat and turned out and divorced all today. She's a vile sinner—brought it all on herself."

If she leaned backward at all, Abigail would plunge into the well. Would that not be an answer?

The blind woman approached, feeling her way along the ledge. When her questing touch reached Abigail, both women flinched.

"I won't hurt you," Leah said.

"I don't want to cause trouble," Abigail said. "It's not for me. It's for my baby."

Leah gently touched the swollen belly and was rewarded with a vigorous kick. "Come with me, sweet," she offered. "Water to wash your wounds and a bit of oil. Had a blessing today. Even have some bread to share. Come on, then. Don't be afraid of Leah. I won't hurt you."

—PP. 16–17

ASK

Why would an outcast—the legless indigent—not welcome another outcast?

_____

_____

_____

What argument does Leah, the blind woman, make to her fellow beggars for showing Abigail kindness?

_____

_____

_____

In what way(s) does Leah go beyond what is expected to help Abigail?

_____

_____

_____

If you had very little to give, would you give to someone else in need? Why or why not?

_____

_____

_____

READ

Without waiting, Romulus swept her up and put her on the saddle. In an instant he mounted behind her. "What is your name?"

"Abigail," she answered, secure between his strong arms.

"Abigail. I've seen you many times in the town."

"Why do you help me? I'm an outcast." . . .

"Even before this I've seen how these women in your town hate you. They hide their bitter words behind their hands as you pass by. It is because you are beautiful."

As if on cue, the heads of her departing tormentors swiveled as Romulus rode away with her. The eyes of Sychar's women widened. Their gleeful outrage echoed against the stone blocks of the city wall.

"They will think you are the father."

"Does it matter?" he asked.

"No. I am anathema." She hesitated.

He laughed. "So how can a Roman make it worse?"

"I meant, I am an outcast and if they think I have—I mean—you are a Roman."

—P. 38

Romulus did not correct the impression that Abigail was his woman. "Then let it be done. Send a messenger at once!"

The innkeeper shouted over the rail, summoning his teenage son to the stair and bawling urgent instructions. "Shechem . . . midwife . . . she'll be well paid. Hurry!"

The clatter of a horse's hooves retreated as Romulus counted out coins for Abigail's care.

"But sir, will you not be here for the birth of the child?" whined Weasel.

"I am summoned to Galilee. But know this: Rome will hold you and your woman responsible for her care and the well-being of the child."

—PP. 39–40

The centurion stood in his stirrups and scanned the faces of the people. He leveled his gaze on Rabbi Tabor. "Your religion is nothing to me. *I* am the law in Sychar. *I* am Rome. You will answer to me if this woman or her child is harmed."

Hatred for Abigail was suddenly overshadowed by fear of a Roman's authority. So it was clear to all. Abigail was the woman of Romulus; this was his child. She was under his protection.

Romulus commanded her, "Go home. No one will harm you. They understand the penalty too clearly."

—P. 91

ASK

In what way(s) does Romulus protect Abigail, even before he takes her into his house?

_____

_____

_____

Why would a Roman centurion protect a Samaritan woman? (Keep in mind that in those days, women were considered possessions of men and not highly regarded.) What did the two share in common?

_____

_____

_____

Why do you think the "pagan" Roman could show mercy to Abigail, whereas her own people were merciless?

_____

_____

_____

Have you ever experienced this lack of mercy from Christians? If so, how did that reflect on your thinking about Christians, faith, and God?

_____

_____

_____

WONDER . . .

"I am praying. Praying. You will see. Our merciful Lord will not let this injustice stand. He will make a way. We must only trust!"
—TZIPPI, P. 144

If you believe Tzippi's statement to be true, how will it help you to trust that God will work everything out for your good, even when you're in the middle of difficult situations?

2 | FOREVER FAMILY

You saved my life. You gave me and Little Bee all your love. I will never forget you.
—ABIGAIL'S LETTER TO TZIPPI AND EZRA, P. 145

What does *hospitality* mean to you? When have you been shown hospitality that went beyond what was expected? Tell the story.

_____

_____

_____

How did this extension of hospitality make you feel? In what way(s) did it influence your view of yourself, others, and the world?

_____

_____

_____

What does *family* mean to you? What people do you think of as members of your family? Why?

_____

_____

_____

Abigail was friendless, husbandless, a new mom, and utterly alone. She, of all people, needed a family to support her and her baby, Deborah. Surrounded by hostile neighbors, she at last makes her way to an inn just inside Sychar's city gate. The Stones of Joshua serves "simple meals, wine and barley beer, and provided a handful of rooms." Its proprietors, an elderly Jewish couple named Ezra and Tzippi, are almost the only members of the Jewish faith in this Samaritan town. Desperate, Abigail shows up at their door, fearing more rejection but driven by the need to protect Deborah.

READ

The door opened, and Abigail recognized the owner. Soundlessly he invited her in and gestured for her to approach a lamp gleaming on the serving counter. Ezra did not seem angry at being disturbed in the middle of the night. Jewish travelers who tried and failed to cross Samaritan territory in one day frequently showed up at awkward hours.

Kind, watery blue eyes studied her. Age had drawn his cheeks downward, but Ezra offered a generous smile for the babe in arms. "I know you. Your name is Abigail, I think."

He did not call her "harlot of Sychar."

"Please, sir," she said, unfolding the pouch of her robe and spreading the coins across the wooden planks, "is this enough for a room for tonight? I have no place else to go."

With the tip of a bent and bony forefinger Ezra pushed the coins around, separating them into two piles. His wife, a short, plump, pleasant-faced woman with her hair wound in tight coils on the sides of her head, padded silently to stand beside her husband.

Ezra's lips pushed in and out in rhythm with his tallying. "Plenty."

Tzippi nodded her agreement.

"Comes with a meal, too," Ezra continued. "No pilgrims this time of year. Too hot. Every room empty." He shoved the second heap of coppers back to Abigail. "A second night if you need it. Come along," he offered, lifting the lamp from the counter. "I'll show you the way."

—P. 106

ASK

How do Tzippi and Ezra respond to Abigail when they first meet? How is their response different from the other townspeople's?

_____

_____

_____

In what way(s) do they go beyond the norm of what innkeepers would do?

_____

_____

_____

How would you respond if a "harlot" showed up at your door with a child?

_____

_____

_____

READ

Tzippi cradled the child against her ample bosom. "Oh, she is a treasure. A treasure! And it's plain to see how much she loves her mother. Well, now. To business."

Abigail reached for her coins. "Oh yes. Another night's lodging."

"Put it away." Tzippi kissed Deborah. "Me and Ezra have talked it over. . . . My daughter died in childbirth five years ago. Her husband remarried and moved on to Capernaum. Twice the work now. Me and Ezra, we're not what we used to be. I was saying just yesterday before you came, I could use help. And then here you are with the little one."

"But I'm a Samaritan. You are Jews."

"You're a mother. You've this little one to care for. I've seen what goes on."

"You know my reputation." Abigail hung her head. . . . "You would take me . . . us . . . in? After everything—"

"I have seen enough." Tzippi's smile did not waver. "But one more question. Will you sing as you work?"

Abigail remembered how the potter's wife hated her singing. "Have I offended—?"

"You sing like an angel. Such a voice! So. That is part of the bargain. You must sing for us."

—PP. 111–112

ASK

What creative solution do Tzippi and Ezra come up with for Abigail's living arrangement?

_____

_____

_____

Why do you think they are so accepting of Abigail, even when they know her reputation?

_____

_____

_____

How does Tzippi allow Abigail to "give back" to her? Why is this dynamic important in a relationship?

_____

_____

_____

Who in your life has been accepting of you, even when you've made mistakes? Tell the story of what happened, how it made you feel then, and how it has influenced your life since.

_____

_____

_____

READ

Abigail waited on tables, did the scrubbing, helped with the cooking, and sang every evening as well. She had never been happier since before her pregnancy became known. . . .

Ezra beamed proudly at Abigail. Tzippi patted her hands together approvingly. She dandled Little Bee on her lap and let the baby tug the ends of her braids.

—P. 113

How she loved this place. Memories flooded her thoughts. Ordinary moments that had passed within these walls were holy in her heart.

She held her clay lamp high and took one last look around. For an instant she saw Little Bee and Grandma Tzippi reading in the corner while Ezra worked on his accounts.

Ezra's eyes crinkled at the corners as he smiled at his wife and the little girl. "A gift. A gift from HaShem," he had said. "An angel from heaven."

How different the old man's heart was from the townspeople's response toward Deborah. The acceptance and love of Tzippi and Ezra had been a shield raised against every unkind remark Abigail had endured.

—PP. 143–144

ASK

How did Abigail's life improve when she stayed with Tzippi and Ezra?

_____

_____

_____

After all the unkindness she has received from the men in her life, how would Ezra's kindness, in particular, have affected her?

_____

_____

_____

When has a person (or people) gone out of his or her way to make *you* feel like a gift? to make you feel right at home—loved and accepted?

_____

_____

_____

How have these people become "family" to you—people you can count on, as Abigail and Deborah counted on Tzippi and Ezra?

_____

_____

_____

READ

Afraid for Abigail's life, Tzippi sat by her bed, stroking her hand and murmuring, "Poor lamb. Poor, poor lamb."
   —P. 137

Abigail left the lamps unlit. The fire on the hearth was cold, gray ash. What did it matter?

   She did not get up to eat. She turned her head away from the spoon when Tzippi brought soup and clucked her tongue for sorrow and for shame.

   "You must eat, my dove, my delight."

   "No." Abigail resisted.

"You'll die."

"Oh?"

Tzippi sternly told Abigail as she held the spoon before her stubborn mouth, "You must live. Fight this thing. The baby is yours. She needs her mother strong and waiting."

—P. 137

"I know. I know, my darling girl." Tzippi came toward her with her arms out. "I miss her too. But we have one another." The old woman enfolded Abigail in an embrace.

—P. 144

ASK

How does Tzippi comfort Abigail in her darkest days—after her daughter is taken from her?

_____

_____

_____

How does Tzippi challenge Abigail?

_____

_____

_____

When has someone both comforted you and challenged you to make the best of a hard circumstance? Tell the story.

_____

_____

_____

READ

[Tzippi] flung herself into Abigail's arms and would not let go. Both women began to weep. "Oh, my angel! My dove. My Abigail!"

"You shouldn't have come here," Abigail protested quietly.

"How could I not come?"

"Please, come in, then."

"I can't. You know I can't."

"Away from their prying stares."

"Let them look! You are a daughter to me. . . . " Panting, Tzippi whirled around, raised her fist to the closed gate, and cried, "You hear me? You viper tongues of Sychar! This is my daughter. My child! Say what you will." She collapsed again in Abigail's arms. . . .

"My own dear Tzippi, mother to me when there was no one. Why did you come?"

"You ran away from me. From me!" Tzippi wiped her tears on her sleeve. "All these years I have loved you until I could not tell the difference between you and my own child. When they stole our darling girl, our Little Bee, my heart broke with yours. And now you've gone!"

—PP. 162–163

The Jewish couple adored the child. In every way they could not have loved or cared more for her if she was their own granddaughter.

When Deborah had been dragged away in the middle of the night, they had been devastated. When they saw how Mara mistreated her, they were appalled.

—P. 174

Ezra asked Cicero, "Where is she?"

"Sir?"

"Our grandchild. Our daughter."

—P. 186

ASK

How does Tzippi refer to Abigail? How does Ezra refer to Abigail? to Deborah?

_____

_____

_____

How does Abigail refer to Tzippi?

_____

_____

_____

How have these four people become "forever family" to each other?

_____

_____

_____

Who has become your "forever family" as a result of your heart connection and experiences, rather than genes? How did this connection form?

_____

_____

_____

WONDER . . .

"If only I could believe," Abigail choked. "The well of my faith is so dry. Oh, Tzippi, if only I could believe. . . . "

"Ask the Lord to give you faith. Meanwhile I will believe for both of us." She cupped Abigail's face in her hands. "Can I ever doubt? Look what the Lord did for me. And for Ezra. We were so alone. And then he brought you and Little Bee into our lives." She kissed her cheek. "What would I do without you? My dove."

Abigail could no longer reply. "For everything . . . thank you. Thank you."
—Tzippi and Abigail, p. 145

Think of the people who have filled the well of your faith, who have believed on your behalf when you couldn't. How might you fill the same role for someone who needs encouragement today?

3 | FED BY HOPE

> Abigail nourished herself with scraps, but she fed on hope.
> —P. 62

What does it mean to have hope? Explain.

_____

_____

_____

How can you tell if someone has hope? Contrast the personality traits, lifestyle, and habits of a person who has hope with those of a person who doesn't. Use examples of people you know (without naming or identifying them, of course).

_____

_____

_____

Would others say that you are a hopeful person? Why or why not?

_____

_____

_____

Abigail had numerous reasons to complain. Life was not going well. In fact, she was relentlessly ridiculed, scorned, physically injured, and gossiped about. Yet Abigail, in spite of her circumstances, managed to feed on hope rather than despair . . . at least most of the time.

READ

There was only one who might . . . who should . . . who must . . . feel pity for her. But Abigail could not go to him, not yet. If he were found out now, it would ruin everything.

She believed he would come to her as soon as he was able. Abigail fixed her hope on that belief, clung to it as desperately as she grasped the post of her shame and punishment.

—P. 15

If only she were brave enough to go to the father of her child and ask for his help. It was the abiding hope that he cared for her, that he would keep his promises to her, that sustained her through the long, long day.

—P. 26

Thanks be to HaShem, the child seemed to be thriving. The little one remained plump and rosy-cheeked, even as her mother spent the coin of her life to keep her so.

Abigail nourished herself with scraps, but she fed on hope. Two things kept her from despair: the overwhelming, all-consuming love for her child and the belief that her lover would come to save her.

Perhaps he would come tonight.

—P. 62

She lived, she had shelter of a sort, she had enough to eat, but what sort of life was this? Was this existence the proof of her *Machama*'s love . . . or of his neglect?

There remained but a slender thread of hope. What if the meager provision was part of a greater plan? What if her lover was hoarding his funds so as to take her away from Sychar and start a new life with her?

That had to be the explanation. She clung to it with desperation, as a drowning person snatches at the most fragile reed.

—P. 71

ASK

On whom does Abigail first focus her hope? Why?

_____

_____

_____

Why do you think she is protective of the person who injured her? What hopes and dreams is she holding on to? What is her reasoning process?

_____

_____

_____

Have you ever held on to a dream that wasn't good for you—either right then or in the long run? What happened as a result?

_____

_____

_____

READ

No more dreams.

No more *Machama*.

Very little hope. Was he to prove faithless after all?

—p. 64

Hope surged through Abigail. Had [Zakane] come to offer mercy? He had always been kind while they were married. Did he know how badly she had been abused and come out of pity?

Most likely she would now live in his household as a servant—as a slave—instead of his wife. But it would be a better home for Deborah than this. . . .

There was no mercy in his hard eyes, no pity on the stern face. . . . No expression of regard for what Abigail faced. No concern for her life or the baby's.

—PP. 85–86

Abigail concluded there was no divine assistance for her. Dreams did not feed or clothe her child. She was beyond HaShem's care, and she knew it. Hope would not be born anew with the dawn. The sun might rise, but Abigail's spirits would not.

—P. 105

In Abigail's dream, Zipporah the Shepherdess had told her that a Redeemer was coming. *"The Lord held all His holy ones in His hand."* How long had Abigail wrongly pinned her hopes of rescue on the rabbi's son? That was over now.

—P. 113

ASK

When her lover proves faithless, who else does Abigail put her hope in? Why?

_____

_____

_____

How do both of these men fail her?

_____

_____

_____

When have you put your hope in human beings, only to be disappointed or hurt by them? What happened?

_____

_____

_____

How does Abigail transfer her experience of rejection by men to her expectations of God? Have you ever found yourself equating human treatment with God's treatment? If so, when?

_____

_____

_____

READ

Where could she go? Who could help her? This was worse than being shunned, worse than being homeless. This was drowning on dry land—each breath more painful than the last and no rescue anywhere.

Without realizing where she ran, Abigail found herself atop the hill looming over Sychar's quarry. The precipice was sheer . . . a drop ten times the height of a man, onto a pile of jagged stones and rubble.

"Why not?" a voice whispered in Abigail's head. *"It's hopeless. You're useless. You can't change it. You can't fix it. There is no help for one like you. You're finally getting what you deserve, and you know it."*

Abigail looked around wildly. What difference would it make to anyone if she stepped forward two paces? The rocks would rush up to meet her, and then all this agony would be over.

She moved up to the very edge. It would not be difficult—not nearly so hard as living without Deborah. Never being allowed to hold her daughter, love her, sing with her.

If all that was gone, then life was already gone. Why not finish it?

—PP. 127–128

ASK

What pushes Abigail to the edge of hopelessness?

_____

_____

_____

How does the "voice" tempt her to hopelessness? In what way(s) does that same voice tempt you during difficult times?

_____

_____

_____

READ

Only one thing held her back. What if Tzippi was right? What if there was the least chance, the faintest gleam of a chance, that Abigail might get Deborah and run away with her? Even slaves escaped their masters. Sometimes they reached freedom. Sometimes there was life after despair.

Romulus, she thought. *What if Romulus can help me?*

To take the tiniest step forward was to deny there was any hope left. One pace would seal her separation from Deborah, who would grow up without her mother.

Abigail backed up a stride, then another. The quarry would still be here on another morning. The plunge to embrace the rocks would be possible another day. For today she would continue to live.

—P. 128

"Don't give up hope. HaShem is keeping watch. You'll see."
—TZIPPI, P. 127

ASK

What keeps Abigail from jumping? What makes her want to live?

_____

_____

_____

Who continually encourages Abigail to hope?

_____

_____

_____

Do you think HaShem—God—cares and is keeping watch over you? Why or why not?

_____

_____

_____

READ

"There is another prophet preaching in the Galil. . . . The Jewish leaders are afraid of him. So is Herod Antipas."

"Afraid? Of a prophet? They come and go."

"This one may be here to stay," Romulus remarked. "I heard him on the last patrol."

"What's different?"

"He gives the people hope," the centurion said.

"They always give the people hope. Always false hope."

"There is truth in what he says. A great orator, perhaps. Reaches the heart of the common man."

—CONVERSATION BETWEEN ROMULUS AND ABIGAIL, P. 151

The truth of Abigail's life was stark and hopeless. Her choices had led to misery. What if everything that had gone wrong could be washed clean? What if there really could be forgiveness—complete, total forgiveness—for her? And what if Abigail could have the assurance of that forgiveness and acceptance?

—P. 208

ASK

What is different about the prophet preaching in the Galil, compared to other prophets who have come and gone?

_____

_____

_____

When Abigail faces the truth about her life, what does she discover? What does she long for?

_____

_____

_____

Take a look at your own life. What is the truth about the way you've lived? What would you like to change?

_____

_____

_____

If you could be completely, totally forgiven of any wrongs you have done, how would that influence what you do both now and in the future?

_____

_____

_____

WONDER . . .

"Abigail was sad and beautiful before Jesus came. Alone. Hoping for something to change even when there was no hope. Nothing has changed. Millions are like her. I see her face every time I step onto the street. The longing lives from generation to generation. Only Jesus can satisfy."
—Eben, p. 222

Are you feeding on hope right now—or longing to be touched by hope? Why not turn to the only One who can satisfy?

4 | CHANGED!

> Walking down Sychar's streets for Abigail was akin to being recognized as a lone spy in an enemy camp. Venom and hatred were still directed at her from every side.
>
> —P. 112

> "You know the little one's the same age as my Susanna," the wife of the tanner replied. "HaShem help her and all our babies."
>
> "Amen. Amen," the other mothers echoed fervently.
>
> —PP. 193–194

Have you ever been on the receiving end of vicious gossip? If so, when—and why?

_____

_____

_____

Why did that particular gossip hurt so much? Was there any truth to it, or was it all falsehood?

_____

_____

_____

Imagine the scene. Your adultery is obvious to all, because your belly is large with a child . . . a child that is clearly not your husband's since he's been out of town for months. Neighbors line the street. Old men look troubled at the sight of you; old women look sad. Young men stare at you or glance away, as if caught in the act. Married women glare at you, their glances full of venom like the strike of an adder.

There is no help anywhere. You are left to bear the brunt of the punishment yourself . . . and the man who got you pregnant is nowhere in sight.

READ

Abigail stood at the center of the square as the crowd dispersed. Some townspeople departed with downcast faces. Others, especially a solid phalanx of married women, displayed satisfaction and scorn.

"But not nearly enough beating," she heard one of them say.

"No matter what that Roman says, this isn't over yet," another added.

Then Abigail was alone. Where was she to turn for help? Where could she go?

It was from her own home—Zakane's home—that she had been dragged by the judges.

The rabbi was her enemy. Even those in the village who had been friendly in the past were cowed by the massive display of hatred against her. At this moment she could think of no single ally in Sychar. No one had spoken up for her, defended her, pleaded mercy on her behalf. . . .

Where was she to go? . . . Where could she turn? So many emotions trampled her thoughts: terror, despair, relief, anguish. She could not think clearly.

—P. 15–16

ASK

Why do you think no one spoke up for Abigail?

_____

_____

_____

If you were one of the crowd and saw a neighbor of yours being beaten, what would you do? What would you say?

_____

_____

_____

READ

The women of Sychar traveled in a pack, so their journey to the well was as much entertainment as chore. . . . Today's subject of conversation was Abigail.

"Now see what her tarted-up ways have gotten her," one said. "Always acting so friendly around the men. My Manasseh says women like her are the pit of destruction." . . .

"Your Manasseh," a friend returned, "used to follow her around your fabric shop with his tongue hanging out." This sally brought a burst of laughter from the group. . . .

"Well," replied the wife of the cloth merchant, "don't we all recall how your Gad went out of his way to help her carry a jug of olive oil all the way to her house? I ask you, does he even offer such a thing to any of the rest of us?"

"Just what are you saying?"

"I'm saying we're well rid of her. She was a wicked, heathen sorceress, if you ask me. Used her wiles to draw men to her . . . all men! Look what happened to all her husbands! Bewitched 'em all . . . only she got caught but good this time!" . . .

"Whose whelp do you think it is, really?"

This question set off a round of speculation. . . .

Every one of the matrons in the discussion vehemently denied her husband's involvement. Every denial had an edge of shrillness, as if not every wife was completely convinced of her man's innocence.

—PP. 24–25

She wondered if the attitudes would change if the women of the town knew about the rabbi's son. Probably not. However horrified they might feel at first, they would quickly coalesce around excusing Saul of any wrongdoing. The women of Sychar might be robbed of an expected prey, but they would have another delicious crime to pin on Abigail.

—PP. 112–113

ASK

How would you define *gossip*?

_____

_____

_____

Who and what are the women of Sychar gossiping about?

_____

_____

_____

What motivations, desires, and fears do you think are behind the gossip?

_____

_____

_____

When you've been hurt by gossip, what motivations, desires, and fears could have caused someone to want to hurt you? Think through a specific situation you've faced.

_____

_____

_____

READ

Hatred for Abigail had worn them out. The wives of Sychar slept deeply beside husbands who did not reach for them.

The flesh and blood of Sychar's menfolk, no longer disguised in the daylight cloak of self-righteousness, was consumed with flames of secret desire. Inner lightning flashed in drowsy male brains, revealing the beautiful image of Abigail. Rabbis, judges, and unhappy husbands murmured in their sleep, dreaming they were kissing the soft lips of the woman they had lately cursed and banished.

Lust for Abigail's beauty had been forged into a determination to destroy what they could not possess.

Who was the lucky man among them all who had seduced Abigail's heart and lived out the fantasies of every man in Sychar?

Who was the father of Abigail's child?

Who was she protecting by her silence?

How could they discover him and destroy his life, as they had destroyed hers?

What cruelty would make her betray the man she loved?

Tomorrow morning works of envy, lust, and hypocrisy would be resumed. For now truth crept in quietly to reveal the secrets of each heart.

—PP. 29–30

ASK

What secrets were in the minds of the men of Sychar when they thought about Abigail?

_____

_____

_____

Why would they curse and banish such a woman?

_____

_____

_____

How do envy, lust, and hypocrisy play a part in how we treat others? Give an example of how you've been on the giving end, or the receiving end, of such action.

_____

_____

_____

READ

Darkness closed in. . . . Abigail touched her own cheekbones. She needed no mirror to know how gaunt she looked. Soon her looks would be no threat to the women of Sychar.

Would they still hate her enough to wish she were dead? With absolutely no reason to judge her so harshly, were they still prepared to be her executioners?

—P. 61

Peaceful days and months at The Stones of Joshua turned into four years more quickly than Abigail could have imagined. The women of Sychar still despised Abigail for her beauty. Rumors about the identity of Deborah's father remained unanswered. After a while the gossips of Sychar almost forgot to ask the question. Time had dulled the raging hatred against Abigail the harlot. There were always new scandals to occupy the women who gossiped at Jacob's Well. Eventually Abigail and her illegitimate child were tolerated—moved down on the long list of offenders or tragedies or unhappy marriages. Among victims gleefully dissected by the sharp-tongued housewives of the Samaritan city were the rabbi's son and his bitter bride, Mara.

—P. 119

ASK

How did the passing of time affect the women's hatred of Abigail? And their gossiping?

_____

_____

_____

Do you believe that time heals all? Or does it just dull the pain? Give an example from your own life.

_____

_____

_____

Why is gossip a constant and growing temptation, with a new victim around every corner?

_____

_____

_____

READ

Abigail held her head high as she swung through the farmers' stalls in Sychar's souk. Four-year-old Deborah followed at Abigail's side. Her right wrist was lovingly secured by a red cord tied around Abigail's waist. Her thick black mop of curls framed a perfect oval face. Wide eyes with long lashes looked every man and woman in the face. Her smile was infectious.

"See! I lost a tooth." Her stubby finger pointed to the empty place where her tooth had been last week.

"And so you have, Little Bee. So you have!" The honey merchant's wife beamed.

"Chewing is . . . difficult," Deborah opined. "It makes me very sorry for old people who have no teeth at all."

Her precocious remark brought laughter from those who heard her. The honey merchant's wife dipped a stick into a honey pot and pulled out a bit of honeycomb. "Then you shall have honey to console your sweet heart."

"*Toda*," Deborah answered her with thanks.

Though the merchants addressed Abigail in businesslike tones, they greeted Deborah with genuine enthusiasm.

No one could deny Abigail's little girl was beautiful and bright. Deborah's smile charmed even the most treacherous females in the city.

—P. 120

Though the little girl was still extraordinarily beautiful, there was no radiance in her features now. The animation that had enlivened and cheered everyone she met was absent. She stared, silent, at the ground, not even acknowledging the cheerful welcome from the date seller, or the offer of a sweet bit of comb from the honey seller's wife.

Gone was the thin scarlet cord of protection by which Abigail had extended love to her daughter.

In its place was a horse's lead rope. Coarse and heavy, it was knotted around Deborah's waist. The slack of the bonds lay coiled at her feet like a length of chain.

—P. 136

ASK

How does Deborah bring healing for Abigail and also acceptance from the townspeople?

_____

_____

_____

Contrast the first passage above, when Deborah was being cared for by her mother, with the second passage, when Deborah was being cared for by Mara. What are the differences in the little girl's behavior and countenance?

_____

_____

_____

READ

"Mama," Deborah cried. "Why don't you help me? Don't let them take me again, Mama. Please!"

Abigail struggled against her restraint. She had to go to her daughter. She must! How could she let Deborah think her mother stood by and let her be carried away? Better to die trying to save her!

Indignant, angry, frustrated, and embarrassed, Mara hauled Deborah from the square like a recalcitrant lamb or an unruly colt. Even after they disappeared, Abigail still heard Deborah's gulping cries: "Mama, please help me. Please! Why don't you help me?"

The charcoal seller shook his head, muttering, "This isn't right."

The honey seller's wife remarked loudly, "That's wrong, that is! What cause do they have to take away her child? Wasn't the babe happy before? Wasn't she sweet and bright, I ask you? Before HaShem, how is this right?"

—PP. 136–137

The women gathered at Jacob's Well past midday fell silent when Abigail approached. Obviously she was the topic of conversation. They stepped back, forming a lane for her to pass through.

She did not look up. She could not speak. The well of her tears was dry. They turned to stare openly—some with pity and others with cool curiosity. . . .

The honey seller's wife whispered, "I gave Little Bee a honeycomb."

Abigail's gaze flitted up to the ruddy face of the woman in thanks. Sad brown eyes gazed back at her with compassion. Abigail was grateful for this small kindness shown to Deborah, but she could not make words form on her lips. . . .

The date seller's wife covered her mouth with her hand and said in a very quiet voice, "So sorry. Know what you must feel."

Abigail's emotions flashed with resentment. How could anyone know what she felt? These women who had hated her for so long? Had they not encouraged this cruelty by their judgment?

—PP. 177–178

A group of Sychar's women was gathered around the water supply. . . .

"Looks like a funeral procession," one said.

"Is the child dead?"

"We would have heard," the charcoal seller's wife returned. "Poor thing! Sorrow heaped on sorrow for her mother."

Suddenly the faces and the voices displayed something Abigail had not witnessed from Sychar before: compassion.

"You know the little one's the same age as my Susanna," the wife of the tanner replied. "HaShem help her and all our babies."

"Amen. Amen," the other mothers echoed fervently.

The consolation she might have drawn from the change barely registered with Abigail.

—PP. 193–194

ASK

What changes in the women of Sychar's attitude, and why?

_____

_____

_____

How did the women try to show compassion for Abigail's plight? Did it work? Why or why not?

_____

_____

_____

If you were in Abigail's shoes, how would you respond? Would you feel resentful, as Abigail did, after the cruelty of the women's judgment over all the years? Angry? Sad? Some other emotion? Explain.

_____

_____

_____

Have you ever had to accept a kindness from someone who has greatly wronged you? If so, how did you handle it? Why is forgiveness so difficult?

_____

_____

_____

READ

Jar on her shoulder, Abigail approached the well with trepidation. . . . A half dozen of Sychar's wives were there, gossiping. . . .

Raising her chin, Abigail parted the Red Sea of Samaritan women and approached the well.

"Let me help you with that," the honey seller's wife declared, letting down the waterskin. "How's the baby? How's Deborah?"

"She . . . she still hasn't moved or spoken."

The charcoal seller's wife said, "We all pray for her . . . Abigail."

"I think about her every time I look at my girls," the tanner's wife added.

"If there's anything you need," the honey seller's spouse volunteered. "Anything at all."

Unnoticed 'til that moment, Mara approached the well. Staring coldly at Abigail, she said loudly, "What's she doing here? What gives you the right to show up here with decent women? Contaminating the—"

"Mara," the tanner's wife said, "be so good as to close your mouth before I close it for you."

"Exactly," agreed the honey seller's wife. "If you weren't so selfish—"

"And so cruel," the charcoal seller's wife noted.

"If you weren't so selfish and so cruel, none of this would have happened," the honey seller's wife concluded. "Is the jar full, Abigail? Come on, let's walk Abigail home. No, no, my dear. We'll carry it for you. We hear you singing to Little Bee. Such a beautiful voice. What are the words to that lullaby? How does it go?"

—PP. 195–196

ASK

How do the women of Sychar begin to show compassion not only in their words, but in their actions toward Abigail?

_____

_____

_____

In what way(s) is Mara's cruelty turned back on her?

_____

_____

_____

Do you think the old adage "What goes around, comes around" is true? Why or why not? If so, when have you experienced it in your life?

_____

_____

_____

WONDER . . .

The townspeople gathered around her as Abigail described her encounter with Yeshua of Nazareth. "He knows everything there is to know about me," she said openly. "Everything I wanted all of you to forget. . . . He said HaShem is seeking true-hearted people to worship him."

"Not hypocrites," the honey seller's wife declared emphatically. "Not greedy priests or cruel rabbis."

"What HaShem wants," Abigail said, "is people honest enough to admit their faults and ask him for forgiveness."

—P. 212

When people experience genuine life change, they become true-hearted people who seek to worship God. Are you honest enough to admit your faults and ask God for forgiveness? If so, you will be *changed* forever!

5 | LITTLE MIRACLES

> Out of the depths of her despair, she had cried aloud to HaShem, and He had heard her.
> —P. 109

What, to you, would constitute a miracle? How would you know it was a miracle?

_____

_____

_____

Do you believe miracles can be little things that happen to us throughout a day, or do they need to be big things?

_____

_____

_____

Have you ever experienced a miracle? If so, tell the story.

_____

_____

_____

Abigail, of all people, needs miracles in her life. Pregnant and homeless, she is flogged . . . until a hated Roman stops the beating. She is taken in by a blind beggar, who tends her wounds, mends her robe, and shares her own meager food reserves. But the next morning she is driven away by another beggar who complains, "We've done nothing to deserve what we are. But she made her own bed of sorrows. She isn't one of us." Going to her husband's home, she is turned away even by the people she has helped in the past.

But amidst all her hardships, Abigail strives to keep her focus on the little miracles that keep both her and her daughter alive during tumultuous times.

READ

Her back and legs ached horribly. She needed rest, she needed water, and she needed food. Her need drove her forward.

"Leah," she called softly as she approached the blind woman's hut. "Leah, it's Abigail."

"I know, dear," Leah replied. "I heard you back in the ravine. Come here."

Almost weeping at the sound of one friendly voice, Abigail met Leah, who was carrying a torn woolen blanket, a bit of heavy sailcloth, a jug of water, and an entire loaf of barley bread. . . .

She passed Abigail the fragments of fabric and meager supplies. "You remember the boulders back in the gully? Where two of them lean close together, you can cover the top with the heavy cloth and plug the entry with brush. There's a bit of clean straw for a bed. Mostly clean, anyway. The blanket is for you as well. I'm sorry it isn't more."

Now the tears did stream down Abigail's face. "No, no! You've helped so much. Thank you! Thank you!" She threw her arms around Leah in a mighty embrace.

Leah returned the hug, then carefully patted Abigail's stomach. "We must take care of the little one, eh? Now go on; get yourself settled before dark."

—P. 27

As if hearing the music of creation's slow dance, the baby tapped a rhythm within her womb. The signal was a reminder: Abigail carried life in her, not death; mercy, not judgment. She placed her warm hand over the infant who shared her heartbeat. Closing her eyes stopped the cold universe's spinning. Abigail regained her focus.

—P. 30

ASK

How does a blind beggar meet Abigail's needs—physically and emotionally?

_____

_____

_____

When has kindness undone your resolve not to cry over your circumstances?

_____

_____

_____

How can a reminder that someone cares help you regain your focus?

_____

_____

_____

READ

He stooped and peered in at her. "You are the woman they were beating in the market square."

She managed to reply, "You made them stop."

"I am Romulus."

"You saved my life."

"Your baby?"

"I am in labor."

"So." He straightened and placed his hands on his hips. Turning his back on her, he surveyed the area for a long moment, neither moving nor speaking.

Would he leave her to face her agony alone? Another pain gripped her. A warm gush of water followed the contraction.

At last he spoke. "Woman, are you able to stand?"

She panted, "A minute more . . . " The pain eased. "Yes, I can stand."
He extended his hand to her. "Come on, then."
  —P. 37

Abigail was seized with panic at the thought that her protector would not stay
with her. "Sir!" she called to Romulus. "Please, sir, don't leave me here alone."
    Romulus entered the chamber and towered over her. His craggy
features softened with pity. "I can't stay."
    "Thank you. Thank you. HaShem bless you. Twice you have saved
my life."
    "Be strong," he commanded. "For the sake of this child."
    "Why . . . why have you been so kind to me? to us? Two lives are forever
indebted to you. Not just one."
    "Perhaps one day I will tell you."
      —P. 40

"Abigail told me how you protected her and provided at the beginning of
our Deborah's life. I am certain you have a good heart."
    "If there is a true God, perhaps he will have mercy on me." Romulus
bowed slightly. "My home is their home. And yours, if a Jewess will stoop
to take shelter beneath the roof of a Gentile."
    Tzippi rolled up her sleeves. "I'm here. I'll stay as long as I am needed.
And I am needed."
      —P. 188

ASK

How does Romulus step in, just when Abigail needs him—multiple times?
What qualities does he exhibit that show her she can trust him?

_____

_____

_____

In what unusual way(s) does a Roman offer a Samaritan and a Jewess shelter? How is this a miracle in that time period and culture, based on the information you've read in this book?

_____

_____

_____

What do Romulus' actions say about everyday miracles? Do you see kindness as an everyday miracle? Explain.

_____

_____

_____

READ

Somehow, this tiny infant made her feel loved. She stroked the downy cheek with her finger as the baby nursed.

"You will be a mighty woman of the Lord, one day," Abigail sang. "Like Deborah, you will be. Fearless and true." . . .

Abigail held her baby close, kissing ear and nose and eyes. "You will be strong and sure. Not like me. No, you will be Deborah!"

Abigail had never known such fierce love. The baby had pushed everyone else into the shadows of Abigail's thoughts.

—PP. 44–45

She glanced up at the last rays of the setting sun and then down at her daughter. *Blessed are you, O Lord, who has let us live to see this day.*

—P. 48

ASK

How can caring for others be a miracle that turns around your own life?

_____

_____

_____

How does Deborah's birth change Abigail?

_____

_____

_____

Are you thankful for each day the Lord lets you live? Why or why not? If so, how do you show that thankfulness? If not, why not?

_____

_____

_____

READ

Abigail prayed, *HaShem! Oh, a place to sleep tonight. A quiet corner where I can feed my lamb.*

Reaching out her hand, Abigail swung a gate wide. The pen was empty. The straw was clean, as if some unseen hand had prepared a place for her to rest. She slipped down to lean against the back wall and fumbled to nurse the baby. Deborah feasted eagerly on Abigail's plentiful milk.

—P. 52

Abigail had made her way back to her little shelter, still intact, among the outcasts of Sychar. . . . Drawing back a corner of the blanket, Abigail lay down next to her child, enfolding her carefully in her arms. For an instant before blowing out the lamp, Abigail studied the precious face. The perfect rosebud lips worked in and out, drawing sustenance in dreams. . . .

The nightingale called. Abigail softly hummed the tune to Miriam's song: *"The horse and his rider He has thrown into the sea."* It was a song of victory, of the triumph of God's Mercy in the face of overwhelming odds.

The fact that it appeared right before the miraculous advent of manna was not forgotten by Abigail either.

—PP. 61–62

It was still true that she had nowhere of her own to go to. It was still true she and her baby had been rejected and abandoned by Saul. It was still true that life in Sychar would not suddenly become easy.

And yet, out of the depths of her despair, she had cried aloud to HaShem, and He had heard her. Being taken in by Ezra and Tzippi without question, without sneering or mocking—to have this safety for even one night made Abigail almost weep with relief.

The room in The Stones of Joshua was simple enough: Pallet stuffed with sweet-smelling straw on the freshly swept floor. Table and stool. Pegs on the wall for clothing.

That was all, but it made for a brighter morning than Abigail had imagined was possible.

—P. 109

ASK

How is Abigail's prayer for a place to rest answered in each of the above passages?

_____

_____

_____

How can an awareness of everyday miracles and an attitude of thankfulness change your perspective—even if the facts still say life is hard?

_____

_____

_____

What song of victory can you sing in the midst of your own circumstances?

_____

_____

_____

WONDER . . .

I will remember Your miracles of long ago.
I will meditate on all Your works
    and consider all Your mighty deeds. . . .
You are the God who performs miracles;
    You display Your power among the peoples.
    —PSALM 77:11-12, 14 NIV

As you look back on your life, what "little miracles" do you see?

6 | WATER FOR THE THIRSTY

"If you knew the gift of God, and who is saying to you, 'Give me a drink,' you would have asked him, and he would have given you living water."
—YESHUA, P. 206

When have you felt so thirsty physically that you could never get enough water to drink? Describe the craving for more . . . and the feeling of never being satisfied.

_____

_____

_____

In what areas of life do you crave more, but still aren't satisfied?

_____

_____

_____

As far back as she could remember, Abigail had longed for steadfast love—the kind of love that is always available, always present, and never changes. Her thirst for it was unquenchable. But she thought that everything she'd done had excluded her from the possibility of that kind of love. Yet it didn't stop her soul's longing for it.

READ

Return, O Lord! How long?
    Have pity on Your servants!
Satisfy us in the morning with Your steadfast love,
    That we may rejoice and be glad all our days.
—PSALM 90:13-14 ESV

Steadfast love was exactly what Abigail craved. She needed it more than food, more than shelter. Her desire for steadfast love was more akin to thirst—burning, intolerable thirst.

How long had it been since she had experienced steadfast love? None of her husbands had modeled it for her.

As a very young child, perhaps she had known it in the home of her parents.

It is, she thought, *what I want Deborah to grow up feeling. Steadfast, enduring, unshakable love. It's what I want her to be certain of always receiving from me. . . . I want her to feel content and safe every morning of her life because of how much I love her.*

I want her to know with absolute certainty that nothing can ever separate her from my love . . . nothing!

But where would Abigail find such love for herself? The hymn spoke of a returning Lord. That must mean when Messiah came—the one the Samaritan clergy called "the Restorer." Was love what would be restored? A belief that such a transient thing as love could actually be reliable? Was there a love so unselfish as to be never failing?

The image of going to the well was somehow linked in Abigail's mind to the psalm. She went to draw water every morning. It was satisfying to fill the water jar and have it fresh and cool to drink.

But each day required another trip to the spring . . . another journey to and from. The satisfaction was real, but it did not last.

—PP. 76–77

ASK

What does Abigail long for the most? Do you think this is something we all long for deep inside? Why or why not?

_____

_____

_____

Take a few minutes to think through your own life. What specifically needs to be restored? How could this restoration—and the resulting satisfaction— last all your days?

_____

_____

_____

READ

He gently asked, "Give me a drink?"

This was so unexpected, so improper, that Abigail . . . stammered, "How is it that you, a Jew, ask for a drink from me, a woman of Samaria?" . . .

Swallowing gratefully, the man's full lips curved in a smile of thanks. He accepted a second offering, then wiped his face with the cool drops that remained. Lifting brown eyes lively with golden flecks, he said, "If you knew the gift of God, and who is saying to you, 'Give me a drink,' you would have asked him, and he would have given you living water."

Living water? Abigail was nonplussed. Was the Jew ill from the heat? Hadn't he just received liquid hauled from the depths with Abigail's jar, when there was no other means at hand?

"Sir," she said, politely pointing out the physical impossibility of his suggestion, "you have nothing to draw water with, and the well is deep. Where do you get that living water?" . . .

The man gestured toward her water jar. "Everyone who drinks of this water—" he glanced over his shoulder at the mouth of the well—"will be thirsty again. But whoever drinks of the water that I will give will never be

thirsty again. Forever. . . . The water that I will give will become a spring of water welling up to eternal life."
—PP. 206–207

ASK

What was improper, in that day, about a Jewish man asking a Samaritan woman for water?

_____

_____

_____

What is the "living water" the man is talking about? What makes it different from the regular water we drink?

_____

_____

_____

READ

She admitted, "I have . . . no husband."

Abigail's heartbeat quickened as the stranger leveled his gaze at her. He seemed to see deep into her soul. The knowledge in his eyes made her uncomfortable.

"You're right in saying, 'I have no husband.' You've had five husbands." She gasped. How could he know this?

He continued, "And the one you now have is not your husband." Drily he added, "What you've said is true."

Not again! When life in Sychar had just gotten bearable, how could it be that her reputation was known to a total stranger? "Sir, I perceive that you're a prophet."

How could she get this conversation to go somewhere else? To what subject could she jump to get off of painfully personal topics?
—PP. 207–208

Abigail was flooded with confused emotions. She had long believed that HaShem was through with her. She felt forever separated from God and unwelcome in His courts. Her thirsty soul had been driven from the well by righteous people. Yet now this stranger seemed to be saying that God was actively seeking her, and that what He valued was not expensive gifts or scholarly achievement but her honesty.

—P. 208

ASK

Why does Abigail try to redirect the conversation? Have you ever found yourself doing the same thing, for similar reasons?

_____

_____

_____

How do you respond when others try to tell you hard things about yourself or the way you relate to others? Explain.

_____

_____

_____

Have you ever felt that God was through with you? that you're separated from God and unwelcome because of things you've done? How would you feel if you knew your life could be wiped clean and you could begin again?

_____

_____

_____

READ

Suddenly Abigail understood what the stranger meant about "living water." But when? Who would make this triumphant transformation true for her? How could all the damaged parts of her life get restored?

—P. 209

This was the third occasion in her life when unbridled, unfettered, expectant joy bubbled up in her heart. . . . Could this be the Messiah? The One she had heard about! Had the One whom Romulus had said turned water into wine asked her for water? What could this mean? . . .

Forgetting her water jar and the errand on which she had come to the well, Abigail backed away, turned, and dashed off toward Sychar. She had to tell Ezra and Tzippi about the stranger at the well. And the honey seller's wife. And the charcoal seller's wife. And . . . and . . . everyone who had ears to hear.

—PP. 209–210

What Yeshua of Nazareth offered was as refreshing as cool water in the desert. He taught—no, more than that—He *showed* that the love of God was reliable and always available.

Like a well that never runs dry!

Even before she reached the inn, Abigail began sharing her experience with the people of the town. "Come with me! You must come back to Jacob's Well to meet a man."

—P. 211

ASK

What was Abigail's immediate response when she believed that Yeshua—Salvation!—was at the well?

_____

_____

_____

If Messiah were to meet you today at the well, what damaged parts of your life would you long to have restored?

_____

_____

_____

WONDER . . .

The townspeople gathered around her as Abigail described her encounter with Yeshua of Nazareth. "He knows everything there is to know about me," she said openly. "Everything I wanted all of you to forget. But here's what he says: 'God's love is steadfast, like living water. Like a spring that gives eternal life.'"

—P. 212

How will you respond to the steadfast love of Yeshua? to His offer of living water? How will you spread the word about the Restorer?

> "O God, You are my God;
>   earnestly I seek You;
>   my soul thirsts for You;
> my flesh faints for You,
>   as in a dry and weary land
>   where there is no water.
> Because Your steadfast love is
>   better than life,
>   my lips will praise You."
> —PSALM 63:1, 3 ESV

Dear Reader,

You are so important to us. We have prayed for you as we wrote this book and also as we receive your letters and hear your soul cries. We hope that *Twelfth Prophecy* has encouraged you to go deeper. To get to know Yeshua better. To fill your soul hunger by examining Scripture's truths for yourself.

We are convinced that if you do so, you will find this promise true: *"If you seek Him, He will be found by you."*
—1 CHRONICLES 28:9

Authors' Note

The following sources have been helpful in our research for this book:

- *The Complete Jewish Bible.* Translated by David H. Stern. Baltimore, MD: Jewish New Testament Publications, Inc., 1998.
- *iLumina*, a digitally animated Bible and encyclopedia suite. Carol Stream, IL: Tyndale House Publishers, 2002.
- *The International Standard Bible Encyclopaedia.* George Bromiley, ed. 5 vols. Grand Rapids, MI: Eerdmans, 1979.
- *The Life and Times of Jesus the Messiah.* Alfred Edersheim. Peabody, MA: Hendrickson Publishers, Inc., 1995.
- Starry Night™ Enthusiast Version 5.0, published by Imaginova™ Corp.

Scripture References

[1] Judg. 5:10-11 ESV
[2] Judg. 5:2, 10-11 NIV
[3] Ps. 23:1-2 NIV
[4] Exod. 15:21 ESV
[5] Ps. 90:13-14 ESV
[6] Ps. 90:16-17 ESV
[7] Judg. 5:22, 31 ESV
[8] I Sam. 2:2-3 ESV
[9] Ps. 136:1 ESV
[10] Ps. 136:2-3 ESV
[11] Deut. 32:1, 3 ESV
[12] Deut. 32:4 ESV
[13] Deut. 33:2-3 ESV
[14] Paraphrase of Exod. 15:21
[15] Taken from Num. 6:24-26 ESV
[16] Deut. 6:4 NIV
[17] From Jewish tradition
[18] Deut. 6:5 ESV
[19] Adapted from Deut. 6:7 ESV
[20] John 2:16 ESV
[21] John 2:19 ESV
[22] Ps. 46:1 ESV
[23] Judg. 5:3, 11 ESV
[24] Judg. 5:12 ESV
[25] John 3:17 ESV
[26] Judg. 5:3, 10-12 ESV
[27] See John 4:5-26 for the biblical account
[28] Ps. 63:1, 3 ESV
[29] John 4:29 ESV
[30] John 4:29 ESV
[31] Isa. 12:3-4, 6, ESV
[32] Exod. 15:2 ESV
[33] Exod. 15:9-10 ESV
[34] Exod. 15:13 ESV
[35] Deut. 18:15 ESV
[36] Adapted from Deut. 18:18 ESV
[37] Gen. 22:8 ESV
[38] John 4:23 ESV
[39] John 3:5 ESV
[40] John 3:16 ESV
[41] Judg. 5:11-12, 3 ESV
[42] John 4:42 ESV
[43] Paraphrase of 2 Peter 3:8

About the Authors

BODIE AND BROCK THOENE (pronounced *Tay-nee*) have written over 60 works of historical fiction. That these best sellers have sold more than 20 million copies and won eight ECPA Gold Medallion Awards affirms what millions of readers have already discovered—that the Thoenes are not only master stylists but experts at capturing readers' minds and hearts.

In their timeless classic series about Israel (The Zion Chronicles, The Zion Covenant, and The Zion Legacy), the Thoenes' love for both story and research shines.

With The Shiloh Legacy and *Shiloh Autumn* (poignant portrayals of the American Depression), The Galway Chronicles (dramatic stories of the 1840s famine in Ireland), and the Legends of the West (gripping tales of adventure and danger in a land without law), the Thoenes have made their mark in modern history.

In the A.D. Chronicles they step seamlessly into the world of Jerusalem and Rome, in the days when Yeshua walked the earth and transformed lives with His touch.

Bodie began her writing career as a teen journalist for her local newspaper. Eventually her byline appeared in prestigious periodicals such as *U.S. News and World Report*, *The American West*, and *The Saturday Evening Post*. She also worked for John Wayne's Batjac Productions (she's best known as author of *The Fall Guy*) and ABC Circle Films as a writer and researcher. John Wayne described her as "a writer with talent that captures the people and the times!" She has degrees in journalism and communications.

Brock has often been described by Bodie as "an essential half of this writing team." With degrees in both history and education, Brock has, in his role as researcher and story-line consultant, added the vital dimension of historical accuracy. Due to such careful research, the Zion Covenant and Zion Chronicles series are recognized by the

American Library Association, as well as Zionist libraries around the world, as classic historical novels and are used to teach history in college classrooms.

Bodie and Brock have four grown children—Rachel, Jake, Luke, and Ellie—and seven grandchildren. Their children are carrying on the Thoene family talent as the next generation of writers, and Luke produces the Thoene audio books. Bodie and Brock divide their time between London and Nevada.

For more information visit:

www.thoenebooks.com
www.familyaudiolibrary.com

THOENE FAMILY CLASSICS™

✪ ✪ ✪

THOENE FAMILY CLASSIC HISTORICALS
by Bodie and Brock Thoene
*Gold Medallion Winners**

THE ZION COVENANT
*Vienna Prelude**
Prague Counterpoint
Munich Signature
Jerusalem Interlude
Danzig Passage
*Warsaw Requiem**
London Refrain
Paris Encore
Dunkirk Crescendo

THE ZION CHRONICLES
*The Gates of Zion**
A Daughter of Zion
The Return to Zion
A Light in Zion
*The Key to Zion**

THE ZION DIARIES
The Gathering Storm
Against the Wind
Their Finest Hour

THE SHILOH LEGACY
*In My Father's House**
A Thousand Shall Fall
Say to This Mountain

SHILOH AUTUMN

THE GALWAY CHRONICLES
*Only the River Runs Free**
Of Men and of Angels
*Ashes of Remembrance**
All Rivers to the Sea

THE ZION LEGACY
Jerusalem Vigil
Thunder from Jerusalem
Jerusalem's Heart
Jerusalem Scrolls
Stones of Jerusalem
Jerusalem's Hope

A.D. CHRONICLES
First Light
Second Touch
Third Watch
Fourth Dawn
Fifth Seal
Sixth Covenant
Seventh Day
Eighth Shepherd
Ninth Witness
Tenth Stone
Eleventh Guest
Twelfth Prophecy

CP0064

THOENE FAMILY CLASSICS™

✪ ✪ ✪

THOENE FAMILY CLASSIC AMERICAN LEGENDS

LEGENDS OF THE WEST
by Bodie and Brock Thoene

Legends of the West, Volume One
   Sequoia Scout
   The Year of the Grizzly
   Shooting Star
Legends of the West, Volume Two
   Gold Rush Prodigal
   Delta Passage
   Hangtown Lawman
Legends of the West, Volume Three
   Hope Valley War
   The Legend of Storey County
   Cumberland Crossing
Legends of the West, Volume Four
   The Man from Shadow Ridge
   Cannons of the Comstock
   Riders of the Silver Rim

LEGENDS OF VALOR
by Luke Thoene

Sons of Valor
Brothers of Valor
Fathers of Valor

✪ ✪ ✪

THOENE CLASSIC NONFICTION
by Bodie and Brock Thoene

Writer-to-Writer

THOENE FAMILY CLASSIC SUSPENSE
by Jake Thoene

CHAPTER 16 SERIES
Shaiton's Fire
Firefly Blue
Fuel the Fire

✪ ✪ ✪

THOENE FAMILY CLASSICS FOR KIDS

BAKER STREET DETECTIVES
by Jake and Luke Thoene

The Mystery of the Yellow Hands
The Giant Rat of Sumatra
The Jeweled Peacock of Persia
The Thundering Underground

LAST CHANCE DETECTIVES
by Jake and Luke Thoene
Mystery Lights of Navajo Mesa
Legend of the Desert Bigfoot

THE VASE OF MANY COLORS
by Rachel Thoene (Illustrations by Christian Cinder)

✪ ✪ ✪

THOENE FAMILY CLASSIC AUDIOBOOKS

Available from
www.thoenebooks.com or
www.familyaudiolibrary.com

CP0064